A Kiss to Wake

MARDA LOOP MYSTERIES BOOK 1

MIMI GUNN

Editing by Jennifer Herrington

Cover design by Claire Brown

ISBN 978-1-0689519-0-9

Published by Petite Press

This book is dedicated to the ones whose voices were silenced

United, our voices will one day be heard.

Author's Note

This book is a contemporary romantic suspense.
It is intended for mature audiences.

Please note that A *Kiss to Wake* contains the following:
Explicit sex scenes
Descriptions of crime scenes
Attempted assault victim/witness testimony
Anxiety rep and panic attacks
A murderer

READER DISCRETION IS ADVISED.

A Kiss to Wake

A kiss to wake,
A kiss to lift,
My eyes are yours alone.
I gaze upon your wondrous face,
And feel like I am home.

Your lips are mine,
My lips are thine,
If dreaming, do not wake.
For within dreams I will reside,
If with you I can stay.

1

"Come to me, sweet, sweet nectar of the Gods," Louise Dubois whispered to her perfectly creamed and sugared cup of coffee as she pressed it to her eager mouth. She loved the tantalizing warmth of the ceramic mug on her lips. She inhaled the comforting scent and glanced toward the welcoming sofa. Watching the morning news under her grandmother's quilt and seated next to her needy grey tabby, Cosette, was her favorite. She waited with bated breath for the irritating woman making a series of inappropriate jokes and announcing the morning traffic to move on and for it to cut to the handsome meteorologist. This is it. This was how she got her kicks these days.

A tiny voice in the back of her mind told Louise that she should date again, if only to stop enjoying the outside world through her television screen. She shook her head. Today was not that day.

The gorgeous man in the perfectly cut grey suit appeared on the screen. Though the meteorologist seemed to announce little more than she could observe on her phone or by looking out her window, she appreciated her five minutes of peace every morning. It was hard to keep her eyes off the thirst trap as he presented his variety of maps and said all charming things as she sipped her coffee. Louise smiled into the side of her mug.

What a perfect way to start the day.

Cosette bumped her elbow, reminding her that she needed some affection and would not be ignored. Louise absently scratched the cat's head as she watched her mother walk up to the main floor from the basement with her slightly stilted gait.

"Did I miss him? Oh shoot. I just wanted to go put a load in the washing machine," Georgie Dubois fretted, walking into the living room. Her eyes trained instantly on the television and their favorite weather personality. "Oh, I like that suit. That color looks so good on him."

Louise nodded in agreement, sitting up and closing her mouth to avoid drooling on her pants. She shook her head.

Yeah, maybe it was time she found a real man.

"Do you think he got a haircut?"

"Yes, finally." Georgie observed. "It was getting a bit long there for a while."

Louise snickered. "Well, enjoy watching. Since semi-retirement allows you that freedom, I have to eat and go," Louise said, as the main anchor duo came back on the screen and the weatherman disappeared. Louise brought her mug back into the kitchen, where she popped her bagel in the toaster and leaned against the counter, waiting for it to surface again.

"What are you doing today?" Louise questioned her mother, who continued to work as a realtor, even though she was getting close to retirement age. After a busy career, Georgie was able to enjoy the fruits of her labor, only working with select clients to maintain her comfortable lifestyle. The house was one of the smaller ones in the neighborhood, but it was all Georgie's, and her mother reveled in that fact. Because of her flexible work schedule, Georgie spent her free time living as a retiree. She maintained a strict mall walking schedule, met various groups of friends for coffee or cards and irritatingly had a much better social life than her daughter.

Louise benefited by living with her mother in the small two-story house in the trendy neighborhood of Marda Loop, in Calgary.

A small chest clutching gasp from the living room drew Louise's attention, and she popped her head in the living room to see what had captivated Georgie's attention.

Louise scanned the words and felt a familiar flutter in her chest. The screen read "Suspicious death in South Calgary." Louise cleared her throat to remind her mother that she hadn't answered her question. Dismissing the news, Georgie quickly bustled into the kitchen, where Louise had gone back to finish eating.

"Oh, I have a few sales to close, but otherwise I'll be finishing my book for tonight. Renée and Verna are meeting me for book club. Maybe you should meet up with your friends, go out and do something?"

Louise shivered at the thought. She rarely went out at night, and only when it was necessary. She was lucky enough to work with her best friends every day at the law office. Her eyes rolled in reaction to the unlikeliness of such an event. Louise had mastered making a bored expression whenever her mother suggested she change anything about her life. She thoroughly enjoyed her work – home routine. It provided a great deal of comfort. Safety.

Her mother shrugged and poured herself another cup of coffee.

"Louise, you need to get out a bit, have some fun," Georgie said, which signaled that it was time for Louise to head upstairs and get ready for work, conversation over. She knew she had pulled back from her life a bit in the last few years, but she had a good reason. A reason she tossed into the box inside her that said "Caution: Do Not Open".

"I gotta get ready for work. Love you, Mum," she said as she climbed the stairs to her bathroom.

In her life, Louise was excellent at two things: bottling up emotions and running away from difficult conversations, as she was proving at this exact moment. Louise rolled her eyes as she gazed at herself in the mirror. She picked up the concealer from her makeup bag and gazed at it dubiously.

"Industrial strength concealer. This should do the trick," Louise said to herself in the mirror. Her under eye bags had bags today. Ah yes, there was another thing she was particularly talented at: not sleeping.

She skipped the thorough facial analysis and dressed in her black tunic top, black blazer, and matching leggings, relying on a bit of red lipstick on her full lips to help add a bit of liveliness to her outfit. Her lips always looked good, no matter how she was feeling. The black clothing matched the state of her mood. Tired, but functioning.

As she walked down the stairs and gazed at the television in the living room, her attention was seized once again by the blinking lights of police cars on the screen. The banner below the image once again projecting "Police investigating suspicious death in South Calgary."

Louise knew she had to get to work soon, but she couldn't help but look at the screen for a moment, her eyes fixated. A wave of cool goose flesh made its way up her body as the familiar sense of dread pooled in her stomach.

Georgie blustered into the room, turning the television off and breaking Louise out of her trance.

"Honey, you need to get to work. Don't look at that, it'll just scare you. We're okay. We're safe. Get going!" Georgie shooed her out the front door as Louise grabbed her purse, raincoat, and keys, then walked out to her car.

Louise would look up more information on this suspicious death once she had time later. There was no way she could keep from following these events happening in her beloved Marda Loop.

She stopped beneath the shelter of their home's front porch to struggle to zip up her snug rain jacket, allowing the cool autumn air to chill her anxiety and fill her with a sense of calm. Her street was safe. Her neighborhood was safe. Marda Loop was the kind of place where people looked out for each other. Whatever happened on the news was a onetime event. And the murder was in South Calgary, a neighborhood next to hers. Not in her neighborhood, exactly.

Her heart was brimming with empathy for the victim, but she could not assume the same would happen to her. Any information trickling from the investigation would help her measure the level of risk and do whatever she needed to keep her and Georgie safe. She would also need a new raincoat, she sighed, as the zipper made its way up to her neck, making her feel like an encased sausage. The only murder she needed to fear was how badly this jacket was killing her self-esteem. She would not let this throw off her workday.

Louise gripped her jacket over her heart and breathed as she had been trained.

Inhale.

Exhale.

One, two, three, four.

She closed her eyes and let the words of reassurance pour out with each breath. It wasn't him. This case was unrelated. It's not him. Too much time had passed. It's not him. Louise chewed absently at her nail as she walked to her car. It's not him. She repeated the mantra until she almost believed it. It couldn't be him.

But what if it was?

2

DETECTIVE BAND WALKED UP TO THE SCENE with much trepidation, his heart hammering in his chest. He knew the area well, having lived there for a few months. Marda Loop was like a small town within a city. A cluster of neighborhoods with cute shops, cafés, and restaurants where people remembered you when you walked in. The area was full of young professionals and families, well-kept homes surrounding rental apartment buildings and condominiums, creating a vibrant place to live with entertaining events always happening.

Detective Band had a lot to prove on this case. He had just been promoted to the role of lead detective and until now he had only assisted on major crimes cases. This time, he had been named the lead and felt personally responsible for it being solved quickly. Nice and tidy, every little loose string tied up. He would be thorough, on top of every detail, and take the necessary steps to get a sadistic criminal off the streets. This case had a lot at stake. He would follow the procedure. Do his job correctly, so that way no one else would get hurt.

He climbed the steps to the two-story walkup with four apartments and noted the placement of the neighbors' doors, and how close each unit was and how plausible it would be to hear sound between units. This was an old building; the floors would be well-insulated and the sound would unlikely travel between units. He nodded at Marty, his partner, who had arrived before him, and sent a detective standing nearby to go knock on the neighbors' doors and question them.

"Give me the deets, Marty. Any spoilers? The initial call to 9-1-1 and it sounds....interesting," Gregory asked, frowning and shaking his head.

Marty waved him into the building with a look that told him all he needed to know.

"This one is bad," he replied, "just downright creepy." They walked up the brown carpeted stairs to a top-floor apartment.

"Better brace yourself, Greg," Marty said, a look of concern on his face. Marty was aware this was Gregory's first major murder case as a lead and his first time seeing a victim in this state. Calgary was no stranger to shootings, gang violence, and drug deals gone bad. From the recording on the emergency phone call, Gregory anticipated this would be different.

"I'm ready. I got this," Gregory said, waving Marty away and walking into the living room carefully, taking in the scene in front of him. The young detective spotted nothing out of the ordinary. He walked gingerly through the hallway to the bedroom.

"She was found by her mother, who had access to her apartment and checked on her when she hadn't heard from her in a few days," Marty explained as they walked. "Her mother could tell by looking at our victim that she was gone when she walked in. She's the one who called it in. The frightened woman was afraid to touch anything and destroy any evidence, which was lucky for us."

They walked into the bedroom where the victim lay. Gregory stilled his stomach, the shock giving him a visceral reaction. He had seen dead bodies before, but this one sent dread pooling in his gut. His pace slowed as his eyes took in the scene.

"Oh shit, I don't like this. She looks so damn…peaceful?" Gregory frowned and shook his head as he dodged the photographers and the technicians collecting various traces of evidence around the room.

"Doreen, what are we estimating as time of death?" he asked.

The coroner, Doreen Heather, responded as she jotted down some notes in her notebook. She was a sturdy, middle-aged woman with bright blue eyes and fuzzy, light brown hair. "I'm thinking sometime between eleven p.m. and one a.m. Cause of death is not obvious right now. She looks asleep, very few signs of struggle. I'll know more once I get her on my table."

Doreen peeled back the blanket as she examined the victim more closely. "No visible traces of DNA," she continued, as she gazed around the room, "but you owe me a drink if I get some touch DNA. We're working carefully to preserve the scene. It's clean. Almost too clean. This killer seems to have dressed her, maybe even put makeup on her."

Gregory shivered and put his hands in his pocket.

So, his first case was going to be challenging.

He shook his head and inhaled, resignation settling in his chest.

"Doreen, I will buy you five damn beers if you find me some DNA," Gregory said, pushing up his dark-rimmed glasses on his straight nose. He turned and called out to Marty, who was investigating some shelves behind him.

"Marty, she looks posed, right? Like she died in her sleep, but not quite?" They both stood back and examined the scene closely.

Gregory pointed to the nightstands. "Look at these books by the bed. They're stacked so neatly. *Great Gatsby*? That's interesting, given the rest of the books on her shelves are romance novels. Seems out of place."

He used his pen to move the book, revealing the one beneath. "*Insomnia* by Stephen King. Definitely creepy. Maybe the killer is sending us a message? Bag these and check them for fingerprints." Gregory raised his eyebrows and turned to look at Marty.

Marty raised his eyebrows in question and shrugged.

"What do you think, Marty? Murder? Suicide? Natural causes?"

Marty frowned and continued to snoop around the room. Gregory furrowed his brow and shook his head.

"This scene makes you almost think she fell asleep and never woke up. She looks too perfect. Posed. People don't sleep with their hands folded angelically beneath their heads like that." He rested his chin on his fist, considering.

The victim was Angela Duffet. She appeared to be sleeping beneath the blanket with her head and arms poking out, hands tucked neatly beneath her left cheek. She wore full makeup. Her hair looked soft and brushed with black curls fanned out on the blanket as though for a photo shoot. The way the bedside lamp was on, her beautiful long, wavy hair was arranged on the quilt, laid out carefully, making her look perfect in death. Too perfect to be natural.

She wore a lacy red slip dress, something definitely suited to the bedroom. Gregory chatted with the technicians, looking for other signs of foul play, traces of blood, things in disarray, anything that would point the investigation in a direction. There wasn't much left behind to tell them the story of what happened.

Gregory walked around the apartment, inspecting all the rooms. He looked at the windows. The curtains were closed. Everything was neat and tidy, seemingly in its place. He looked forward to getting more information when he talked to Angela's friends and family. He walked into the kitchen, trying to trace Angela's final steps that night. Two glasses of wine on the counter, lipstick on one glass, dried up traces of red wine at the bottom. The second glass was clean. Immaculate. The counters were spotless, indicating they may have been wiped. If this was a homicide, this might be another message from the killer. The scene had been scrubbed. He looked under the kitchen sink for a garbage the bin was there with the bag removed.

"Hey guys, have all the garbage bags been removed? Let me know if anyone sees one. All signs point to a very thorough clean up," Gregory called out to the team. He could hear Marty's footsteps coming from behind.

"What's your gut telling you on this one?" Marty piped up. "Something unusual about this crime scene, don't you think?"

Gregory paused to ponder for a moment.

"Well, I want to see more of the results from the evidence we've collected. I also want the phone and computer analyzed before I make any call, but the whole scene is suspicious. I have to look at our files. Maybe even some older ones. I can't remember there ever being a homicide like this in the city."

Marty nodded in agreement.

"The killer took a lot of care and pleasure in setting up the scene. He seems to have left us only what he wanted us to find. When a killer is this playful, it makes me think this is not his first time and it probably won't be his last," Gregory added.

* * *

He finished his shift at the office, looking through paperwork and trying to find more information about Angela Duffet. The victim had a clean record and worked at a school close by as a grade two teacher. Gregory had made the difficult visits to her family and had arranged to come interview them once they had had time to process the information.

When they unlocked her phone, nothing seemed suspect. However, Gregory knew it was possible that someone could have erased messages, so he expected to see more from the digital forensic analysis of her computer and phone. He removed his dark brown rimmed glasses and ran his hands through his carefully combed and parted blond hair. It was the end of his shift, so he no longer cared about keeping his appearance neat. He pinched the bridge of his nose to ease the tension headache that was forming. His phone rang right as he was packing up his files to take home to read and saw it was a call from his supervisor, Antonio.

"Greg," he started, "Tell me you've got some leads on this case."

Gregory shuffled his papers nervously, looking at his files. "Yup, I've got some strong possibilities. I'm waiting on some DNA results, and I'm eager to see what's on that phone so I can get cracking on sketching out her last few days."

Antonio paused on the other end of the phone line. "We have to keep this one under wraps for now. It might scare the public. Keep the details quiet until we know if there's something the public needs to know."

"Of course, no need to frighten people for nothing."

"Listen, Greg, let me know if this case is too big for you. I have faith in you, but I'm also aware that you're new to this role. This is a big leap from traffic policing."

Gregory paused to gather his thoughts and find a way to reassure Antonio. "Don't worry, man. I have a lot of stuff to work with here, and I'm confident we can get this case solved quickly. I'm interviewing a few witnesses, and I know I can lean on Marty if I need to. I can handle it. I've got this in the bag."

Gregory frowned, thankful he could not be seen by his supervisor and knowing he definitely did not have this in the bag. They hung up, with Antonio sounding reassured and Gregory feeling like his neck was out more than ever with this case.

He climbed into his car and drove home, looking forward to studying his notes and catching up on some TV. As was his habit, he drove slowly by his crime scene, seeing the lights were out and gazing out of his car windows to inspect the area around. He had an eerie feeling there were eyes watching him as his car crept past the site. His gut did not usually lead him astray, so he kept a close eye on the property, hoping someone would be loitering around the scene, maybe even his suspect. There were no unusual agents out on this night, so he continued driving on to his apartment building. He sighed, thinking he would be eating another microwaved burrito tonight.

Gregory lived alone and kept only minimal groceries on hand, since his shifts were always unpredictable. He relied heavily on takeout and frozen meals to give him the energy he needed to keep going. When he was a child, it seemed as though meals with loved ones were sacred, an essential part of their daily routine. As a big family, they ate, laughed, and talked about their day. It was truly a time he treasured, now that he entered his sparsely furnished apartment.

Gregory went into his bedroom, changing into comfortable charcoal sweatpants and a grey t-shirt. He laid out his files on the table and quietly ate his warm, soggy burrito.

As he gazed around him, then down at the files he would be working on, he realized that despite his work keeping him always busy, his life, like his apartment, seemed empty. He blew a pent-up sigh over his burrito, watching the steam as it danced away in front of him. His life had everything he needed in it. After all, his only focus was solving this case and earning his place in the major crimes department. He had little time for anything else. His hands scrubbed his weary eyes, then he straightened his spine and returned to his meal. This break couldn't last too long, he had to get back to work. The files needed his careful perusal. The victim needed him to be on guard and fight for her. A killer was walking the streets of Marda Loop and there was no way of knowing if or more likely, when he would strike again.

3

LOUISE LEANED HER HEAD AGAINST the cool leather headrest, eyes closed.

She was safe.

Inhale.

Exhale.

One, two, three, four.

Her beloved community was safe.

She didn't live alone.

No one was coming for her.

Her eyes flicked open, and she took in her surroundings and sighed. She loved her neighborhood. She felt a deep appreciation for Marda Loop's unique vibe, as well as its warm and welcoming businesses. She knew her local coffee shop owner and all her favorite workers at the grocery store. Everything about the area filled her with the sense of safety for which she longed. The fall season changed Marda Loop into a stunning mélange of orange, yellow, red, and maroon leaves bursting between the houses on pathways and in parks.

The day was damp and fresh because of the previous evening's rainfall, and Louise breathed in deeply. The intoxicating air after autumn rain was a comforting odor that filled her with calm.

She was stronger than before.

She had walked through the fire and survived.

She turned around and looked at her mother's adorable home, Cambrai Cottage as Georgie called it. The cottage was a small two-story home with white siding, black shutters and roof, as well as a bright red door. It was a beautiful and cozy home that Louise had made her own after the worst night of her life. Her mother had encouraged her to take what felt like a step backward, moving to a safe haven in order to help her heal. Georgie was a source of strength and comfort for Louise.

Each day required some effort, but she was not raised to live anything but a full life. It had been humbling to take that step back in her productive and successful life. It was hardly the ordinary suburb where she had grown up, in the time when her parents were still married. When her parents divorced, she was in her early twenties, renting a small townhouse in Marda Loop. Her mother decided she wanted her new life to be in this vibrant, bustling part of the city. When she at last found the Cambrai Cottage, Georgie felt alive again, like she could breathe freely in a way she hadn't for thirty-six years of marriage. Georgie had made herself whole and was living the busy and fulfilling life she wanted. Louise had hoped that by living with her mother she could absorb some of that resilience and strength. Perhaps she could unlock some of the fearlessness she had possessed before he had entered her life. Perhaps she would feel whole again one day as well.

It took her a moment to notice that she would have to scrape the windshield because it had frosted over from the night before. The gloomy cloud and fog that covered Calgary in the fall had a certain charm. Gone was the intense and relentless heat of summer on the prairies, as well as the smoke from the surrounding forest fires that occurred every year. The air was clean and crisp and the colors vibrant. She cursed herself for not wearing gloves, for it seemed premature in September. Yet here she was, grumbling as she scraped her lousy windshield for the first time this year.

She arrived for eight in the morning at the law office of McCarthy and Braithwaite, a criminal law firm located in busy downtown Calgary. Louise worked as a law librarian, in charge of fact-checking, research, and acquiring the information for the lawyers in the firm.

She came out of the parking elevator and scanned her key card to get the security gates to open, which would allow her access to the rest of the building. This was a benefit of her job — she felt secure and safe thanks to the high level of security in the building.

To access the upper floors, one had to scan to get through the main floor gates, then tap a key card to go to their elevator floor in the building. She nodded to the guard as a brief thank you for performing his duty. The elevator took her to the thirty-eighth floor and she walked to her clean, sleek modern office. She shared a large room with multiple large desks neatly arranged in rows with her best friends Anika Sharma and Simone Cormier. Louise also had access to a large library with floor to ceiling law books and various other textbooks pertaining to their research.

Since their adjacent library was missing the tome she was looking for, Louise made her way to the secondary library in the office, where the overflow books were stored. Louise's work environment was most likely a product of her passion for books. She was most comfortable surrounded by them and they spoke to her in a revealing and non-judgmental way. Touching the embossed spines and smelling the delicate pages evoked a calming sensation inside Louise. Books were quiet companions, speaking very loudly only when called upon to reveal their secrets.

Since the night she had been assaulted in her old townhome, she prayed that something would occur to expose her attacker, though the absence of clues was disheartening. She seldom traveled back to that night in her mind, knowing it would create an emotional storm within her that she had trouble controlling. Louise had a hard time shaking the guilt, feeling she could have done more to fight back, remembered more details during the investigation, or been stronger for herself. She was also reminded that her attacker was still out there.

Louise sighed loudly as she gazed sightlessly out the window. Those thought patterns ended up nowhere, except getting her a lecture from her mother and a few nights with less sleep. The first thing she needed for justice was a few matching cells of DNA. They had the evidence, yet no one to whom they could connect it. Only a match with a living, breathing human being would bring her the true feeling of safety and peace she sought.

She jumped as her phone rang and she picked up, seeing it was Simone calling. Louise smiled seeing the screenshot that popped up when she called. Louise gazed at the photo of them at the bar, taken about five years ago, when they were celebrating some university friend's birthday. They looked so hot and so carefree. And totally drunk. It seemed like a lifetime ago.

"Hey, where the hell are you? Anika and I are waiting in the lobby for you." her friend asked.

"I'm in the Carmicheal Library, what's going on?" she said as she glanced at the clock in the room. "Oh my gosh! Sorry I am missing our lunch date. On my way!" She hung up and dashed to meet her friends in the lobby. They walked to Cucina, their favorite lunch spot, where their usual table was waiting for them.

Louise and her friends glanced at the menu, though they always ordered the same items. Louise opted for a goat cheese and beet salad with a side of grilled chicken. Simone ordered her grilled cheese and soup, and Anika got the fresh homemade pasta with tomato sauce. They all shared a carafe of bubbly water, avoiding the glass of wine they were all longing for, since they had to go back and finish their work at the law firm.

Anika got their attention with a radiant smile and a hand she brought up to her face, which sparkled with a new diamond ring. Simone and Louise gasped in unison.

"Well, ladies, I have an announcement," Anika shared while Louise and Simone looked at each other in surprise, "Tom and I are getting married!"

The ladies all gave each other hugs around the table, rejoicing at the happy news. Anika and Tom had been dating for nine years, since they had all hung out together in first-year university.

Anika continued, her face glowing with happiness: "I have a second announcement: You are both going to go broke because I cannot imagine anyone else being my bridesmaids! It's going to be a destination wedding. Buckle up, ladies, we're going on an adventure!"

Louise and Simone cheered and clapped together.

Excitement flared up inside Louise, living vicariously through her dear friend, glimpsing an old part of herself, thinking of the events that would be planned for Anika and the fun they would have. She loved throwing parties at one time in her life. Her friend's joy made her long for the free, carelessly joyous person she had once been. The person she could be again, if she just tried. It was heartening to see her friends moving along on their life paths, Anika getting married, and Simone articling and preparing for her bar exam next fall. Tired, Louise felt like she was standing still, no relationship, no apartment, and no travel or future plans to prepare for. If you googled "things that will never change", the name Louise Dubois would be sitting there between the sun rising and setting and the past.

In fact, it was best to forgo that particular google search, it was a downer.

"Loulou...hello?" Simone chirped testily and waved a hand in front of her. She had zoned out completely. How rude.

"Louise, we are talking to you right now. Listen.... Anyway, I'm going to ask you again. Could you host an engagement party at your place? My place is under renovation until January, so it's a mess," Simone asked. "Plus, I live above my parents' garage, so it's not exactly a place to host that many people."

Louise nodded, and smiled, attempting to appear extra attentive, after being caught daydreaming.

Wait. Did she want to host an engagement party at Georgie's?

"You know, I haven't hosted anything in a long time. I'm not even sure I know where to start, am I the right person for this?" Louise said nervously.

Simone rolled her eyes. "O-M-G, Loulou, you have thrown so many parties. I just know you'll figure it out. And I'll be here to help too. Eek, I'm so excited, Ani!" Simone said with great confidence and determination as Louise just sat there, mouth agape for a moment then rolled her eyes and nodded in silent agreement.

"Let's just wait and see how big the guest list is. We can only fit so many people at my mom's place," Louise said.

She had a strong urge to not have anyone invading her space, but it was overcome by her love for her friends and wanted to take part in celebrating this wonderful occasion. She convinced herself she could be enthusiastic, masking her inner reluctance. Her mother's mantra, "fake it until you make it" rang in her ears. It brought a willing smile to her face and helped her to play the well-adjusted human while masking the turmoil that festered inside most of the time.

"Sure, let's write up a guest list and see if it'll work," Simone said.

"Sounds good," she told her friends, "I can host the engagement party at my mom's house." She feigned embarrassment for still living with her mum and shook her head, giggling with her friends. "Won't be awkward at all, ha ha…" Louise said with a straight face.

Louise wasn't sure whose bag the notebook came out of, but their fun lunch was soon taken over by list making, requests, and possible businesses to contact for the party. They settled on having an engagement party soon, a bridal shower in the new year, and later on they would plan a low-key bachelorette.

Louise was sure Simone would make that bachelorette glamorous and memorable. Life was propelling Louise back into the activities she had previously enjoyed. Upon leaving the restaurant, a tingle of joy and excitement for the celebrations to come reverberated through her. There would be plenty of occasions for Louise to flex her party planning muscles again and maybe, just maybe start living her life again on her terms. Nothing would get in the way of her pseudo-comeback, because whether or not she was ready, it was happening.

4

PATIENCE. THIS WAS ONE OF THE WORST PARTS OF THE JOB. The patience required when the crime scene had been processed and Gregory had to twiddle his thumbs, waiting for more information to trickle in. He had thoroughly researched Angela Duffet's life, a seemingly innocuous existence as a teacher, lots of positive interviews with her friends and family seemed to add a layer of challenge to the investigation. There were no obvious enemies, no clear motives or concerning actors in her life, save an ex-boyfriend who, on the surface, seemed to have very little motivation to kill the victim. He clearly still loved her. Nothing would be ruled out this early, though Gregory felt at a loss for which avenue to pursue next. He had scanned his crime scene photos — they were so clean — and reviewed his interview notes. He emailed the various departments processing the evidence and was put off, once again.

Gregory scratched at the edge of the paper coffee sleeve on his cup and dug deep staring sightlessly at the drink. He loved puzzles. This one was missing some pieces, which they almost always did at first.

"Nice to see you working hard, Greg," a voice startled the young detective out of his pensive cloud. Tony's dark eyes were judgmental as he crossed his arms over his generous midsection. His supervisor always wore brightly colored golf shirts that were clearly chosen by his wife. Tony brought his hand to rub his close-cropped beard as he considered Gregory carefully. A raised eyebrow made Gregory stutter nervously.

"Ah, I'm just…Just putting the pieces together in my head, Tony," Gregory explained, hoping his embarrassment wasn't as evident as the flush that was creeping up his neck. Something about Antonio always made Gregory feel like a screw up. He was a fair, but very demanding boss. He instilled a desire in the young detective to measure up to his high standards every time.

"Greg, I want an update on this file. The news wants an update, and I don't really want to release any information until we've got a suspect or something. People are going to freak out."

Gregory sighed. He scoured his mind for updates.

Did he have updates?

He thrummed his fingers on the desk and glanced at his screen.

He was still obsessively scanning his inbox for DNA results, fingerprints, or digital forensics analysis, but nothing had come in yet. He cleared his throat.

"I've interviewed friends and family, no huge vibes there, but I'm keeping the ex-boyfriend in my sightlines, since two-thirds of the time, it's an intimate partner." He rested his face in his hand, as disappointment etched itself on Tony's face.

"People are going to want more sure leads than that soon, but I'll put them off. Gregory, this case is in the news and there are a lot of eyes on it, don't screw this up." Tony stared at Gregory until their eyes locked and the young detective nodded eagerly.

Gregory gave his supervisor a thumbs up and a nervous smile. He scrubbed his face and left his face in his palm, digging for more ideas in his brain. Tony grumbled, then walked off and Gregory released a nervous exhale.

He read his notes about the killer once again, seeing the profile that seemed to lift off the pages: sexually motivated, the killer liked to establish dominance over his victim. The killer dressed and posed the victim for his gratification, or possibly to shock the ones who found the body. Gregory had never seen a case like this before, even in his past local case studies. One thought nagged at him. If he hadn't killed before, could the killer have found his gratification in other ways prior? The answer, according to Gregory, was a resounding yes.

The killer had premeditated the murder, that was evident to Gregory. The killer found a way to subdue the victim and established communication prior to committing the act. Of course, his damn digital forensics were still being processed. Gregory rubbed his chin while he stared at his computer screen. If the killer spent anytime stalking or seducing his victim, he could be very experienced in hunting, following women. Gregory typed a few related keywords into his search bar.

His page filled with cases that had occurred in the Calgary area in recent years, mostly unsolved peeping and assault cases. Gregory felt a tingle of energy in his fingers as he scanned through the various files, looking for similarities to his case. This could be promising.

He narrowed his search to start looking at cases that had occurred in the South-West quadrant of Calgary, near where his murder had occurred, and was rewarded with a smaller list of cases to review. He eagerly jotted down the case file numbers and went to track down the physical copies in the storage room.

The file room had a smell of old paper mixed with new paper, as well as aging boxes moldering on the shelves. Gregory ran a hand on the tops of the boxes as he read their assigned numbers. He could feel the accumulation of dust, rough beneath his fingers, and immediately pull his hand away. He located the three boxes he would begin combing through, looking for something — anything that might be familiar, or something that might speak to him. He placed them on the empty table in the storage room.

The first file seemed to have a scene that didn't match his current crime, the behavior of the suspect unlike his current perp. The scene was too bloody. The attacker too overtly aggressive. Gregory cracked open the second box, waving his hand in front of his face to disperse the cloud of dust that came bursting forth. After a coughing spell, Gregory cleared his throat and examined the files contained within the box. A gusty sigh escaped his lungs as he perceived the crime to be slightly too old.

The scenes were similar, a bit messy, though he was a firm believer that repeat offenders learned from past experiences. His killer could have been refining his practice, endlessly seeking that gratification. But the case was ten years old.

Gregory noted some items that could be flagged for a deeper examination later. He wouldn't dismiss the case out of hand or would place a sticky note in his brain to examine it later, when he wasn't in such a rush.

His third box had a thinner layer of dust, aged only from three years ago, which was promising. It suited his timeline much better. He scanned the initial call information, and the photo of the victim slipped out, fluttering silently to the ground.

Shit.

He had to treat his evidence more carefully.

Double shit.

A shiver ran through him, his hand shaking ever so slightly.

No, it couldn't be, could it? Calm down, Gregory.

He opened the manila folder from where the photograph slipped out to read the personal details of the victim and his stomach dropped. His finger traced the glossy finish of the photo paper. His chest ached at the sight of the familiar hazel eyes, the flat mouth that always glowed from within when she smiled, and the long silky light brown hair that she had imprisoned in a tight bun. Gregory clutched the photo to his chest, needing a moment to collect his thoughts and emotions.

This was the girl he dated in university.

He still held a place in his heart for her — the one that got away. He shook his head.

This wasn't about his dating history. *Get it together, Band.*

She was a survivor, and her case might have links to his current one.

His fingers tingled where they touched the photo, an electric instinct telling him he needed her for this case. His gut never lied.

He packed up the box and signed it out, knowing he needed to look at it. He had to help Louise, regardless of what secrets the box in his hands held. He would examine the evidence and if it didn't align with the case he was working on, he would at least give it a long perusal in his free time to help Louise.

It was the least he could do, for someone who was once so special to him.

He cleared the files off his desk, reserving a special place for the Marda Loop murderer case in the corner. Gregory made sure his inbox didn't contain any new and breaking information, a sigh escaping as he scrolled through the messages.

Nothing new.

He made space for the box and began pulling out each file, each scribbled note, and each photograph, to be thoroughly examined. Gregory wasn't sure what he was looking for, but his eyes sought feverishly for more puzzle pieces. Her interview read like a thriller, sending more chills rippling through his body. Gregory was disgusted at what her attacker had done. He kept analyzing each piece of her interrogation, looking for tie backs to the new case and finally, he saw it. It was so quick; it could easily be missed.

Louise Dubois: He said something about seeing me in a red dress, that's when he knew he wanted me.

Detective Langley: Do you know which red dress he was talking about?

Louise Dubois: I guess…I only had one, and I had worn it, but it's been a while.

Gregory slammed the file shut. This was big. This was huge. Would he be able to prove that this killer had been previously roaming the streets of Marda Loop? He called Marty to discuss his next move, which he knew already, of course. They both agreed his hunch was worth exploring.

He had to talk to Louise Dubois.

Gregory picked up his phone and quickly dialed the number listed in the file. He tried to calm his breathing. Why was his heart racing like he had just finished a 5K run? Was he feeling nervous? Of course he was. If his hunch paid off, this could be huge. It would expand the scene of his crime, there could be Louise's case, as well as many more. His search hadn't been thorough and hadn't included every quadrant of the city.

The phone rang until the answering service picked up, and Gregory left a message, telling her to call him back as soon as possible. He wondered if she would remember him; it had been almost a decade since they had seen each other. Did his voice really tremble nervously as he spoke? Hardly the reassuring presence of the upstanding detective he tried to be. Ugh.

Adrenaline coursed through him as he put his jacket on and checked his phone. It was midnight. Of course she didn't pick up. He would call her again. It was imperative that he hear Louise's story for himself. It could be a matter of life and death.

5

LOUISE OPENED HER EYES AND SIGHED DEEPLY in relief to be awakening on a day where she did not have to face people or get out of bed if she was not inclined to do so. She turned to her side, closing her eyes once more to the light penetrating beneath her eyelids.

At moments like these, she wondered how she had allowed him to bring her so low, in this endless pit of despair, which left her feeling empty and entirely void of joy. One would think she was depleted of emotion after all this time, but she did feel. She felt a fear that stalked her every move, tiptoeing lightly behind her, her faithful companion in all her endeavors. Fear, like a poisonous hand gripping her heart and influencing her daily decisions. She saw her therapist regularly to talk through her troubling thoughts and worked hard to keep the toxic fear at bay, knowing that it hindered her ability to live a fulfilling life. At this point in her recovery, she was mostly able to keep the constant worry and fear at bay.

As her mother often said, "if you stop living because of this, then he wins," and the thought played often in her head. It reminded her the importance of not giving up on her goals. Or at least the importance of making goals. Did she have goals?

She wanted to live — to cast off these dark robes and open herself up to living brightly and feeling deeply. The fear drained her, and she fought every day to push past it and have fun. Feel joy. Find meaning. Taste adventure.

She hoped to move out of her mother's home and have her own apartment. Louise longed to go out at night without constantly looking over her shoulder. Something within her always held her back, telling her it was too soon to let her guard down.

When she picked up her phone to check her social media and emails, a message popped up indicating she had a voicemail from the Calgary Police. Louise shivered. What could they possibly have to talk to her about? It had been years since anyone had wanted information on her case. The familiar gathering inside of her chest nearly overwhelmed her. The knot pulled and squeezed within her. She realized she had stopped breathing and released a few deep breaths to center herself. She calmly listened to the message, her thoughts racing when she heard a familiar voice.

Gregory.

She inhaled.

Exhale.

One, two, three, four.

Gregory Band.

The name made her heart squeeze in a completely different way.

Detective Gregory Band.

A soft slippered foot walked on the carpet outside her room.

"Loulou? Are you awake?" her mother whispered, startling her as though she was being caught doing something terribly naughty.

"Yes, Mum. I'm up," she answered.

"Oh good! Waffles are ready for you, sweetie. Come on down when you're ready."

Louise could hear her mother go down the stairs in her usual stilted gait caused by lingering hip pain, from where she could hear the muffled sound of *Father Brown* playing in the kitchen.

She had to bring her racing heart back under control.

Her mother would know she was upset.

Inhale.

Exhale.

One, two, three, four.

Breakfast first, deal with Gregory later.

She devoured Georgie's delicious cooking. Living with her mother definitely had its benefits, besides saving money by sharing living expenses and having someone always taking care of her. Walking into her mom's home after her short time in the hospital three years ago had felt like a homecoming. Even though it was not the house she had grown up in, it was permeated with the scents and feelings of comfort she attributed only to Georgie. Georgie had purchased the home after her divorce from Louise's father, a messy affair she would sooner forget. Louise had not been close to her father since, though it bothered her. Her relationship with her dad would be something she would have to sort out eventually.

Every element of her mother's home, from the cozy furniture, to the lovingly arranged antique knick knacks, to the walls filled with books, embraced her with a sense of healing and comfort. When she moved in, she brought her cat, her clothing, a few precious objects, and her toiletries. Her family and friends had helped her clean out the rental townhouse, it being unimaginable to return to the scene of the attack. Every other part of her old life seemed tainted, even her old furniture and belongings associated with terrifying memories. Louise imagined she would have to buy all new furniture eventually. Start fresh.

Louise's mother made her way out early to go grocery shopping and run some errands, as she did every Saturday morning. Louise switched from the wholesome British mystery to the news channel to change up the comforting background noise and drown out her thoughts during her meal. She enjoyed her breakfast, looking out onto the colorful fall garden, covered in brown, yellow, and orange leaves and a layer of frost that dulled the colors to muted tones. She resolved to go rake up the leaves once she had finished eating. Her mother's backyard was low maintenance, with large flowerbeds edged in stone which lined a stone path that connected the house to the garage.

The cozy fleece of her moss-green sweatshirt cascaded down her back over black leggings. Her bra was considered, then rejected, because bras were torture. She stuffed her feet into some thick socks and her warm brown ankle booties. Finally, she completed the outfit with her knee length sherpa jacket and black tuque to keep out the fall chill in the air. She was relieved when this jacket zipped up easily, since it was stretchy and had always been a favorite. It would survive another season. She grabbed her earphones and sought the refuge of her favorite music while she raked and swept the yard, then threw the leaves in the green city composting bin.

She needed the time to think and raking gave her space to get her thoughts in order.

Louise would call Gregory, of course.

When she returned inside, she was thoroughly chilled, and

decided to take a break on the sofa beneath the warm blanket lovingly quilted by her grandmother. She prepared a cup of orange pekoe tea with milk and sugar and placed it next to her on the side table, along with a couple of cookies. Louise perused the channels, stopping for a quick news update, where she saw the banner at the bottom of the screen reporting that police were seeking information on a suspicious homicide in the neighborhood adjacent to hers called South Calgary.

Police were not releasing any details at the moment, though they encouraged anyone who had witnessed any suspicious activity or who had any dashcam or doorbell camera footage to contact their tip line. Murders were not commonplace in her affluent area and the words "suspicious homicide" sent a chill down her spine. She waited for the banner to pass again to ensure she had read it correctly.

The urge to know more pounded in her chest and she fought against the impulse, knowing it might work against her and feed the fear and paranoia she worked so hard to control. She changed the channel aimlessly, her moment of peace shattered. Louise glanced at her phone, thinking it might be a good time to call Gregory. Her bravery disappeared, and she shook her head, thinking to avoid the call for a little longer.

She got up and slowly trudged up the stairs, deciding to put on her gear and go for a jog. Though she had no clear idea where she would go, her feet led her, as if on auto pilot, on her regular path through the neighborhoods she like to look at while she ran. She had a mapped out five-kilometer jog that she always did and stayed on her usual path.

As she jogged block by block, she subconsciously searched for clues that would lead her to the neighborhood crime scene. She had caught a brief glimpse of the street on the news and recognized a few of the homes. A glimmer of her old self was returning…she was curious…and nosy. The feeling of her feet pounding the sidewalk and sweat dripping down her back was empowering.

She was gonna snoop.

Since the incident, she had relied on self-defense courses and fitness to help her feel strong and capable. Regardless of her fitness level, she still despaired at the extra weight she had gained since she had entered depressed isolation. Her deep appreciation for wine and beer, as well as good food and desserts, meant she would never be skinny. Louise didn't rely on her jogging for weight loss. She simply wanted to be able to outrun any future attackers with strength and stamina. Jogging made her feel breathless and strong. Made her heart race for reasons other than fear.

She squeezed her eyes shut momentarily, thoughts of Gregory flashing in her mind. First, she would snoop the crime scene.

Then she would call Gregory.

6

"Loulou? Loulou?" Louise jolted out of upright in her bed, aware suddenly that she had fallen asleep curled up in a ball on her side, on top of the covers on her bed with her clothing and headphones on. Her brain was foggy, as one did after falling asleep at a strange time during the day.

Her mother called her down for dinner, as though Louise was a child, and she once again felt her old yearning for independence. She made her way downstairs, observing the evening news on the living room television as she made her way to the tiny dining area off the kitchen.

"Mum, can we give the news a break?"

Her mother shut off the television, shrugging as she sat down at the table to eat her meal. Louise filled her plate with meatloaf covered in a brown sugar sauce, roasted baby potatoes, and broccoli.

"I can't believe they found a body in South Calgary," Georgie said, her eyes glowing with curiosity. "The reporter said the death is suspicious, not a lot of details yet though. I wonder what happened."

Louise rolled her eyes. "Well, I probably shouldn't think about it. It makes me paranoid."

Georgie reached across the table and grabbed her hand reassuringly. "You're safe here and no one is going to get you. They'd have to get through me first and I am one tough cookie."

Louise snorted softly, believing her mother, in spite of her misgivings. "Okay well, I did happen to jog by the site today. I just stumbled upon it totally by accident," Louise lied, since she had been actively looking for a large mass of police presence on a street. "It was very quiet, almost spooky. The police tape was up, and a few cruisers were parked out front of the house. I don't want to speculate but it looks like a doozy."

Georgie smirked. "That's my girl. You can't ignore this true crime stuff, it's in your blood!"

Louise smiled lovingly at her mother and chuckled in agreement, getting back to her meal.

Louise had grown up watching *Murder, She Wrote* with her mother and had graduated to the true crime shows she found appealing today, like *Dateline*. She enjoyed the mystery of a crime, especially when she wasn't the targeted victim. The true crime shows were always interesting because the different ways the police officers went about solving a case. They provided a sense of comfort for Louise, which some would consider unsettling, but she wrapped herself in it like a blanket when she was feeling lost. Which was more often than she cared to admit. One never knew what interesting piece of evidence would crack a case. She hoped that watching them would help her find a solution to her own case. Her investigation had technically gone cold, though she hated to admit it. She would have to work up her courage before calling Gregory, since every time someone new was assigned her case, they were always hopeful.

Until they weren't.

The disappointment was crushing.

She would need time to prepare herself emotionally for the call.

* * *

The following Monday, Louise had put away all thoughts of the South Calgary case when she entered her office building and smiled, eager to see her friends. They attended a morning meeting and began working on some new files that had come in. Anika and Louise were assigned to begin work on research for the new case while Simone continued to finish up a few cases that were requiring some final details. Louise lost track of time trying to finish a report that was needed the next day for trial work. She seemed to have looked up and suddenly everyone around her had left for the day, except Anika, who was packing up her things.

"Not sure how to keep up this schedule when I'm so tired. Wedding planning is hard work," Anika said, yawning. She sighed deeply and put on her jacket. "Don't stay too late, Loulou. I can help you in the morning to tidy up any loose ends." She shut off her desk lamp and headed to the elevator.

Louise nodded absently and looked back at her computer screen. She checked her watch, eager to be done, but knowing that she needed more time to finish her notes. The trial was tomorrow, and everything had to be perfect for Braithwaite. He liked his notes organized a certain way and if she didn't follow his exacting demands, she would feel like she failed. She had worked at the law office for long enough that she had almost memorized the different partners preferences. Louise prided herself in always getting it right.

"I'm almost done, it won't be long now," Louise said, turning her attention back to the computer. She felt safe, since some of the partners were still working late as well.

After what seemed like only a few minutes but was actually two more hours. Louise looked around and was suddenly aware of how alone she was.

Louise took a deep breath and told herself everything was fine.

Don't panic. She packed up her things and put her jacket on. A familiar tingle on her skin spread as she braced herself against her desk.

Pack up your things and leave, Louise.

Inhale.

Exhale.

One, two, three, four.

The office was completely silent, save for the constant hum of the ventilation system combined with the sounds of cars outside. She instantly felt the weight of her mistake and started her self-talk to calm down. Her skin crawled, and the hair stood up on the back of her neck.

The stupid sensor lights in the office came to life as she walked toward the elevator, but the darkness before her was suffocating. Louise clutched her bag to her chest and dug through it for her cell phone.

What a dummy.

This hadn't happened in so long, that she had gotten cocky.

She had created a situation and needed her mother. Louise rolled her eyes, ashamed to be scared of the dark, the empty space, and the feeling that he could be hiding. Anywhere. Which was ridiculous.

There were security guards to prevent that exact thing.

She pressed the number to call Georgie.

"Mum?"

"Yes, dear?" Georgie replied.

"Can you walk with me to my car?" Louise asked, her voice small and scared.

"Of course, dear, don't fret. I had wondered why you were out so late."

"I was working on some research and lost track of time."

Georgie, used to Louise's panic attacks for some time, clearly recognized the tone in Louise's voice and worked to keep her talking. It was only seven p.m. and at this time of year everything went dark around six thirty p.m. Normally, Louise took her car home without incident. At this time of the night though, the parkade silence would be deep enough to reach into her soul. This evening felt different, for some inexplicable reason, and she needed a rescue. Perhaps she was more affected by the news reports than she had thought.

She pressed the down button multiple times and impatiently waited for the numbers count up to her floor. Louise knew her sudden attacks of fear and panic were a normal part of her recovery and to be expected, though it was hard when they snuck up on her. She dug around in her purse for her anxiety pill, prescribed by her doctor for sudden attacks and swallowed it with water while still staying on the phone with Georgie. Georgie stayed on the phone the entire time Louise waited. She slowed her breathing to work her way through the attack.

Inhale.

Exhale.

One, two, three, four.

The doors pinged as they opened before her and Louise rejoiced as she stepped into the elevator, pressing the lobby button and then the close door button repeatedly, as though it would make the door close faster. Somehow, the elevator was safer. No quiet and empty corners. She arrived at the lobby quickly, since the elevator made no other stops on the way down. She nodded to the night guards that sat in the black leather chairs and then took the stairs to the parkade. As she walked up to her car, she spoke to Georgie.

"I'm sorry to do this, Mum. I just get so scared sometimes."

Her mother hushed her and reminded her gently. "Do not ever hesitate to call, I will always be here to walk with you when you need."

The click of her own footsteps echoing in the parkade startled her, and she looked behind her. Her heart raced at the haunting sound.

Louise jumped in her car quickly, as though someone was truly chasing her, and locked the doors right away. As soon as the doors locked, she said goodbye to her mother and reassured her that she was on her way home. She clutched at her chest and practiced her breathing to ensure she would be able to drive calmly. Louise drove out of the parkade, breath still shaky in her chest, admiring the reflection of the streetlights as they rolled past her window. She should have left with Anika, knowing that when night fell, and the office emptied out she might be triggered. She had been caught off guard by the way she could almost feel him, as though he was with her, watching. She shook her head, trying to loosen the hold he had on her, and to not feel so afraid.

When she got home, she hugged her mother tightly, saying, "I wish I could shake this hold he has one me."

Georgie hugged her back almost painfully, as if to replenish her strength. "Now, Louise," Georgie replied, "you come from a long line of strong French-Canadian women. You have the courage of generations of settlers flowing through your veins. Rough nights happen. You are strong, and you made it home."

Louise nodded slowly in response to the speech she had heard before.

"We will get past this," Georgie continued. "This murder that has happened nearby must have upset you more than you thought. Did you take your pill?"

Louise nodded again. Her medication made her feel a little groggy, but calmer.

"Good," Georgie said.

Louise warmed up some leftovers, enjoying a late supper and covertly looked up more information about the South Calgary death on her phone, thinking that perhaps if she knew more information, it would calm her nerves. She needed to know what happened in order to be sure she had nothing to worry about. More information would help her confirm there was no possibility that her worst nightmare could be happening: the monster was back roaming the streets of Marda Loop.

7

LOUISE SHOWERED AFTER DINNER, as though to wash away the feeling of her skin crawling, which came every time she thought about him. She watched *The Bachelor* episode she had recorded on the PVR and was subjected to Georgie's inevitable disdain for the show, since she considered it "soft porn". Maybe that's why I like it, Louise thought to herself, at least somebody is getting some action.

It was the best distraction from her earlier episode. There was no way she could sleep, regardless of how well her pill worked. Lingering traces of nervousness ran though her body like electrical currents.

She sat on the sofa surrounded by her warm quilt and flanked by the soft puddle of her grey tabby cat, Cosette. Her gaze traveled outside her window at the empty pools of light on the sidewalk and wondered again if he watched her. If he was lingering there, in the alleys of darkness between the shards of light. A shiver ran through her body as though she knew the answer to her questions. Cosette nudged her insistently, begging to be petted, and Louise's hand automatically rubbed the cat's head, eliciting a soft purr. Her body sank deeper into the sofa, trying to move away from being visible in the window. Feeling paranoid, Louise settled with lowering the curtain to increase her comfort. Louise fantasized about how lovely it would be to be ignorant of all the monsters that lingered in the shadows.

Her phone pinged and brought her back to reality once again. She looked at the message, grateful for the distraction.

Simone: "Bitch, get ready I'm calling you."

Louise snorted with laughter. Just what she needed.

Before she could finish reading her message, her phone began to ring. Louise answered, a smile on her face.

"Hey, Simone. You feeling spicy tonight?" Louise asked.

"As usual," she answered. "I'm calling to speak to the bad bitch that lives inside you. I need a break from studying."

"Alright, give me a second and I'll see if she can come to the phone…." Louise paused for dramatic effect. "Hello? Bad bitch speaking, how can I help you, Simmie?"

"Come be my dance partner. I'm going to the Wild Rose Saloon this weekend and I need a hot girl with stellar dance moves to come with me."

"When?" Louise asked.

"Saturday," she replied, "and don't even try to say no. I know you don't have plans. Ha ha. You've been hiding for long enough. We are getting back out! Don't make me call Georgie to convince you."

"I had a rough night, I can't even imagine going out," Louise said, still feeling weak from her panic episode.

"Perfect reason for a change of scenery. I'll be with you, and we'll change up your routine a bit. It'll be good for you Loulou, trust me," Simone insisted, her skills of persuasion hard to resist. Her friend was close to becoming a lawyer and it showed.

"I don't know, Simmie. I feel so gross and fat now. What would I even wear? None of my party outfits fit anymore. It's been years since I've done anything remotely like partying." Louise despaired; a familiar heaviness settled in her chest. Crowds. Eyes. Exposure. Happy people. All things she dreaded.

"Listen, I don't know who this lady is on the phone, but I want the bad bitch back," Simone demanded playfully.

"Okay. I'll put her back on," Louise answered in a breathy voice with a small chuckle.

"Listen, you are going to go online right after we hang up, order a gorgeous tight, sexy western dress, in a color please. None of that black shit you're always wearing. Put on your cutie boots, because I know your feet didn't gain weight, and rock that body you got. You are not fat and stop calling yourself that. You're just normal. Just buy something cute and show off that body you've been hiding. Got it?" Simone demanded. "Oh, and make sure you eat a good supper because we're getting drunk." As though to punctuate her sentence, Simone hung up.

Louise tried to look up a few online boutiques where she could find a dress and some new makeup with only a few days' notice. There was a beautiful dress shop in Inglewood that she loved, only she hadn't been there in a while, thinking she looked horrible in everything. Trying things on felt like an ordeal. This would take some real effort, Louise thought, tapping her phone to her chin. She would find some dresses and return whatever didn't feel good. She hadn't cared about her appearance in so long, or gone dancing, that she kind of enjoyed the idea of the challenge.

How LONG COULD ONE AVOID their old university fling turned detective?

Certainly, he could wait a few days while she emotionally prepared herself.

Digging back into her memories was such an exhausting exercise. And for what?

Was it worth getting excited about someone working on her case, since the last few times had been dead ends? Louise opted to avoid reality — and her thoughts — within the pages of her latest romance series about a coven of witches. Romance and magic was just the cure she needed for her uncomfortable thoughts.

She would call Gregory tomorrow.

Avoiding this conversation would have been something the old Louise might do, but she was looking to change her old habits and start living her life.

Stop being frozen by those old thoughts and memories.

It was time for action.

So she would call Gregory.

Tomorrow.

She wore her favorite sweatpants and an obnoxious sweater that made Georgie rolled her eyes, which filled her with a bit of satisfaction when she wore it. It read "A LOT GOING ON AT THE MOMENT", which Louise found deliciously ironic. She usually had nothing going on in her life besides the daily routine of work, dinner, television. She chuckled, even though perhaps it wasn't funny. No one could tell her that inside jokes with herself weren't hilarious.

The sudden trill of her phone ringing jolted her out of her reverie. Phone calls always made her feel vulnerable and jittery, though she knew there was no danger in answering. She saw the caller identification labeled "Blocked ID", which made her wary. Allowing her curiosity to get the best of her, she picked up the phone.

"Hello?"

"Hello, may I speak to Louise Dubois, please?" a deep masculine voice asked. Louise squeezed her eyes shut.

Shit.

She knew that voice.

The time for action was now, whether she liked it or not.

"This is Louise. Hi, Gregory."

"Hey, long time no chat. I'm working as a detective with the Calgary Police Service these days, and I'm wondering if you might be able to help me answer a few questions. Are you available sometime soon?"

Louise felt a blush creep on her cheeks at the sound of the familiar voice having such a professional tone. The last she had seen him, he had been a nerdy but adorable university student, with a charming grin that made her heart beat faster.

"Detective Band. Impressive. Good to hear from you, Gregory. I'm not sure how to be of help," she replied.

Louise broke into a quick sweat, suddenly a bit nervous, it had been so long since she had spoken to Gregory Band. Nervous butterflies fluttered in her stomach, or was that nausea? She hated talking about her case with anyone. The feelings of shame and crippling fear always floated to the surface. Imagine spilling her guts to the guy she dated briefly in university? She'd probably rather die. His voice interrupted her walk down memory lane.

"I'm working on a case in your neighborhood and chasing a possible lead. Call it a hunch," he explained.

Louise's eyes widened at the thought of being involved in some way in a case happening in her neighborhood. The confusion muddled her thoughts. She reminded herself that in a phone conversation both people had to talk, so she put together a few words.

"Uh, I'm not sure how I can help," she replied lamely.

"Actually, I'd like to go over your file with you. I've been looking at your case from about three years ago and I'd like to hear what happened in your own words. I know you previously gave Detective Langley your statement, but I want to get it fresh from you." Gregory paused, the silence stretching awkwardly between them.

Louise cleared her throat to give herself more thinking time. "My case? Oh…" She laughed nervously. "I didn't think anyone was working it, it's been a while." She rolled her eyes. Why was she laughing? This was the most embarrassing conversation.

"I've been looking over some cold cases trying to come up with some leads in a hurry. Will you meet with me down at the station? Or I can come to you, if that's easier. I'd like to go over a few details. I had a few questions after reading your file."

Louise sighed rather loudly and may have uttered a quiet, "Oh God."

She sucked in a breath before she spoke aloud. "I'll be honest with you, it's really hard for me to talk about it. I spend so much time kind of…suppressing what those memories make me feel. They haunt me."

She could feel her throat become thick and her eyes fill as she touched the place where her memories hid, ever so briefly. Her hand trembled lightly, adrenaline surging in every part of her body. Every time she traveled back in time, there was a physical cost. She already felt exhausted. And cold, she shivered inside her black sweater.

"I'm sure it does," he replied, "you've been through a lot. I understand that it's hard to relive these memories, but I'd love to catch this creep and see if we might be able to finally get you some justice."

Her mouth would not produce words. She was too afraid to touch that part she kept closed off, to make others think she was moving on — to convince herself she could move on. It was easier to make people think she had recovered from the attack, to avoid making them uncomfortable by showing the turmoil that lived within her. Very few people saw the effects of the attack she still endured every day. Even Georgie had to be protected from some of it.

"I can meet with you tomorrow, I'm not sure what I can add at this point, seeing as so much time has passed, but I'll do anything in my power to find this guy."

"Great. I just have a few questions about specifics. I won't keep you too long," Gregory said.

"Okay, I can help with that. I'll meet you at the station," she replied, reluctant to let anyone enter her home, her sanctuary.

They arranged a time to meet, and Louise began to contemplate what she would wear. It gave her pause to think why she felt she had to look good for this outing, but she ignored any rationale behind that niggling thought.

Simone told her it was time to pay attention to her looks again, to treat herself well, and join the land of the living. That seemed like reason enough to make sure she paid extra attention to her appearance. She did not want to piss off Simone. Besides, there was nothing wrong with leaving her hair down instead of doing her usual tight bun, or applying a bit of mascara or choosing a new lipstick color. Nothing.

* * *

Louise was tapping her phone and staring at the interplay of weathered light grey and dark pewter vinyl composite tile in the waiting area. Gregory was fifteen minutes late from the time she had planned on meeting him. The agony of stretching out her nervousness almost made her get back in her car and leave. Her heart raced almost painfully in her chest and her fingers traveled to her mouth, as though a quick nail bite might alleviate the tension she was steeped in. She saw the handsome detective walking down the hall toward her and as he got closer, her mouth parted, mesmerized. She hadn't known she had missed that face until she saw it. Louise swallowed and took her hand out of her mouth, placing them in her lap. She swallowed as Gregory's mouth split into a huge grin.

Damn.

The years on the police force had clearly agreed with him.

"Gregory. Long time no see," she said, slightly startled by his appearance.

How on earth did Gregory get more attractive? It wasn't fair. There was a good chance it was the uniform, but his dark blond hair with a slight curl, parted and combed to one side and his ocean-blue eyes made her mouth go a bit dry. Even his dark-rimmed, rectangular glasses were hot. She coughed. Must be the dry air at the police station, she surmised.

"Hi, Louise. I'm sorry for the reason I had to call you, though I have to say I was a little excited to see you again. It's been so long. Can I hug you?"

Taken aback, Louise nodded slowly and was rewarded with the most incredible feeling of a hug. Had his arms always felt this warm and comforting? Her eyes closed of their own volition. Her rapid heartbeat instantly slowed, and she pulled away quickly, reluctant to savor the foreign feeling. It was a lot.

"Can I get you some water or coffee or something?"

"No thanks," she cleared her throat and coughed. "I'm good. I really want to get this over with, I've been dreading it."

He nodded. His expression turning serious and his demeanor dripping with sympathy. "Understood, sorry for the wait. If you'll follow me into this room over here."

"Sorry, it's just the longer I waited, the longer I stressed about the interview," she explained. Her hand rested on her chest to still the fast tempo that had recommenced.

"No worries. I get it," he said, a look of non-judgmental understanding in his eyes. His presence made her relax, even though he was virtually a stranger, it had been so long since she had seen him.

He gestured to a small, carpeted room with a navy-blue leather sofa. She placed her purse and jacket next to her. Gregory sat on a chair across from her, next to a table and a second chair. She could see he had a few files stacked on the table. It was disheartening to think an event that made such a powerful impact on her life could be reduced to a small stack of papers in a manila file folder. Gregory shuffled a few papers searching for a particular sheet, his eyes darting over the information.

"Would you like me to get another detective in here? A woman? I want you to feel completely comfortable."

Louise couldn't imagine talking about that night with more people. It was her secret shame, and she wanted the least number of eyes on her as possible. She shook her head, her eyes widening in fear. "I just want to get started."

"So, let me explain the reason we're here today. First, I'm re-examining a few cold cases in your area that might be tied to another case I am working on. I'm sure you saw it all over the news this past week. I can't give you information that pertains to that other case, but I can reveal that I'm looking for evidence that might connect the cases."

Gregory paused, to give Louise a moment to absorb the information. "We've had multiple assault reports in your area over the last few years. Some have been solved, but I'm wondering if we might be able to dig a little deeper and connect your case with some other ones that are eerily similar. I'm trying to find a pattern of behavior, something that would shed light on what's happening in Marda Loop right now."

Louise rubbed her hands together, considering the information. The sudden knowledge that there could be others like her filled her with desolation.

"I can't confirm I'm a victim of a sexual assault though," Louise said, gazing at her hands as she stilled them in her lap.

"I'm not here to compare you to other victims. You were attacked by a horrible person, a dangerous man. You are a survivor." He looked at her and reached over to place his hand on hers.

She flinched momentarily, recoiling at the touch when she was so preoccupied and unused to being touched. She raised her gaze to his and felt comforted by the warmth in his eyes. He looked like he would truly do anything to bring her a sense of peace.

Gregory continued in a soft voice. "I need you to think back to that night and tell me everything you can remember about your attack. Can you do that for me? I'll be recording this conversation, so I don't miss a single thing."

Louise realized in that moment that she had to be brave to achieve the sense of peace for which she longed. Her eyes fixated on the surface of the wood laminate table. She exhaled the breath she had been unknowingly holding, then began her story. Closing her eyes, she could remember the night as though it happened yesterday. Her hands rubbed her arms subconsciously as her body began to feel the impact of her thoughts. As she traveled back in her memories, she felt cold, surrounded by the chill of that October night two years ago.

"I MET MY GIRLFRIENDS FOR OUR WEEKLY yoga night and then we went for a beer after class, around seven. It was a super chilly night, so we went to Marda Loop Brewing for that drink because we did not want to be outside more than necessary, and it was close to the studio. We were giggling because Simone had definitely farted during our yoga class, but she was denying it, which was so hilarious." Louise smiled, thinking of her friends and the laughter they had shared.

She put her head in her hand as she chuckled lightly. "We spent a couple hours there just chatting about work and life. You know, gossiping about guys we were dating, mean bosses, life being expensive, just a bunch of nonsense."

A small smile tugged on her lips when she thought about her how simple their lives had been back then. She had enjoyed her yoga nights and couldn't understand why she never resumed going with her friends. She made a mental note to think more about this later.

Louise sobered as she continued. "The walk home was absolutely wonderful. The air was so crisp with the leaves rustling in the wind and the moisture in the air. It was a pretty typical fall night in Calgary, as you can imagine. I had no issues walking home. I did the walk from Marda Loop Brewing to my house almost every Thursday night. I'd never felt unsafe before. I got to my place, which was a small rental townhouse I had near my mum's house. The house was dark, but that was normal. I had forgotten to leave lights on for myself when I went out. When I unlocked the door, I don't know why, but it felt weird in my house." Louise looked up at Gregory to ensure he was still following. He nodded for her to continue.

"I guess I should have listened to my gut, but I didn't. I noticed that my cat was hidden, which was weird. Cosette usually welcomed me at the door when I came home. Regardless of that, I ended up having a snack in the kitchen, looking out at the backyard. You know, eating and staring out the window, kinda lost in my thoughts. I locked my doors and went upstairs. I got ready for bed the way I normally do, nothing strange. I went to the bathroom, washed my face, brushed my teeth. I was planning to read in bed, which was my normal routine. I stood by my bed, folding the clean clothing I had left on my bed and fussing over a pile of clothes that was sitting there. Sorry, I need a minute…"

Louise swallowed and closed her eyes, placing her head in her hands for a moment, taking her practiced deep breaths to cope with her anxiety. She then rubbed the sides of her neck as her body filled with chills at what was coming next in her story.

"Please keep going, I know it's not easy," Gregory said, as if he sensed she was struggling to continue.

"It's hard because I feel the goosebumps and the hair standing up on the back of my neck like I did at that moment…There was a split second where I know my body sensed the danger, but it was too late. His hands were on me at that moment. He wrapped his arms around me lovingly and smelled my hair. I'll never forget him smelling my hair. It was so surprising…and so revolting. He mumbled something like 'you smell better than I imagined'. I didn't know what to do, so I struggled to get out of his arms, but he was just too strong and had planned everything. He grabbed my hands from behind and zip tied them, which hurt so much. I screamed and screamed, and he flipped me over and placed a sock deep in my throat, so I was choking on it. He tied my legs together, so I wouldn't be able to fight anymore, and covered my face with something like a shirt or dress or something. Once I was completely immobilized, he took his time. He would softly pet me all over my body, almost worshipfully. He rubbed my legs up and down, spent a lot of time kissing my neck and just kind of feeling me all over with his hands and his mouth. Meanwhile, I was bucking and trying to get the sock out of my mouth. I tried to use my legs to kick him, but he was just so heavy he held me down like I was nothing." Louise paused as she watched as Gregory was writing notes on his paper.

"It was seriously like I wasn't even there," she continued, "it was just him and my body. He murmured things like 'I have dreamed of this night' and 'If you just give in, we can have a wonderful time'. Meanwhile, I was trying to figure out what I could use as a weapon. I didn't have anything nearby. After a while he got angry with me, like I wasn't doing what he wanted. I wasn't playing along, or I wasn't behaving. He said if I didn't lie still, he would make me stay still. That was kind of the last thing I remember him saying. Everything happened really quickly after that. I managed to get the gag out, I rolled over fast and screamed. I jumped up to my bedroom window, screamed out the window and banged my head on it, hoping someone would hear me. He grabbed me and threw me on the bed violently and put his hands around my neck, squeezing until I passed out.

"Maybe he thought I was dead, I'm not sure, but I remember waking up on my front lawn, lying on the gurney with an oxygen mask on my face. I was shivering with cold, and I was so groggy. I saw Mac, one of my neighbors, but I'm not sure where he lives. He was talking to the police and there was no sign of the guy who had attacked me." Louise looked down at her hands and sniffed, chilled by the flood of painful memories. She rubbed the arms of her light cotton sweater, trying to warm herself despite the comfortable temperature of her surroundings.

"Who found you?" Gregory asked in a quiet voice, seemingly worried about startling Louise. She had submerged herself so deeply in her haunting memories.

"I had opened my window a crack earlier in the day, when it was warm and sunny and had forgotten it. Mac heard me screaming and yelled from the back door, checking in on me. They told me that my assailant ran out the front door, knocking Mac over and disappeared into the night."

"You were very lucky your assailant was interrupted. Did you get the impression he would have let you go after? From what you described, it doesn't seem likely," Gregory inquired.

"It seemed like he was oblivious to me and got very upset when I fought back. He wanted me still and silent. When I wouldn't obey, he got really pissed and took it to the next level. I think I survived because we got interrupted and because I passed out. Once I wasn't fighting back, he could do whatever he wanted." As she spoke, Louise touched her throat in the spot where no visible scars remained, but the feeling of breathlessness would never be forgotten.

"I know your memory is patchy, but do you think he raped you?"

"We did a rape kit to check, and the nurse collected DNA from various parts of my body where he touched. They also collected the zip ties, but he wore leather gloves. I could smell them, so I wasn't surprised when there were no fingerprints left behind or anything by his hands. My rape kit came back negative for semen, though DNA from his mouth was collected from where he put his mouth on me. When I woke up, my throat was sore, but I didn't feel any-thing suspicious down there really. He made his intentions quite clear." Louise breathed deeply and looked at Gregory who was still furiously jotting notes. He glanced up and nodded for her to continue.

"I could tell you with utmost certainty that he knew my routines. He knew I kept my back door unlocked if I went out. Ugh, it's so stupid now that I think about it. He said he loved my yoga pants, but he planned on me putting on my red dress for our first special night together. He said he knew when he first saw me in my red dress that he would make me wear it for him. I had enticed him and when he saw me in that dress, he knew I was meant to be his. It makes me sick to think how long he would have been watching me. I couldn't even remember when he saw me in my red dress, so it had been a while." Louise looked away shamefully, mortified in the retelling of her tale.

"Can you remember any more physical details about him? I know it was nighttime, and your eyes were covered from what I read in the report, but I'd like you to close your eyes and describe what you can remember about his appearance to me."

Louise closed her eyes and saw him only in brief flashes. "He had dark hair and was very clean cut. Orderly. His hair was held down by something, gel or some product. He was clean shaven and wore dark clothing. I felt his leather gloves on my body. His jacket was stiff, so maybe also leather jacket or a bomber or something?"

Gregory asked if she remembered any details about his face.

"I remember he rubbed his face on mine and inhaled deeply. I only saw him briefly from the side, then he put me face down and had my face covered for the time I was with him."

"What did his face feel like," Gregory asked.

"It was baby smooth," she replied.

"Were his cheeks kind of chubby or slim? Was he bony?"

"No, he was trim. Fit, I'd say. He was very strong. I fought back, but it was absolutely no effort for him to hold me down. He must work out a lot. Every part of him was hard, muscular," Louise replied. "He was average height, not too tall. He wasn't towering over me or anything."

"What did he smell like?"

Louise paused, since she hadn't thought of that detail the last time she was interviewed. She closed her eyes, leaned back and inhaled. Touching those parts of her brain that held her scent memories. She could hear her screams, feel his painful grip, and the tight squeeze of the zip ties. She could smell...what was it?

"He smelled like a combination of mint, but not like any mint I'm super familiar with." She inhaled again. "I could also smell a vanilla cupcake, maybe? He smelled strongly of mint and very sweet vanilla."

"Can you guess a brand, maybe? A gum, a mint, something like that?" Gregory persisted.

"I can't say. I don't really know any. It was strong and unusual. Mint and vanilla. Yep, definitely mint and vanilla. It smelled like an unusual combination to me for a man," she replied pondering the question in her mind.

Gregory paused after her response. "Okay, this might sound strange, but it could be significant. Have you ever smelled products to try to figure out what it might be? Or tested different mints?" Gregory asked. "I know, not exactly what you want to be doing after a trauma, but your nose could be a pretty powerful witness. It has been a long time, and it's hard to say if you'd be able to nail that down to any degree of specificity, but maybe?"

"No, that never occurred to me, I guess I could try," she offered. Her curiosity was piqued at the idea that there was something she could do. Louise curled her hands in her lap, her mind racing with how she would begin such an investigation.

Her own investigation.

It was empowering.

"Well, don't feel any pressure, I'm just thinking out loud. Do you think he lives in your neighborhood? Have you ever seen someone similar since?" he asked.

Louise paused to consider. "No, I haven't. But I will say, even though I moved, I still live near the original house and sometimes I worry that he's watching me or looking for me. I probably should have left town or changed neighborhoods, but I feel safer living with my mum. And in this neighborhood, I know a lot of people and feel like my neighbors are always watching out for me. They were so good to us when everything happened. Pretty much the day I was released from the hospital I was living with my mum. My family and my friends cleaned out my house and moved me out while I recovered. My neighbors brought over food and really took care of us."

Louise neglected to add she had yet to feel completely safe in any surroundings since that night. She may not have seen him, but she always felt his presence around her. Knowing her attacker had never been caught left her forever looking over her shoulder, waiting for him to come and finish what he started.

Louise cautiously asked Gregory why he had decided to look at her case at this time. He explained that he was revisiting some old, but similar cases to see if he could make any connections between them. He cautioned her that he was working on a hunch and could be wrong. It was too early to get their hopes up, and DNA testing took time to get results.

Louise nodded in understanding, feeling the tiniest ray of hope begin to flicker within her. She felt her knees come up to her chest and hugged them to her, trying to keep the hope sheltered deep within her. As though sensing she had had enough, Gregory told her she had answered all his questions for that day.

He stood and Louise was relieved to see the interview was over.

"Well, Louise, it was great to see you again. Thank you so much for coming into chat with me. I really appreciate you going through all this for the sake of this case. I want you to know I'm working hard for you. We're examining old evidence, comparing old files and trying to make connections to see if we can get a break in the case."

He took her hand as she got up and squeezed it reassuringly, then reminded her to give him a call if she thought of anything else that could be useful. She marveled at the warmth she could feel emanating from his hand as his thumb carelessly brushed the top of her hand. It was so soft and comforting. She stared at their interlocked hands for a moment before pulling away.

Gregory walked her back to her car and waved her off once he saw she was safely buckled in. Louise smiled as she backed out of her parking spot. The presence of Gregory in her rear-view mirror filled her with a foreign sense of warmth and comfort. She truly believed he had the power to solve any case to which he devoted himself. What would it mean to be working so closely with him again? Would she even see him again? Louise struggled to decide how she would feel if she did.

10

SATURDAY ARRIVED and a tremendous amount of trepidation burned in Louise's chest. She fretted over her preparations for her first night out in what seemed an eternity. Why had she even agreed to this? Oh yes, she wanted to live again. Do stuff. Be interesting. Going to the Wild Rose Saloon seemed like starting off by jumping into the deep end. She had to do everything in her power to keep her intrusive thoughts from holding her back.

It had been a while since she had put effort into her appearance, and she walked back into it like riding a bicycle. It felt nice. When she finished getting ready, Louise looked in the mirror and gasped at how different she looked. She had transformed herself with the help of a beautiful burgundy mini dress dotted with a soft antique floral in a mixture of pink and dark green tones and enhanced with a layer of tulle beneath and puffy sleeves. She touched a lock of her soft, light brown hair, the long curls resting upon her shoulders. She hadn't curled her hair in such a long time. Louise used to spend hours doing her hair and makeup.

It was nice to have a reason to do that again. She even delighted in her cleavage, which reminded her that gaining weight wasn't all that bad. Her curves looked amazing in the adorable dress she had picked from Adorn after much hesitation. She couldn't remember the last time she had browsed a boutique, looked at a few styling videos and enjoyed trying on beautiful outfits.

Louise dusted off that part of her French-Canadian roots, which insisted that she always look stylish, regardless of her size. It would not do to punish her body by shunning its new appearance or cloaking it in dark swathes of clothing. Louise had been so obsessed with being the woman she had once been. She had forgotten about the amazing person she was becoming despite her history.

The focus of her life could not be events from the past, for their all-consuming power would drain her of the ability to live. She looked at the beautiful twenty-nine-year-old woman in the mirror and realized she was much stronger than who she had been in the past. She had survived trauma and was rebuilding her life and reveling in a new strength and resilience.

Telling Gregory her story had been exhilarating. Even the thought of catching the man who had attacked her filled her with drive. It was time to start looking at that woman in the mirror with more love and respect for all that she had overcome. And what she was going to accomplish. She giggled and twirled in the mirror, enjoying the feel of the silky fabric and the rustle of the tulle skirt instead of her usual trusty cotton. She spritzed herself with her favorite Jo Malone perfume in the red roses scent and walked downstairs to wait for Simone. Georgie had tears in her eyes when she walked into the kitchen.

"Wow. Louise, you look so beautiful, you are glowing. I love seeing you so happy. You are going to have so much fun!" Georgie brought her hands to her mouth as she scanned Louise from to toe. Her mother nodded in approval. "Call me if you need a ride or anything and I'll come."

Louise checked her purse for her pepper spray and keys, as well as a credit card and her favorite Bobby Brown Parisian Red lipstick. The bright red hue was the final piece of her armor that would help her get through the night. *Be normal. Have fun. You can do this*, she thought to herself.

She hunted in the closet for her black pea coat, since the nights in Calgary were always chilly when the sun set in the fall. The jacket she put on was a little tight, so she left it open. Simone entered the house like a gust of wind, looking gorgeous in her black patent cowboy boots and belted plaid shirt mini dress. She undid her buttons down to almost her belly button letting her lace bralette peek through, which did not shock Louise.

By this point in their friendship, Louise accepted Simone's appreciation for showing excessive cleavage when going out socially. Simone had left her long blond hair loose and wavy, flowing down to her mid back.

"Lou, you look amazing! I can't believe how long it's been since I've seen you in beautiful colors. You are so adorable!" Simone exclaimed as she took Louise's hand and twirled her to better see the entire outfit. "That dress is so gorgeous! I see you understood the assignment, my friend."

Louise positively sparkled in white cowboy boots and her mini dress. A few impulse buys, some curls in her hair, bright lipstick of course, and she felt like a different person. The friends climbed into an Uber and giggled with new excitement. Louise looked at Simone with gratitude for forcing her out of her comfort zone. It had been a long time since they had done something so fun and frivolous together.

A familiar wave of heat whooshed across her skin as she entered the Wild Rose Saloon. The air was thick and humid with the crush of people dancing and talking. She recognized the familiar tangy scent of beer taps and bar cleaner. She had spent many nights here in university and came back yearly when Calgary Stampede rolled around. Simone grabbed her hand and led her through the bar. Her friend looked around after reading a text on her phone, as though searching for someone, which lead Louise to suspect they were not going to be just the two of them. Simone turned, taking Louise's hands in hers, and gave her a mischievous look. Louise was instantly on edge.

"Don't be mad, but I have a surprise…"

Louise hated surprises. She frowned at Simone, trying to guess what a surprise might be.

"I invited some guys to hang out with us, but you know them already, so no stress, okay?" Louise felt her mouth flatten in response. The idea of hanging out with guys was so foreign to her these days, she would have to pivot.

Was she ready to pivot?

They walked toward a booth and Louise's stomach dropped to her feet as she saw who was sitting at the booth waiting for them. Louise pulled Simone aside as they walked to the booth.

"Simone, I can't believe you would bring me here to meet with these guys. I just spilled my guts to Gregory and now I have to hang out with him? So cringe," Louise whispered to her friend as she sighed in a peeved manner.

The last person she wanted to see; after telling him her deepest, darkest secrets was Detective Gregory Band.

Simone shrugged in response. "It'll be like old times. Aren't you trying to be more outgoing? What better way to practice then with guys you're already somewhat comfortable with?"

"Just answer me this," Louise asked, "why is it that I don't see this guy for nine years and now I see him twice in one week! It's so crazy!" She groaned silently.

Simone gave her a stern look, as though to remind Louise she had to behave. "Forgive me, Lou," Simone replied, "but you'll just have to be a good sport tonight. If I told you in advance, you wouldn't come. I want to make it a double date with Roger on purpose. I think I like him, but I'm not interested in anything serious. We recently reconnected, and he's a fun hang. He's newly divorced, so I know he won't bug me to be his girlfriend or anything. So what if he's friends with Greg? You don't have to hang out with him at all after tonight, I promise." Her friends voice switched to a high pitch as she greeted Gregory and Roger in her bubbly and enthusiastic way.

Louise groaned inwardly but forced a small smile and a weak "hi."

Louise slid into the booth and sat waiting with Simone for the guys to fetch some beers at the bar. She was struck by how much this reminded her of their nights partying in university. Only Anika and Tom were missing to round out the group. Her smile returned as she remembered their wild nights blowing off steam.

"What happened with his wife Bianca? They were stuck like glue in university," Louise asked with curiosity. "Spill the tea!"

"I don't really know yet," her friend replied.

Simone held a hand up, mouthing a silent "later" and watched the men as they approached with four frosty mugs of Budweiser. It was Saturday night, and Louise was much too happy to be out and much too thirsty for this beer to turn back now. Besides, she looked hot and felt slightly powerful tonight, like she had put on her armor before battle.

Louise grew concerned as she noticed Simone and Roger seemed to down their beer alarmingly quickly, as the four of them enjoyed light conversation. Suddenly the other couple was getting up and enthusiastically joining the other partiers on the dance floor. Louise rolled her eyes inwardly with frustration and glared at them, knowing she had been abandoned with Gregory.

"So, how is the investigation going?" she asked, attempting to initiate conversation using a safe subject.

"We're still in an information-gathering phase, following whatever leads we find. Have you remembered anything new?" he prodded gently. "I'm off the clock, but I'm always here to listen."

She shook her head, spinning her beer and focusing on the label to avoid his gaze.

"We can be normal with each other, right? I know we did that interview, and it was stressful, but I hope we can still be friends," he said. "Can you believe it's been almost a decade since we dated? University seems so long ago now."

"Yeah," she said, laughing softly, "I guess things have changed since then. I'm pretty awkward at social interactions since I don't really go out much these days. Just work, home, work, home, on an endless cycle." She looked away from him regretfully, feeling she sounded like a loser. Gregory cleared his throat, probably feeling that the energy had changed.

"Want to dance? Or should I get us another round of beers? We've got a lot of catching up to do," he said.

"Sure, let's have another beer. I'm not quite ready to dance yet." A clutch of nerves gripped in her chest, as she was always hunting for normal answers to normal questions. *Have I really forgotten how to human?* She scanned the dance floor and was amazed at how life could be so simple. People would just hear the music and move, have fun, no hang-ups getting in the way. A surge of something like envy filled her. If she wanted to be normal, she had to try. Push herself out of her comfort zone, especially when she was surrounded by people that made her feel so comfortable.

Simone and Roger came back giggling and thirsty for more beer. They sat down with them and joined the conversation yet again. Simone seemed to be her usual flirty self, which worried Louise only a bit, since Roger was just coming out of his divorce and might be more vulnerable than Simone anticipated. Roger married Bianca, his college sweetheart, right out of university. Louise didn't know any details about the breakup, but she could imagine it might still be a sore spot. Simone had whispered only that it was messy and had left their friend very bitter, so it was best not to ask him about it tonight.

Louise recognized that if Simone thought a date with Roger was a good idea, she would have to trust her friend. Louise had enjoyed hanging out with Roger and their group of friends in university. They always had fun when they partied together. Now that they were all adults making their way in the world, all with their own challenging experiences under their belts, it was like getting to know each other anew. Conversation came easy and helped Louise to paint a better picture of what the men's lives looked like now. She was glad the men had remained close, and that boded well for them maybe reconnecting their circle of friends.

It only took a bit more convincing to get Louise to join her friends on the dance floor. To her dismay, they arrived just as a song was finishing and a romantic ballad began to play. All the couples around them began to dance and Louise looked at Gregory like a deer in the headlights. Her face burned with embarrassment. She could feel the nervous flush coloring her cheeks. Just be normal, she kept telling herself.

Gregory shrugged and wrapped an arm around her waist and grabbed her hand on the opposite side. Louise scoffed inwardly at the way her body warmed once again to his touch. She hadn't been touched in such an intimate way in a very long time.

The feel of his hand splayed around her waist sent a tremor of longing through her. Her heart began to race again. Why did her heart always race when he touched her? She wondered if it was the unfamiliar and, until now, unwanted touch of a man that sent her body into an instant flush of warmth. Unbelievable.

"Is this okay?" he asked, feeling her hesitation as they began to dance. Her breath hitched with every new touch.

"Yeah, it's okay," she replied. *Act normal*, she kept saying to herself in her head. *Have fun. This is what fun is supposed to feel like.*

She could hear the low soulful voices of the band filling the dance floor and felt herself relaxing in Gregory's arms in spite of herself. Her head fit perfectly on his strong shoulder, and she inhaled the scent of him, alarmed at how deliciously comforting his scent was. From their few dates together, she could remember how good he always smelled. Her entire body become heavy, as though filled with a calming drug and connected to the rhythm of his breath in his chest.

For all the awkwardness she was displaying, he had a way of calming the nervous tingles in her body and quieting her constant survival mode, replacing it with a happy haze.

"You know, it's been really nice seeing you again. When I changed schools, you know I had my reasons. It was a hard time, and I missed our friendship. This has been… fun," he said carefully.

She looked up at him and leaned her head back against his chest. "Yeah, I was pretty bummed," Louise agreed with a smile. "But I wasn't looking for anything serious. It made sense at the time. It's too bad we lost touch. I'm not glad I'm involved in this case, but I'm happy it kind of brought us back together."

Perhaps it was the cloying warmth of the bar or the delicious smell of his Old Spice deodorant or maybe it had been so long since she had welcomed the feel of another's arms, but she was feeling overwhelmed by the sensations inside her. He made her feel sleepy while simultaneously awakening a chaotic jumble of need within her. She peeked up at him to see if he was suffering in this bliss as much as she.

I missed our friendship.

Friendship.

Louise shook her head, trying to distance herself from where her thoughts were heading. Her gaze fell upon his soft, generous mouth and felt her insides puddle with longing. Had his eyes always looked this blue or were his dark brown glasses accentuating them? Louise had missed his friendship too, but she was feeling certain less than friendly feelings toward him. She closed her eyes to break the contact they had with his skin, his mouth, his warm gaze. She wondered if there was a way she could stop the feeling of heat radiating from each spot where his hands were touching. It was all too much. She was broken. Plus, she had been down this road before with Gregory and it ended painfully. She didn't want more pain; she wanted life, excitement, goals. Not more pain.

She started to breathe heavily as though having a panic attack and looked at him in alarm, her eyes a plea for help. Then she walked off the dance floor, away from the crush of people. She ducked away in a side hallway and pressed herself against the cool slate-grey colored wall, breathing heavily and trying to compose herself. She placed her hands over both sides of her face, as if to block out the sights around her and closed her eyes. Gregory followed her out, seemingly oblivious to his effect on her and put a hand gently on her elbow to assess what was wrong. Louise inhaled then let her breath out slowly.

One, two, three, four.

It's okay.

Inhale.

Exhale.

One, two, three, four.

You can do this.

She looked up at him.

"Are you okay? What's going on?" he asked.

"It's just too much for me out there. I just needed a breather," she replied. "I mean, it's so hot and this dress is so tight, and I am not used to having fun anymore, I guess." She looked down at her hands, struggling to explain the turmoil she felt within.

"Want me to get you some water? A cold drink maybe?" he asked, a worried look on his face.

"No, I just haven't been held like that in a while. It's been a long time, it felt...weird. No. Different..." She looked up at him with a chagrined look, knowing she wasn't making any sense. "There are just so many people here." She was failing abysmally at communicating in this moment.

"Sorry I made you uncomfortable. I didn't realize." He took his hand off her elbow reflexively.

"No, it's okay. I just need time to adjust." She shook her head, hardly understanding her own reaction.

Inhale.

Exhale.

One, two, three, four.

Louise brought her gaze up to look at his eyes as her breathing calmed and she shrugged. "What can I say? I'm complicated now. More than I was when we were in first-year university. But I like being close to you. It's comforting. I missed being with my friends more than I thought I did."

She wrapped her arms around his waist and rested her head on his chest again, enjoying the comfort of his proximity. He brought his arms around her and gingerly pressed his hands into her back. Holding Gregory felt like a return to something, to normalcy, to wanting something that was possible and maybe, just maybe, having that something within her reach. She breathed in deeply, inhaling his essence and letting it fill her with a rush of…safety.

His mouth came closer to her ear, and she wondered if he was going to kiss her cheek. "Let's go back and finish that beer," his voice reverberated against her chest. "I feel like you need to fill me in more on these levels of complexity you have achieved since we last saw each other. They sound intriguing," he said playfully. He grabbed her hand and led her through the dance floor to their booth.

Louise wondered how Gregory managed to do that so easily. He led and she followed. He smiled, and she knew she would be alright. Her heart was still pounding, and she questioned whether she was still feeling the lingering effects of the panic attack or if holding Gregory's hand was giving the blood-pumping organ another reason to beat, besides fear.

11

THE FOUR FRIENDS SPENT THE REST OF THE NIGHT dancing and enjoying a few beers while the country music floated around their shoulders like a comforting blanket. They attempted a classic western line dance, where most excelled and Louise laughed as she messed up constantly. The dancing emboldened her, and she even joined in when they were all singing along to their favorite country songs. This was fun. Louise could have fun. She felt all at once strong, sweaty, and powerful. Gregory was smiling and looking at her and she suddenly felt self-conscious, knowing her hair was drenched at the temples and her forehead was so sweaty. She touched her hair and blushed as they made eye contact. He looked at her as though she was the most beautiful thing he had ever seen. Louise was grateful when Simone grabbed her hand and pulled her toward the ladies' washroom.

"Whoa, I needed to pull you two apart. I was melting from those looks between you two," Simone said, elbowing Louise in her side. "I thought *I* was the one that was on a date, Loulou!"

Louise rolled her eyes. Gregory's look had been a bit heated, but could that just be the night, the dancing, the happiness at being all together again?

"I'm sure I don't know what you mean. You are so silly. We must have looked downright ridiculous belting the music at the top of our lungs like that. Of course he was staring."

Simone gave her a raised eyebrow, showing Louise exactly what she thought of that look. Simone enjoyed drama and was not immune to making some up if she thought it might cause a situation. She was a hopeless romantic and clearly liked the idea of setting Louise up with someone that might take good care of her and put that spark back in her eyes.

"Well, I'm seeing a lot of meaningful glances going on. I would not be surprised if you hooked up."

Louise shivered at the thought. Imagine hooking up with someone. How preposterous!

"Not likely," she asserted.

Simone pushed open the greasy bathroom door and pulled Louise by the hand into the washroom.

"Look, it's nice to see Gregory again. We were good friends before we dated, remember? He's a nice guy. He's cute too, I guess. But I'm not looking for anything like that right now. I need to get my shit together before dating anyone."

They both checked out their appearance, fluffed their sweaty hair and reapplied their lipsticks. Simone turned her gaze to Louise in the mirror, tilting her head with a sympathetic look.

"Honey, you don't have to have your shit together to date someone. Maybe dating someone could help you, you know, sort the pieces and put them back together. Wouldn't it be nice if you didn't have to do it alone?"

Louise left the mirror and went to dry her hands under the ear-splitting hand fan. With all the technology we have in the world, why hadn't they invented a quieter hand dryer yet? Louise rubbed her hands and avoided looking at Simone. She hated how her friend could look so deep inside her and spread her insides out for her to look at, figuratively. But Simone didn't know everything she had gone through. She couldn't possibly. Her friend only saw what Louise chose for her to see.

"Simone, please remember this if you start getting any ideas. I'm not looking for a boyfriend. I can barely handle my own emotional issues right now. I am not relationship material." Louise looked back at the mirror and wiped a bit of lipstick that had traveled to the sides of her mouth.

"You're not broken, Lou," Simone said. "If you like a guy, just go with it. Have a bit of fun. It won't hurt, I promise, if you keep it casual like I do." Simone winked and raised an eyebrow suggestively, to which Louise couldn't help but release a laugh. Simone was pure gold. She rubbed Louise's shoulder and pulled her into a sweaty, disgusting hug.

"I love you," Simone said. "I'm so happy you're here tonight."

"I love you too," Louise replied, her eyes watery. She blinked away the sensation, determined to end this night on a high note. Louise considered Simone's words as she gazed at her reflection and pretended to adjust her hair once more. Their eyes met in the mirror.

Simone turned to her friend and took her hands. "Listen, I know this is going to sound shitty, but I really want to get a ride home with Roger. We'll share an Uber or something. Would you be okay with Greg driving you home? I know I'm springing this on you, but I think you can handle it," Simone said, winking. "You're a big girl."

Louise held her breath, then exhaled with a nod. Of course she could survive a drive home with Gregory.

"I guess that would be okay," replied Louise. "I trust Gregory, and I can't feel much safer than with a cop, right?"

Simone smiled at Louise. "You wicked thing. Just try to not have sex on the first date, okay? Make him work for it a bit," Simone said.

Louise pulled back, mildly disgusted. This night out was not a date.

"Ugh, Simone, this was a girls' night, if anything. NOT a date. Yes, I'll get a ride home with him, and YOU try to behave with Roger, okay? *You* need to make Roger work for it," Louise said, pointing at Simone.

"I promise nothing," Simone said as she giggled and grabbed Louise by the hand, taking her back to the booth where the guys were waiting. Simone asked Roger back out onto the dance floor for another spin. Gregory got up with his jacket.

"Hey, Roger let me in on the shady plan, so, I'll drive you home? I would prefer to go now because I need to work early tomorrow, but I can stay longer if you'd like," Gregory said.

She shivered at the thought of being alone in a car with Gregory. It brought back memories of their nights out in university. But times had changed, and she had changed. Louise was more than ready to leave. That was enough excitement for one night. She picked up her jacket and purse from the booth and walked outside with him into the frosty night air.

It was a big difference in temperature from the sweaty dance floor, and Louise shivered. Gregory slipped his jacket around her to warm her as they walked to the car. He walked ahead slightly to open the door of the small SUV and Louise sat down in the passenger seat. For some reason, she appreciated that he had a nice, sensible car. It seemed like a very safe choice.

They enjoyed a friendly chat on the drive back to Marda Loop. Gregory shared a little about his journey to becoming a detective in the major crimes department of the Calgary Police. Louise could tell how passionate he was about his career, and she realized that it was smart that he had changed programs in university. He was where he belonged. Louise described her job as a law librarian, attempting as best she could to make it sound exciting. Which it wasn't really. That's what she liked about it.

"I work pretty much behind the scenes. It's the research I'm passionate about, really. Finding those old laws or statutes that can bolster an already solid case. The partners are the ones fighting the fight in court, I just play a supporting role."

"When I signed up for this job, my goal was to never put anyone in jail that didn't deserve it," Gregory explained. "I've seen some cases like that and they're tragic. People's lives are ruined by a miscarriage of justice. It's cool that we both play an important role in the world of criminal justice."

"Yeah, we ended up having careers that kind of work against each other, in a way. You help get the criminals arrested and, I'm helping criminals with their defense. Awkward, ha ha…" she said as she gave a light chuckle. "White collar, finance crimes, but still…"

"I guess," he replied. "But you don't get them off if the case against them is solid. If we have a strong case, we don't miss our shot."

Louise stared out the window, enjoying the city lights at night. The colors were so bright against the relentless darkness of the sky.

"Makes sense. How often do you miss your shot?" she asked.

"Well, I haven't worked on many cases where we don't get the guy. Cases like yours are the ones that piss me off. I feel everything is there to solve the case, we just need a break to get us moving in the right direction. I will do anything to make sure we get a clean shot at the guy."

Louise looked absently out the window as they turned into Garrison Woods, her neighborhood. She smiled to herself, feeling the little flicker of hope within her gain a little more strength.

"Full disclosure: we do work on corporate law projects and litigation too. I get my little hands in everywhere."

Gregory seemed to quieten. "I'm not surprised, you always were way smarter than me," he said with a quirked eyebrow.

"I don't know about that, but maybe," she replied, giving him what she hoped was a warm smile. The compliment seemed to warm her from the inside. He sobered as he gazed at the road in front of them, as though he was contemplating something.

"I'll be honest with you, Louise," Gregory said, "I'm worried about the murder in Marda Loop, which is a few blocks away from Georgie's house. You need to be careful. We've got a clean scene in both cases, a really slick guy who thinks he's so clever."

Louise turned and looked at Gregory. "Wait, you think both cases are connected?" she asked, her curiosity piqued.

"It's not impossible, right? It's still a hunch, but I feel safe telling you my theory because I know you won't tell anyone. Right?" He glanced at her, his eyes questioning.

"Duh. First rule in an investigation, only tell the public what they need to know. I'm no amateur."

She gave him a conspiratorial look, and he seemed reassured.

"They really go all out for Halloween here, eh?" Gregory said as they passed by the spooky decorations on the homes as they drove through the neighborhood.

"Oh, yeah, Marda Loop takes Halloween super seriously. They even hand out drinks for the adults walking on the night of Hallow-een. It's like a street party on some roads. Very cool. Georgie and I walk it every year. It's so festive, in a way."

"I'll have to check it out. Police are always out doing extra patrols on Halloween. It's a night well known for mischief."

Louise gripped the bottom of the seat, her body thrilling at the idea of mischief. There was something terribly alluring about picturing Gregory upholding the law and keeping the streets of her neighborhood safe.

They drove through a traffic circle and passed by the beautiful two-story homes on Garrison Boulevard, which were a mixture of Victorian townhouses, Georgian and Tudor style single-family homes. Gregory parked his car in front of the Cambrai Cottage, and Louise could feel the silence around them thicken as she raised her eyes to look at him.

"Well, thanks for driving me home. I was a bit surprised to see you at the bar, since it was supposed to be girls' night, but it was good to catch up." Louise said.

Gregory reached over and touched her cheek. "You know, I was glad to see you smile tonight. You've been through so much since we first knew each other. I love your smile, and it made me sad to think someone had stolen it away from you."

"Well, life is full of twists and turns. I'm hoping to change the direction mine is moving in and stop living in fear. Taking baby steps, of course," Louise replied, her eyes captivated. The place he had touched on her cheek tingled and Louise was unable to pull away, even when she knew she should.

"You have so much strength and courage. I will hold some of it in my heart as I go back to your case and fight for you." He placed his other hand back on his chest, as thought to show where he would keep them. Louise leaned into the hand on her cheek. How had she forgotten how nice it was to feel a hand on her face?

"Thanks, I miss the girl I used to be when we first dated, but you're reminding me that parts of her still exist. Like the part of me that thinks it's charming when you say things like that. Are you my knight in shining armor, Gregory?" she whispered as her gaze traveled up his lips to lock with his ocean-blue eyes.

"I would love to be," he said as he moved in a fraction closer.

It was funny to think of Gregory as a prince, such as the ones she knew from the fairy tales. They could rescue a princess with a mere kiss, thus was the power of their connection and their love. As her gazed traced the shape of his lips, Louise wondered if she might want to be saved with a kiss. A ribbon of desire curled within her, fed by the way he looked hungrily at her own mouth.

"If only I could be so easily saved — a kiss to wake a princess. How lovely would that be?" she mused. "But, life is not that simple."

She pondered for a mere moment how heavenly his lips might taste, then panicked at the chaos that would ensue if she acted on her thoughts. Would his lips taste the same as when she kissed him in university? Or would their kiss hold more wisdom, experience and in her case, a hint of desperate longing for closeness. Imagining the torrent of need that would be unleashed made her reach for the handle behind her. She couldn't imagine revealing so much of herself to Gregory.

"If we catch your dragon, then will you believe in fairy tales?"

She looked back up at him, shaking her head. "Then I might

believe that a knight in shining armor can save a damsel," she said with a smirk. "Fairy tales are bullshit and very problematic if analyzed with a critical eye."

Gregory chuckled, faking a blow to his chest and rubbing his injured heart. At that moment, his phone startled them both by ringing. Louise took the opportunity to escape before falling for any of Gregory's charms. She mouthed a goodbye and waved, a rush of relief filling her as the car door closed behind her.

She ran into the safety of her mother's warm and well-lit home and looked back only to see him speaking to an unknown person. Louise thought she had made a narrow escape, though as she rested her body against the door and closed her eyes, she pondered what exactly she had been running from. The thought of Gregory's kiss wasn't all that repellent to her, in fact, it was downright tempting.

Therein lay the problem.

12

LOUISE SEEMED ALMOST THANKFUL that the bright trill of the phone had interrupted their unexpected moment of intimacy. Was it intimate? Gregory pondered as he pressed the green button on his phone screen.

"Talk to me, Marty."

"Hey, Greg, I need you to meet me at the Rockyview Hospital. We got a call about another victim. They've got someone we need to talk to," Marty said. "Hurry."

Gregory could feel the familiar flutter of nerves in his stomach. He gave Louise's house a parting glance as he chewed at the inside of his lip. Another victim. Not what they wanted, but if she's alive, that was good news for many reasons.

Finally.

A new development.

Gregory's chest filled with hope. Meeting Marty at the hospital wasn't usually a good thing, but this could be a break in the case, and he was more than ready for it.

He pulled into the designated police parking area of the hospital and walked with a brisk pace to find Marty inside the bustling front entry. Gregory ambled up to this partner after sanitizing his hands and pulled him aside.

"What's going on, Marty?"

"We've got a new case. Antonio handed it to us because he wants to verify it's not the same guy we've been chasing. We need to talk to her and see if the MO is the same."

Gregory nodded and indicated to Marty to lead the way with a wave of his hand. His partner had already obtained the room number from the information desk. They walked directly to the emergency department and learned that the victim had been transferred to a quieter floor. Once they arrived, they had a brief chat with the nurse about her condition, only the details the nurse was able to share.

The victim had been through a horrible assault but was eager to share her story and catch her attacker. The nurse pointed them in the direction of her room and the two men made their way to their interview.

A fist gripped Gregory's heart painfully as he opened the door and saw the back of the woman's head, which was facing in the direction opposite them, looking out the window. It could have been Louise lying there — the long, light brown hair laid upon the pillow.

Shit.

Gregory attempted to calm his racing heart by reminding himself that the attack could prove to be unrelated. He couldn't imagine knowing there was a predator out there looking for victims that resembled Louise. He pressed a hand to his chest to still the storm brewing within. Seeing the woman, a visceral emotion shot through his body. What if that had been Louise? He knew she was safe, but fear clawed at his insides. He sensed some foretelling in the picture that lay before him, and he didn't want to acknowledge what it might mean. He needed more information.

He knocked on the door softly to alert the woman without startling her. She turned and Gregory's stomach dropped. The woman had brown eyes and remnants of red lipstick staining her lips.

At that moment, Gregory knew. He pulled out his small notebook and pen from his jacket pocket.

"Hi, Elaine. I'm Detective Band, and this is Detective Tall. We're here to ask you a few questions, if you're comfortable with that."

Elaine's hands, visibly trembling, came together over her stomach. She stared at the wall beyond her feet and took a few deep breaths. Gregory held his breath, waiting for her to respond, trying to quell his eagerness to speak to her and uncover all the horrific details of her night. He could already see the telltale redness of ligature marks and bruising around her neck. Elaine gave Gregory a brief look and a small nod, then turned away.

Signs of strangulation.

Check.

Red lipstick stain.

Check.

Elaine cleared her throat. Her voice came out raspy and hoarse as she kept her gaze focused on the wall in front of her. Marty and Gregory sat in chairs near the bed, far enough away not to crowd or frighten the victim.

"Tell me what happened tonight, as best you can."

"I was on a date with a guy. He seemed really nice and normal. We'd been chatting back and forth for a month. I felt comfortable with him." The woman paused to clear her throat and reached next to the bed for her cup of water. Gregory grabbed it and handed it to her. She sipped through the white straw and swallowed. She handed Gregory the cup.

"I invited him in for a drink," she said, with a thick voice, her eyes shiny with tears. She closed her eyes and rubbed them with one hand. Gregory recognized the signs, and he instantly wanted to comfort her. No victim would ever feel shame for being attacked if he could help it. It was a typical reaction to being assaulted, yet no blame should ever fall on the shoulders of these women, who were simply living their lives.

"Elaine, this wasn't your fault. Let's be clear on that."

Elaine nodded, though Gregory could tell she was still battling a surge of emotions on the inside.

"I don't know when, but I know he put something in my drink. I felt woozy and went to lie down. I asked him to leave, but all I remember him saying is 'I've waited so long to be with you. I've dreamed of you.' Then I blacked out," Elaine barely whispered the final words.

Gregory looked at Marty with a shake of his head. They could only imagine what had happened.

"How did you meet him?"

"We were chatting on a dating app called Meet Cute."

Gregory scribbled notes in his notebook. "What did he look like?"

"He was really fit and muscular. He has dark hair parted and combed to the side. Very clean and neat. He smelled good. Tall, tanned. Dark brown eyes, almost black."

"Do you remember what he smelled like?" Gregory asked, his pen scratching the paper furiously. Elaine paused, her brow furrowing in consideration. She closed her eyes and inhaled, then shook her head.

"He smelled sweet, but I can't remember like what exactly. Sorry."

Gregory scanned Elaine's face to assess if it was time to shut down the interview. It had been a rough night, and her recovery was only just beginning. He tried to think of any final questions that would help them connect the cases further.

"Who found you?"

"My roommate, who was supposed to be away for the night. She had a fight with her boyfriend. She came in and found me, I think she scared him off. Our back door was left open," she said. "She called 9-1-1. I was completely knocked out. It was so strange, but he dressed me. And put makeup on me. I wasn't wearing what I had on for the date."

Gregory looked at his partner, awareness in both their regards. Elaine's eyes were overcome with shame and regret, the tears that were threatening finally streaming down her face. Gregory stood and walked up to the bed, looking directly in Elaine's eyes. He handed her a tissue.

"Thank you for telling us your story. You are so brave, and your information will help us catch this dangerous man."

Elaine held his gaze, then turned back to looking out the window. Gregory could tell she was tiring. There would be more time to question her later.

"Elaine, if you remember anything, please call me at this number." Gregory left a card on her bedside table and gave one last long glance at Elaine. As if he didn't know already, she was a stark reminder of who he was fighting for. If the Marda Loop murderer wasn't stopped, there would be more victims. It was only a matter of time. The duo exited the hospital, feeling the rush of the cool damp autumn night as it washed over them.

"So, have we got any DNA on this perp, Marty?"

Marty shrugged. "It's in testing right now, they did a test kit on her when she arrived." Gregory glanced toward his car as Marty walked toward his police cruiser.

"Marty, what was she wearing when they brought her in?"

"I have a feeling you know what she was wearing."

Gregory's mouth flattened as he sat in his car and stared at the patients and visitors milling about the hospital at night.

Chills ripped through him as he considered the repercussions of his interview tonight.

The killer had sought out another victim so quickly.

The killer was shortening the time between attacks.

The killer had a type.

Gregory leaned his head on the back of his seat and closed his eyes. Of course, he knew what Elaine had been wearing when they brought her in and put her in the light blue hospital gown.

She was wearing a red dress.

13

GREGORY TOOK THE STEPS UP TO THE LAB two at a time, rushing to confirm his suspicions. The hospital evidence bag sat on the counter, waiting in the queue to be examined. Gregory could see the color of her clothing through the clearly labeled bag. It was a grim confirmation of his suspicions.

He waved to the tech as he left, leaving the evidence in the lab to be processed and reminding the tech to send him the results when they came in. He took a cursory glance at his inbox before leaving the station, since it was technically still his night off. No new information.

Gregory hopped back into his SUV and began the drive back to his apartment. He now had potentially two victims from the same perpetrator. The first had died, the second had survived. Were they truly the first and second? His gut was telling him that there were more.

Louise's case had some similarities that could not be ignored. The attacker had strangled her, leaving her for dead before he was interrupted. The attacker had fantasized about Louise in a red dress…

Louise. What was he going to do about Louise?

He scrubbed his hand down his face, recalling how close he had come to kissing Louise. How unprofessional. He wasn't exactly working on her case, so it technically wasn't his assignment, but he certainly shouldn't be kissing a witness that could be valuable in his current case. He cringed at the memory. Would she know he thought about kissing her? She must be horrified. She practically ran away as he attempted to get closer. Of course she did. He was a brute pretending the past had never happened and making advances on Louise, who had survived a brutal trauma at the hands of a vicious attacker. Gregory smacked his forehead in embarrassment.

No matter. It wouldn't happen again.

He would keep his hands — and his lips — to himself.

Forget how her dewy skin and tempting lips drew him to her like magnets.

And forget how much he wanted to touch her hair again to see if it was still as silky as it had been when they dated in university. Gregory groaned again, thinking of what a doofus he had been in university.

He had broken up with her at the time he had made the life altering decision to become a police officer. It was a terrible time in his life. He had dashed his parents' dreams of him being an engineer, working in a booming oil and gas industry. How his mother had cried when she told him he had a dream he could no longer ignore.

"But Gregory, it's so dangerous. I would be worried about you getting shot or something. You can't do this," his mother, Sheridan Band, had said. "It would break my heart." She looked up at his father, as though he would be able to change Gregory's mind.

"Son, I have connections that could help you be very successful once you get that engineering degree." His father stood, staring grimly as Gregory sat at the kitchen table, holding his mother's hand.

Gregory had finished his first year of university and started planning his exit strategy. His heart just wasn't in it. His only regret had been that he had to break things off with Louise. Stop seeing her before things got too serious and anyone got hurt. Or that's how he thought it had happened. He had begun withdrawing from her well before she knew what was happening in his life. The weight of disappointing his parents had doubled the pressure to be successful.

Since he was crushing the dreams they had for him, he needed to be successful, no matter what the cost.

"Louise, I'm changing programs to join the police academy. It's always been my dream to be a police officer," he'd confessed to her as he had caught up to her in-between her classes. "I'm really sorry."

"Oh," she said in a small voice. He could hear the surprise and worry in her tone. "What does that mean for us?"

"Louise, I've had fun with you, but I'm not ready for anything serious right now and I need to focus. I can't screw this up."

Confused eyes stared back at him. Her voice silenced by disappointment. She nodded in understanding, though her expression gave him the impression she wanted to run away.

"Okay." He placed his hands on her shoulders, but then instantly pulled them off, seeing her physical reaction as she backed away.

"I just know if we stay together, it'll be more than I want in my life right now from a relationship." She chewed her lower lip.

"I just want to be friends," he said.

Louise frowned, her shoulders drooping slightly.

"It's probably best if we don't see each other again, Gregory,"

Louise finally said in a soft voice. She adjusted her backpack straps and started walking away.

"Wait, can we be friends? One day maybe?" He instantly hated the desperation in his voice. He knew he was doing the right thing for himself, yet why did it feel so wrong? They had only dated a few times after hanging out with their group of friends that school year. It wasn't like they were even boyfriend and girlfriend. Louise shrugged and shook her head, the idea distasteful, judging by her scrunched-up face.

"Too soon, Gregory. I gotta get back to class."

His eyes followed her as she walked away, admiring how cute her butt looked in those jeans. Damn. Gregory had a sinking sensation in his gut that he had made a mistake, but he ignored it. His focus couldn't waver between a woman he had a crush on and his education. He had already messed up by quitting his current program. A year of preparation for the career he actually wanted had been lost. He needed to get his life together before ever diving into a relationship again. This was the best decision for him, and Louise. Yes. Louise would thank him one day.

Gregory sighed at the memories. He had let everyone down that day. It had been hard to have the conversations, while also harboring secret joy that he had been accepted into the police academy. He had furthered his education by doing a degree in policing part-time and continued his training to feed his fascination with criminal psychology and forensics.

Thinking back, Gregory was confident he had made all the right decisions for himself. His parents were now fully supportive of his career, and somewhat comfortable with the level of danger he faced in his line of work.

Gregory was grateful for the path he had chosen, for it had led him to this moment. Now, he was in a position to save Louise and to prove himself to her. He would be her knight in shining armor. His investigation would be so perfect, he would catch the killer and prove to her that he had made the right decision all those years ago. If he did his job well, a monster would be off the streets of Calgary, and Louise would forgive him for hurting her all those years ago. But he needed to keep his head on straight. No enticing distractions. He had to focus. There was a predator out there, looking for victims and they all had features in common that lead Gregory to believe they were substitutes for a bigger target.

14

LOUISE WAS IN BIG TROUBLE.

She had seen this one in a Hallmark channel romantic movie before. Girl meets ex, girl realizes maybe he's not such a bad guy, in fact, he's a cop now (in the movie he worked at a dog shelter, sigh) and of course she finds herself falling for him. It was all a big misunderstanding or something.

No.

Louise shook her head as she pulled up her favorite stretchy pants.

No way.

This was not happening.

She pulled on her sports bra to strap down her boobs. She always had to get the extra strength bras which were a workout in themselves just getting on. Louise decided a jog might help rid herself of all the passionate thoughts inspired by a certain police officer. Work out her sexual frustration or something like that.

Was she sexually frustrated? Louise scoffed.

No.

Absolutely not.

She dealt with her sexual frustration very well, on her own, and never sought the comfort of a man.

Running filled her with a sense of strength and power. Exercise cleansed her mind and changed the pattern of her thoughts when they snowballed and became overwhelming. Jogging helped her solve problems in her head. She put her headphones in and turned on some upbeat music to help her keep her pace and distract her mind off any pain the jog might be causing in her body. She took in the stunning colors of the fall around her, breathed the fresh cool air which filled her lungs, and attempted to forget that Gregory ever existed.

The air burned in her lungs as she sped up for a particular song that made her want to run for her life. She slowed her step as soon as it became intolerable and walked some of the way as she continued her usual path. The burning had temporarily helped distract from the mess she had become in such a short time.

Had she almost kissed Gregory?

She cringed at the thought.

How desperate.

Imagine, going years without ever craving the touch of a man and suddenly, Gregory appears out of nowhere, well, straight out of her past, really. Damn him for still being so damn adorable. His boyish grin, and the thick glasses that did nothing to hide the warmth in his blue eyes. Perhaps it was a consequence of being alone, of having isolated herself for so many years. She had summed up the things she was good at in her life and left out any possibility for flexibility, or for change. Was being safe truly the only goal in her life?

She was an amazing law librarian who worked hard and always produced top notch results. There was no bit of research she couldn't find for the partners, no matter how deep she had to dig. No fuss, no muss.

But being social? Feeling human? That was a part of her skill set she long thought dead and buried. How could she be capable of loving a man properly if she was afraid of him? She liked being alone. She bristled at the touch of others, the suffocating crowds, and failed to make conversation properly unless with the right people or smile at the right times.

Or did she?

Did she bristle when Gregory touched her? Louise rolled her eyes. No. When Gregory touched her, she felt... tingles. His smile never failed to beckon the same from her lips. She felt so much when she stood in his orbit.

Warm.

Safe.

Known.

Gregory had a perspective that no one else could. He knew her before, but he understood what she was going through now. He didn't tiptoe around her like she was overly fragile, or incomprehensible. He made her feel like a living, breathing woman.

Alive.

Her skin tingled at the memory of being wrapped up in him on the dance floor. The unfamiliar feeling of her skin warming, not from the heat of the dance floor, but from her cells awakening beneath the feel of his arms. Her breath became deeper, slower, as though she wanted to inhale more of him; fill herself to the brim his reassuring essence.

Louise pressed her hand to her chest, as the memories made her heart race, not from anxiety, but from... longing. Perhaps if she clung to Gregory, she could expose the human that lived inside her. Release the pressed down emotions and free them. Let them go. Louise shook her head.

No.

It was too soon. She was definitely not relationship material.

And neither was Gregory, if the past was to be kept as a lesson. She had cared for him, and he had let her down.

Sure, theirs had been a budding romance, yet she couldn't shake the feeling that if things hadn't been worth fighting for back then, how would it be any different now? She could recall the dull ache in her chest as she walked away from him, seemingly rushing off to class after he had told her he was leaving their university to enter a new program and follow his dream of being a police officer. Louise didn't fault him for leaving to pursue his dreams. These things happened. But she did still feel the lingering sense of abandonment. Collateral damage.

Her father had abandoned her mother, having affairs behind her back, and treating her love and devotion with a careless disregard. Louise vowed she would never be with a man who didn't give her all of himself. She would rather be alone than in a loveless relationship. And that was before her attack had even occurred. Now, she had such thick protective walls built around her that she was safe, yes, but the loneliness was sometimes breathtaking.

Simone was busy with her career, passing the bar this fall and studying, studying, dating, working, and studying some more. Anika was living her dream of marrying Tom, after so many years together. Her friends had big bright things to look forward to. Louise was content. And safe. Or maybe not so safe now that there was a killer on the loose. Were those truly the only things she ever wanted?

Had Gregory found a tear in her armor?

A flaw that revealed her as not so immune to the passion that arose between lovers. She felt that familiar ache in her gut.

This wasn't a good idea.

This was a terrible idea.

She made a frustrated sound and wiped the top of her head of the sweat that had accumulated there over her sleek ponytail. A lady out watering her pots turned and looked at her with concern (one must not make such noises when jogging, apparently) and a lightbulb went off in her brain. If she deviated from her usual jogging route, the old path would still be there, and she could resume it anytime.

So, maybe she would change course.

Slightly.

Louise took her cool down walk a little further than usual to the grocery store. Her curiosity had been piqued at the thought of doing her own investigations for her case. It had never occurred to her to go test a bunch of mints, or smell hair products. The idea seemed so simple; she was angry she had never thought to do it.

She combed the candy aisle for various mints, gum, and Tic Tacs. There were many to try, so she grabbed them all to take them home with her. She was not completely satisfied with the selection of mints at the local grocery store, so she then drove to London Drugs to explore their selection of more exotic mints. She devoted some time to smelling men's hair products, though she had trouble finding anything made for men that smelled like vanilla cupcakes. She wondered if maybe she would have to check out women's products in her next investigation. It could be like finding a needle in a haystack, since every salon could also have another selection of products to test.

In a moment of weakness, she sniffed a few Old Spice deodorants,

under the guise of research. She happened upon the "Swagger" scent
and felt her body warm with recognition. Why did everything about
him make her body tingle? It was so embarrassing. She purchased
a few more types of mints and stopped at the nearby coffee shop,
Distilled, for a treat before returning home.

Upon entering the café, Louise was greeted by Logan, the owner
of the coffee shop and spa. Distilled was a cool modern place with
French bistro styling. Beautiful, modern brass light fixtures were offset
by white marble tables and light wood benches. The gorgeous grey
and white tile elongated the space and a black metal framed wall of
windows with a brick base separated the café and spa.

Louise loved their lattés the best, as well as the friendly faces that
always welcomed her when she arrived. After she had been attacked,
this had been one of the places she felt she could come and hang
out without feeling afraid. The place was always bright and busy,
the seating area was perfect for having a coffee, reading, or doing
some work on her computer. She loved that she had several exits
if she encountered a person that made her uncomfortable or if she
felt herself having a panic episode. She stood at the till ordering her
coffee and chatted up Logan. They always shared an easy banter; he
enjoyed walking around the café visiting patrons and getting to know
them better. If ever she and Georgie sat outside and it got chilly, he
would bring them blankets to keep warm. Georgie adored Logan and
his willingness to partake in a neighborhood gossip session anytime.

"Hey, Louise, what are you up to today?" Logan asked, an easy
smile on his face.

"Well, I just had a jog and did some grocery shopping. Now I
think I'll just go chill at home," she replied. She ordered a latté and
a sugar cookie shaped like an orange leaf with gold detail.

"I hope you're being careful. There's a creep running around out there," Logan said, handing her the cookie in a bag.

Louise nodded seriously. She paid for her items, then went to the end of the long bar and waited for her drink at the end. A sunny, brown-haired girl took over the till and Logan came to make the latté and continue chatting with Louise in his friendly manner.

"You know, if you need a jogging buddy, I'm around. Just let me know. I hate to think of you taking risks and jogging alone," Logan said as the milk heated in the stainless-steel container with a slight screech.

Louise looked away, feeling slightly taken aback at his suggestion. Was Logan asking her out in a roundabout way? She looked at his bright blue eyes and his curly short dark brown hair. Louise pondered her response as someone came into the coffee shop and caught her attention. She could feel her face turning red as she saw the true object of her desire walking in, innocently walking up to order a coffee at the front of the bar. After paying, Gregory made his way to where she was standing and greeted her with a shy smile.

"Hey, Louise, long time no see," Gregory said, his boyish grin sending a fluttering sensation beneath Louise's heart. She hoped she affected him physically as he did her.

"I didn't know you got coffee here," Louise responded, using her fingers to brush her hair behind her ears. "It's literally the best."

Gregory nodded enthusiastically in response, rubbing the back of his neck. She glanced up at Logan finishing up her coffee to avoid staring too long into the officer's dreamy, light blue eyes.

"What have you been up to today?" Gregory inquired. Louise turned back to him, remembering with enthusiasm her secret mission.

"I bought some mints to test to see if I could identify which type of mint the guy used," Louise said quietly, feeling slightly embarrassed by her personal investigation. Gregory leaned in; his interest piqued.

"You're going to let me know the results, right?" he said eagerly.

Logan reached toward them to hand Louise her latté. "Here you go, Louise. Don't forget to let me know if you need a jogging buddy. I can make myself available," Logan reminded with an easy smile and a wink.

Louise panicked, thinking Gregory might get the wrong impression from that comment. She thanked Logan for the coffee and placed the cup on the bar, emptying a sugar packet into the creamy white foam. She picked up a spoon and stirred her coffee and brought the spoon to her mouth to lick the foam. She loved the sweet foam so much. Her glance traveled to Gregory's eyes, which were fixated on her mouth. *Oops*, Louise thought, *maybe that's a gross habit*. Now Gregory was going to think she was even more imbalanced than he already did. Louise shrugged.

"Yum. Nice to see you again," she said, her chest flooding with embarrassment. As she rushed past him to the exit doors, Gregory touched her arm.

"Hey, you and Logan jog together or something?" he asked, and Louise panicked.

"Ah, no, ah, maybe?" she responded awkwardly. "Bye, Gregory. I'll let you know about the mints!"

Louise walked briskly out of the coffee shop, then stood outside for a moment, trying to catch her breath. How could she have been so awkward with both of those men? Maybe she needed to role-play some human interaction scenarios with her therapist, because clearly, she needed practice. She tucked her cookie in her grocery bag and hustled to drive back home, worried Gregory would catch up to her and she would be subjected to another uncomfortable encounter.

When she arrived at Cambrai Cottage, Georgie looked at her funny as she walked into the kitchen and spilled out the contents of her bags on the kitchen table.

"Honey, what on earth are you doing?" Georgie questioned.

"I'm testing some mints. Gregory asked me if I had ever looked for the kind of mint that my attacker smelled like, and I realized I had never even thought to research it. How remiss of me."

Georgie responded with a "hmm" and sat at the table with her. She began opening the bags with Louise and they pulled the mints out one at a time to smell and taste them. Georgie and Louise seemed to enjoy playing at being detectives, though by the time they got through the entire pile of mints, Louise was feeling discouraged.

"I don't know what I was expecting. That was such a waste of time," she grumbled.

Georgie shushed her. "Now don't get discouraged, I'm on Amazon right now and there are tons of mints we haven't tried. I'll keep any eye out when I'm shopping too, and we'll find some more to try."

Georgie reached over, putting an arm around Louise, who rested her head on her mother's shoulder. If they had learned anything from watching Jessica Fletcher on *Murder, She Wrote* for years; it was that one tiny clue could break a case. Solving crimes was all in the details. Louise considered her mother's words and reminded herself the investigation was not over yet. It had only just begun.

15

THE INVESTIGATION HAD FAILED. No new pieces of the puzzle had been discovered. Louise stared at the white, red striped, green striped, circular, chewy, pink, and green pile of candies in front of her and wondered if she would live long enough to eat this many mints. It was such a disappointment to try to fail so abysmally. The pieces of the puzzle would stay lodged in her mind for now.

Louise texted Gregory that evening to let him know about her unsuccessful mint investigation. He was pleased with her research and wanted to see the mints she had been testing. Though it seemed like a lame reason to come over, he was very insistent about stopping by check on Louise. They had unfinished business, she imagined.

Louise had taken the time to put on a clean sweatshirt with the words "All Peopled Out" on it, a bra, and jeans before Gregory came over, though her hair was a lost cause and would have to be saved by a brush and a scrunchie. Louise snickered to herself as Georgie asked her to change her sweater, but there was not much else she had time to do. How was she supposed to get over this guy if he started dropping in whenever he wanted?

"Louise, he's going to get the wrong impression from that shirt," Georgie bemoaned.

Louise shrugged, accepting whatever fate the sweater created for her. Funny sweatshirts were part of her armor. Her mother waved a hand in frustration and walked back upstairs.

"It's too late to change me, Mum. I like funny sweaters," she called out, as a knock sounded on the door. "Plus, I'm okay with him getting whatever impression he wants. We're just working on a case together. Nothing more."

When the detective walked in, he was in his civilian clothes, looking handsome and cozy in dark jeans and a navy-blue zip up hoodie. Louise put on a mask of indifference and casual conversation, when really, she was dealing with an uncomfortable level of attraction churning inside. Her stomach dropped to her loins. She somewhat regretted not putting something more attractive on, but only a little. They looked over the mints that she had tested, and Gregory discussed the next steps in her research.

"I'll take photos of what you have tested already, so we can keep track of what mints are not the ones you remember. I'm sure we'll come across some more in our travels. The important thing is that you are taking charge. I'm so proud of you. I know it's not easy."

Louise blushed and Georgie came downstairs and interrupted their conversation.

"Gregory, is that you?" she asked. "Wow, it's been a long time since I've seen you." Georgie reached out and patted his shoulders affectionately. She looked between two and smirked. "Are you here to take Louise out? She would love it if you did, I'm sure. I'm on my way out to my play cards with my friends. You'll take care of her, right, Gregory?"

Gregory stumbled on his words and mumbled something sounding like "uh..."

"I hear there's a killer out there and want to know my baby is safe." Georgie shivered in a theatrical manner. Louise rolled her eyes, not buying the act.

Gregory opened and closed his mouth, looking from Louise to Georgie, clearly searching for a response.

Louise was ready to dig her grave and climb in, she was so mortified by her mother's desperate attempt to get her to go out. Georgie went into the closet, taking out her coat and handing Louise hers.

Louise looked at Gregory, her mouth agape as she automatically put on her jacket.

"I guess we're going out too," Louise said.

Georgie almost pushed them out the door and locked them out, waiting on the sofa for her friend to come pick her up. Louise and Gregory laughed over the awkwardness of the moment as they wandered down the street from the house.

"Sorry, my mum is so crazy. I really need to get my own place, so I don't get tossed out like that. I am so embarrassed," she said walking along the sidewalk in the cool night air. Her cheeks burned with humiliation.

"Don't worry about it," he said. "I know she means well. I'm glad we get to chat alone."

Louise was nervous at the thought of being alone with Gregory, even if they were walking outside in a public place. The streets were painfully quiet, which highlighted to Louise that she had no place to hide, no place to avoid his gaze or his questions. They walked along for a few blocks, past the lovely brownstones with festive Halloween decorations, bright decorative blow ups, and cobwebs strung along bushes and fences. When she wasn't alone, the outside didn't seem so scary.

"You know, it's really nice being outside at night. I kind of stopped going out, especially alone, at night. It made sense at the time, but now that I'm out here, the air is so fresh, the decorations are so cute and spooky. I don't know what I was so afraid of. My community is so special. It comes alive at night and looks so different. So pretty. I just love it out here."

Gregory agreed with her, giving her a meaningful gaze that she chose to ignore. "What did you need to talk about, Gregory? I'm sure there haven't been any developments in the case that you can tell me about."

Gregory cleared his throat nervously. "Nothing really, I just felt bad about what you said the other night and I wanted to make sure I cleared the air," he said. "I'm sorry I hurt you back when we dated in university. Like really sorry."

"Gregory, it was a weird time for you, I get it."

"Yeah, I had just disappointed my parents by changing programs and leaving town to complete my degree in policing. I was hyper-focused on my goals. I was too oblivious to notice I was hurting you. Can you ever forgive me?"

"I can understand that. I mean, I had my own goals too. And Georgie always told me to never let a man get in the way of my career."

She shrugged it off, as though to indicate it was water under the bridge. She had no reason to cling to the anger, given that so much time had passed, and they were very different people now.

They walked further along the well-lit streets of Garrison Boulevard, ending up in a large field attached to a playground. The area had few streetlights, which made it gloomier to walk through than the streets. Louise shivered, unable to hide the effect the darkness had on her sense of security.

"I'm glad you're here with me. This place is creepy at night," she said shivering, but not from the cold, and looking up at Gregory as he kept the pace next to her. He put out his elbow and Louise looked at his arm for a moment not understanding. Gregory grabbed her arm and put it in the crook of his, so she could walk closer to him. She was startled at how cozy and safe that small adjustment made her feel. She leaned into him a bit more, unable to resist the closeness.

"What makes you afraid of this park? It's so nice here." Gregory questioned gently. She looked around at the shadows cast by the streetlamps, the places someone could hide, the silence. She shook her head.

"Parks at night are terrifying. There are too many places for him to hide. I feel watched," she responded. "I've felt watched for a long time now. Like until I know he's been caught, he's trying to find me."

Louise looked at him, feeling uncomfortable when relaying the true depth of the fear she contended with each day. She found it hard to share this truth with another human, to trust him to protect her, thus allowing him in her pitifully small circle of safe people. She hoped he could somehow understand.

"I'll never feel safe in the dark again," Louise continued. "When your sanctuary is violated, it seems impossible to ever feel secure anywhere. If home is not safe, how is any place anything but dangerous? Threatening?"

Gregory glanced around the park. Louise followed his gaze, taking in the beauty of the trees and grass, the golden yellow moon shining above them, the stillness of the night.

"I see this place differently. Yes, it's dark and maybe too quiet for some, but in my line of work, I love to hear a place that is peaceful," he noted.

"I guess, it is different when I'm not alone. It's nice. Intimate," she agreed.

"Are you saying that right now, you could feel safe, with me?" Gregory asked, pressing her to reveal more. He raised his eyebrows and smiled playfully.

"I guess I should say, I do feel a bit safer in this moment, because…" She looked up at him, a reluctant smile appearing on her face.

"Because I'm here?" he finished her sentence optimistically placing a hand to his heart.

"Not exactly. You have a gun, right? I feel way safer when my friends are packing heat," she said and giggled, enjoying his insulted expression.

"Actually, I don't carry a gun when I'm off duty. But I do want you to feel safe; I'll protect you."

They paused in their walk and turned to face each other. He placed his hands on each of her shoulders reassuringly, as though he understood the privilege it was to have her trust. She placed a hand on his chest and rested her head on the other side, feeling an irresistible urge to hear his heartbeat again, as though it would give her strength to challenge her boundaries and perhaps allow for a door to be opened in her protective walls. Or maybe, just a crack, where she could glimpse what she was capable of emoting.

He carefully rubbed her arms as though to warm her, and leaned forward to press his face in her hair, as though breathing her in. It made her blush to think he was enjoying her scent the way she did his. Louise was afraid to look up, to see what might be waiting for her in his eyes. She turned to keep walking, hoping that would break the tension of the moment. Their hands brushed as they moved, sending a shock of desire to Louise's core. She inhaled sharply.

The silence stood thick between them, with Gregory making her feel safe and cared for and Louise trying to suppress a desire that had long been dormant within her. She wanted to kiss Gregory. But she was afraid to kiss Gregory.

What if he rejected her? What if she kissed him and remembered what it felt like to want something so badly, she could taste it? Would she be cursed with a desire that could not be fulfilled by anyone? Louise felt like a coward.

So, she looked up at him. "What are you thinking about now, Gregory?"

"You don't want to know."

Louise's mouth curved into a lopsided smile as she tilted her head. "Try me."

He stopped walking and passed a hand through his hair as if there was a battle warring within. He brought his hands to either side of her face, his gaze intense.

"I'm thinking I want to kiss you and that would probably be a bad idea, you know, because of the case and all that."

"Sounds like a big decision, I wonder who's going to win? Officer Band or Gregory." Louise gave him what she hoped was an inviting gaze. She was admittedly horny, after all. She wouldn't mind that kiss.

"Would you like it if I kissed you?"

Louise felt a familiar gush of warmth in her chest — or was that nausea? No, it was longing. Louise instantly knew she was in trouble.

Good trouble.

"I think I would," she whispered.

She tilted her face up as he leaned down, and their lips met in a tentative, gentle kiss. They both pulled back for a moment, each assessing the reaction of the other for a mere second, though irresistibly drawn back together for another taste. Louise reveled in the softness and warmth of his mouth on hers, an uncomfortable curl of desire collecting in her abdomen and sudden tears formed in her eyes. He pulled away from the kiss and lay his forehead on hers.

"Was it that bad?" he said, his brow furrowed in concern.

She sniffed. "I never thought I could kiss anyone again. You could practically bury me, Gregory; I feel so dead inside sometimes. And here you show up in my life and all I want to do is kiss and touch you."

A tear rolled down her cheek, betraying the intensity of her feelings and she pressed her face in his chest as though to hide her face shamefully. He gently brought her face up by placing two fingers beneath her chin and lifted her face back up to look at him. He ever so slowly kissed one tear, then another.

She released a sob, overwhelmed by the excruciating sweetness. He then pressed his salty lips to hers, causing a surge of intense fire to rise in her chest, filling her with a painful hunger. She could devour him he tasted so good.

He pulled back and smiled.

"Welcome back to life, Snow White. You feel plenty alive to me. And damn you kiss good." He rested his forehead on hers.

"Normally I would object to the reference to Snow White, since I have concerns with the lack of consent and the allusion to necrophilia, but I'll allow the comparison this once," Louise said with a chuckle.

She buried her head in his chest. He wrapped his arms around her and held her close, allowing the silence and the intimacy of the night wrap itself around them. If kissing Gregory was a huge mistake, Louise had never wanted to be wrong so much in her entire life.

16

THE HARVEST MOON GLOWED ABOVE, as though to heighten the intimacy the darkness had provided them. A cool breeze tousled the leaves in the branches around them, shaking Louise out of her love haze. She wondered who this person was, that had come to life so suddenly within her, and why that person seemed to act so impulsively.

After a moment, they lifted their heads, unable to resist the temptation presented before them. Gregory claimed her lips once again and Louise gave in, a warm, drunken feeling overcoming her senses when his tongue slipped between her lips. He tasted like jellybeans. She should have known he would taste like candy. She pulled back, a concerned look on her face.

"We can't linger here too long, people could be watching us," she worried.

They looked around, seeing the park, a small field with a giant tree in the middle and the playground to the left of them. It was deserted at this time of night, but the well-lit homes that surrounded the area reminded them that people were home and could spy them making out in the park. Gregory leaned into her, nuzzling her neck.

Perhaps he was reluctant to abandon the closeness, like her. An intimacy she had not felt with anyone in a long time.

"You're right. Let me walk you home, maybe Georgie will let us come in now," he said as he grabbed her hand, and they walked back the few blocks to her mother's house.

When they arrived at the cottage, they could see the house was dark as they walked up to the door. Louise refused to let go of his hand, even when she turned herself and he pressed her up against the door to kiss her goodnight.

"My mum should be out late playing bridge. Want to come in?" she asked. She turned the knob behind her, and the red door opened into the small foyer and the living room. They took off their shoes and coats, draping them on the sofa. Louise walked into the kitchen, turned on the lights, and asked Gregory if he wanted a drink. He walked up behind her, trapping her against the small kitchen island. She turned around in the circle of his arms.

"Later," he said, "I think we have some unfinished business. I'm not done kissing you yet."

His lips possessed hers once more, stoking the fire that was burning deep in her loins. She pulled away and took his hand, leading him upstairs to her bedroom. She was suddenly mortified, since she was bringing him to a bedroom filled with her childhood furniture and decor, complete with frilly lacy bed linens and a creaky three-quarter antique bed.

"Sorry if this is a bit cheesy. This is my old bedroom stuff, which my mum kept after the divorce, and I haven't done much to update this room. I didn't really plan on staying here long term."

Gregory chuckled softly. "I think these frills are hot. You look good covered in lace I bet."

He placed his cold hands up her shirt to warm them up and brought them onto her back as she yelped at the surprise. Their lips met in a deep kiss, both uncaring about the surroundings all of a sudden. She placed a hand on his chest, pausing the action for a moment.

"Listen, I'm not sure what you've been up to these past nine years, but I want you to know it's been a while for me," she admitted.

Gregory groaned. "Okay, that's hot. I can go as slow as you need. We can just make out if you want. Trust me, I feel like I took a vow of celibacy when I became a cop."

She stood by the bed as he took off her shirt and she attempted to undo his belt in response, but he stilled her hand.

"Don't," he whispered. "I need to touch you. We can take care of me after, but I need to have my hands on you right now. May I?"

Louise nodded. He kissed her gently and pulled off her pants, leaving on her full brief tan cotton panties and nude bra. She lay on the bed, grateful for the low light her bedside lamp provided in the room, because she had not prepared for this at all and was not in love with her underwear choice for the evening. It wasn't even her lacey nude bra.

He lay on his side next to her and unclasped her bra at the front, laying her breasts bare for him to enjoy. He buried his face between them and inhaled.

"What is that delicious scent? Roses? I could just lay here and smell you all day." His hands bunched in her hair as he slowly kissed his way to each nipple, taking one into his mouth while using his finger to circle and pinch the other simultaneously.

She moaned at the sensation, not having felt this aroused in so long. Her hand, unable to resist an exploration, unbuttoned his shirt and went inside to feel his warm stomach, reveling in the softness of his skin beneath her fingers.

She continued her one-handed exploration by unbuttoning his jeans and rubbing the hardening length of him beneath the cotton fabric of his boxers. He moved his lips down to her stomach, essentially blocking her access, but she wasn't complaining. She was near to bursting with arousal and had missed feeling this kind of closeness with someone. While he kissed her stomach, his hand slid beneath her underwear and between her legs, where she knew he encountered an ocean of desire pooling there.

"Can I touch you? I don't want to move too fast," he said.

She nodded helplessly and shrugged, looking at him as he brought his lips back to her mouth and gently probed her nether lips with a finger to feel the level of her arousal. He groaned as he encountered her excessive moisture level. She jerked at the invasion, her body awash in pure hot sensation as she melted on his fingers.

"Is that okay, Louise?" She nodded in response, her entire body trembling at his touch. "Tell me it's okay."

"I love it, Gregory. I want more."

"I can't just leave you like this," he said as he slowly pressed another finger into her and began entering her with gentle strokes.

Louise kissed him like her life depended on it. Their tongues greedily exploring each other's mouths. She lifted her hips to meet his hand, eager for the release that was building within her. He kissed his way down her neck and vigorously kissed and sucked on her nipples while she squirmed beneath him. She felt a huge wave of release as she came powerfully on his hand, barely able to catch her breath as her body contracted on his fingers.

"Woah, that was… a lot," she said, panting and smiling up at him as he brought his fingers up to his mouth and tasted her. "I want more, Gregory."

"Mmm, you taste so good. I can't wait to be inside you and feel all that honey on my cock," he said. Louise gasped and blushed at the mention of his arousal straining against the zipper of his pants.

She pulled off her underwear and giggled as she knelt before him eagerly to unbutton his jeans. They heard the front door downstairs open and close. Louise gasped and her heart sank.

"Shit, Georgie's home," she whispered.

Gregory pulled back and quickly started putting his clothes back together. They could hear Georgie calling out to Louise, who ran to quietly close her bedroom door and started looking around the room for her robe. She sat on the bed with a book as Georgie made her way up the stairs. Her mother knocked on the door as Gregory stuffed himself into her closet. Georgie came to check on Louise, as was their nighttime routine.

"Hi, Loulou, all ready for bed? You look so cozy there," she said.

Louise nodded in response, barely able to speak yet. She desperately hoped Georgie would not see how flushed her face was and how fast her heart was racing. She was tingling all over.

"Did you spend most of the night at home?" Georgie asked. "You really need to get out more than your old mother. It was so nice to see Gregory again. He's so nice. And pretty good-looking too, eh?"

Louise rolled her eyes impatiently, suddenly noticing Gregory's hoodie hanging on the end of her bed. She eyed the sweater, opting to pretend it wasn't there so that maybe Georgie would think it was one of Louise's castoff garments.

"I guess he's alright. Did you have fun playing cards, Mum?" she inquired, trying to distract her mother. Had she heard a small snorting noise coming from the closet?

"Yes, I did, and I had a few glasses of wine. Eleanor drove me home. I am so tired now. Have a good night, sweetie."

Georgie exited the room and closed the door behind her. Louise let out the breath she had been holding and got up, trying to figure out how to get Gregory out without Georgie seeing him. She investigated the hallway and crept out when her mother had finished using the bathroom. Before letting him out of her room, she shut the lights off in her bedroom to make it easier for them to get around without being seen. The dark startled her, but she felt safe when he was with her. The doorknob turned quietly in her hand as she looked into the hallway to make sure the coast was clear. She opened her closet and let him out. He put his arms around her and pressed her against the wall to kiss her deeply one more time before they entered the hallway.

"Just alright, eh? I'll show you who's alright next time," he whispered as he gazed at her, intense blue eyes gazing into hers. With a cocky grin, he grabbed his sweater, then tiptoed down the stairs with her following behind him.

Louise went to the kitchen to get a glass of water and to create a reason for being back downstairs. Holding the glass to her chest, she sighed as she watched him leave and locked the door behind him. Gregory had awoken a hunger in her, and she did not see herself being satiated anytime soon. Watching out the window long after he left, she was aware of a sense of dread overcoming her. She could not let herself get too deeply involved with that man. His love hurt too much. They had to slow down. She took a sip of her water, suddenly feeling excessively thirsty. If his love hurt so much, why did her entire body feel so good?

17

Louise smiled as she watched Simone come up her walkway to the house. She grabbed her jacket and went out to join her before Simone had the chance to ring the doorbell.

"Thanks so much for coming to do this with me!" Louise said as she wrapped her arms around her friend. "I'm kind of excited and kind of scared but I think it's time."

They walked east from her mother's home and continued on a sidewalk which brought them through a gorgeous arch of trees bursting with bright burgundy- and yellow-colored leaves.

"Hey, do we need to drive there or something? My car is actually parked that way," Simone asked.

"Nope," Louise replied. "It's a few blocks away and I'm hoping you'll be excited because if it's good, this apartment will really facilitate our nights of drunkenness." Simone connected the dots in her mind.

"What are you saying? Is this place close to Marda Loop Brewing? That would be too great!" she said hopefully.

Louise smiled at her, nodding enthusiastically. "Yep, it is! I'm super excited but we have to be open-minded. It's cute from the outside, but you never know what's inside," Louise noted.

After her temporary madness with Gregory, she needed a distraction that would help her move forward and give her more options now that she clearly had a desire to get back in the dating game. The rental market in Calgary was a crazy competition. You had to line up to see places and if you were not ready to make a move, offering to sign papers and give deposits right away, you risked losing the apartment. It was an environment ripe for gouging monthly rents and sometimes rental scams.

When her mother's friend had given her advance notice that her rental unit would be available in a few months and asked her if she wanted to check it out, she was ecstatic. Louise had a list of requirements a mile long, though her main priorities were pet-friendly for Cosette and two bedrooms, so that she would have space to sometimes work from home or host guests. She had also decided that it would be best if the unit was on an upper floor, so as not to have easy entry points for intruders. Though it was her goal to move on from her past trauma, she was not forgetting to set herself up for the safest possible future. Her attacker was still out there, and it would not do to be living in constant fear of being watched. Louise smiled at Simone, excited to check out this place and, if necessary, pass their bitchy judgments on the apartment, should it not meet their stringent expectations.

They walked up to the building called "Marda Point" and saw the owner of the property, a shrewd older businesswoman dressed in high-rise dark jeans, a white blouse, and bright pink blazer.

Myrna had short grey hair, bright pink lipstick and chunky

colorful matching jewelry. When they walked up to the entrance of the building, they could already tell it was a well-kept property, very clean, very beige, with cream-colored tile hallways and cream walls with white trim.

There were easily accessible mailboxes with a cute table beneath them for package and food deliveries. The artwork could best be described as generic hotel artwork, with abstract prints in muted colors. They followed Myrna into the elevator and went up to the third floor.

They entered unit 328 right into a cute kitchen with modern light wood grain cabinets with stainless-steel hardware matching the stainless appliances. There was a roomy pantry, where Louise could put all her food and small cooking appliances. The floors were a dark laminate throughout, which complemented the cream paint and white trim colors. The bathroom was painted a garish orange color, but she could always brush a coat of paint in there.

Louise had no problem doing a few projects to make the place truly hers. The bedrooms had enough space for a bed and dresser and Louise nearly swooned when she saw the walk-through closet which led to the master ensuite. She morbidly considered it would be hard for someone to sneak up on her from there and smiled to herself. It seemed like a perfect apartment.

They finished the tour with seeing the small second bedroom and laundry room, as well as stepping out onto the terrace, which overlooked the courtyard and made her feel like she was in the canopy of the colorful, leafy trees that she loved so much in her neighborhood.

Myrna explained that the unit would be available January first, and she would be putting it on the rental website soon.

"Thanks for showing us this wonderful apartment, Myrna. I

really appreciate you giving me the first look."

The older woman smiled. "You know I love your mother and when she told me you'd maybe be looking for a place, I knew you would be a wonderful tenant. I'll need you to provide some paperwork, sign a contract, and provide first and last month's rent if you end up wanting the place. Get in touch with me either way," she said.

Myrna walked them out and then went back in, having parked her car in the apartment parking spot. Another bonus about the place.

Simone and Louise walked away from the brick building and decided to have a beer at their favorite place, which was right across the cobblestone street. They sat down at a high-top table with booth seating and ordered their favorite seasonal pumpkin spiced ale. They giggled at their passion for pumpkin spice anything. The first sip was cold and slightly spicy. Louise moaned at how good it tasted.

"So, Loulou, what did you think of that apartment? How are we apartment hunting right now?!" Simone asked.

Louise could not help but smile nervously, hesitant to be open about her desire to move. "Well, I feel like living with Mum is getting old or is aging me. I'm not sure which. I kind of had a close call when my mum almost walked in on me with a guy and it just kind of motivated me to start planning my next move!" she revealed.

Simone gasped and had a mock fainting spell, with the back of her hand on her forehead. "What? Do tell. You're getting hot and heavy with a man? I thought you'd be in a relationship with your vibrator for the rest of your life, and that was it!"

They both laughed uncomfortably at the thought, though at times it did seem like a definite possibility for Louise's future. Louise continued, ignoring Simone's request.

"You know, I'm feeling stronger and happier these days, and

it's time for me to get on with my life. I can't let my past leave me frozen in place forever."

Simone nodded in agreement and raised a glass to cheers her best friend. "Amen, sister. Anika is getting married, you're getting a new apartment, I'm having so much fun sowing my wild oats... and you too, maybe? The future is looking bright for us, baby!"

They clinked their pints again and finished their beer with an order of fries. Simone, clearly unsatisfied by the way Louise had dodged her earlier question, tried to ask it again.

"So, tell me more about this guy you're seeing. Is it Gregory? Cause you guys were positively eye fucking the whole time we were at the Wild Rose."

Louise raised an eyebrow in response.

"Oh really, we were not! We've known each other for a long time, and maybe I like him? He's really hot and... Ugh, I don't know we just get so hot when we're together and I'm not even sure who I am when I'm with him," Louise paused to think, unsure of how much to reveal to Simone, though her friend would dig until she revealed all. "Simmie, it's like my sex drive was asleep and now it's awake, and I can't stand it!" Louise dug her hands in her hair and exhaled.

"Wow," Simone interjected. "You got it bad."

Louise sipped her beer before continuing. "He's all I think about. And we literally have never even been on a proper date," Louise said, fanning her face with her hand to emphasize the heat Gregory was generating within her. The change in her life was difficult, but necessary.

"Anyway," Louise continued, "we were getting frisky, and I mean FRISKY, like we were going to maybe, you know... Then Mum comes in the house, and we hear her. He hid in the closet, and it was so embarrassing. I snuck him out, but seriously, I felt like a horny teenager, and it was just too much."

Simone placed a hand on her chest, aghast. "Lou, my heart is racing! You have to work on finishing the job with him. I mean, only if it feels right, of course. I know he flaked out on you in uni, and I have not forgotten that slight. He will have to earn his place not only in your heart, but mine as well."

Louise nodded and smiled in agreement, not really sure she was all in with Gregory by any means, which reminded her that Simone had been on a date with Roger. She was more than happy to switch the subject.

"Wait, how did things go with you and Roger when you dumped us at the Wild Rose? Did you guys...?" Louise raised her eyebrows meaningfully. She was used to her friend giving guys one or two dates at most, so it would be unusual for anything to actually develop with Roger.

Simone winced at her memories and took a sip of her beer. "Ugh, no, he's sweet, but he's not ready for a relationship. We went back to his apartment and the topic of his ex-wife came up. Once we started talking about her, things went off the rails," Simone said, inching closer to Louise as though telling her something in secret. "Loulou, he literally cried. Ugh, I cringe thinking about it. Like he misses her or is definitely not over it. I think she hurt him really badly. Needless to say, I ended up cuddling with him on the sofa and we fell asleep. We're better off as friends. I'm looking for something easy and fun, not some sad guy obsessed with his ex-wife. Too much baggage. Please let's change the subject. What do you think about the apartment?"

Louise replied that she really liked it and would have to think about if she was prepared to take this step in her life. There was much she admired about the place and loved the proximity to her work and family.

Simone pulled a journal out of her purse and brought up the engagement party they had both committed to planning. Though Louise felt overwhelmed at the time crunch, the party date was decided. They came up with a tentative guest list, including their family and friends, as well as the guest list Anika and Tom had sent them. They put out a few calls and organized most of the party from their table.

Once they looked at the huge guest list, they decided their venue would have to change and they thought up a few new options. They both agreed the party was going to be special once everything came together. Simone and Louise ordered a second beer to celebrate their happiness, and both felt the joy of possibility simmering within them.

.

18

THE ENGAGEMENT PARTY was planned for the middle of October, before too many Halloween parties sprouted up. Louise gave herself a final glance in the mirror, pleased with her outfit of choice for the evening. She wore a navy velvet dress she had purchased for the occasion and loved feeling its softness against her skin. It was a luxe V-neck dress with a wrap neckline, slim-fitting arms and pleat detailing that gave her curves a sexy spotlight. She finished the look with black tights and black pointy heeled ankle booties. She smiled at herself in the mirror, loving the look of her burgundy lipstick, which added that final touch to the outfit. Simone was really good at encouraging her to dress her body beautifully and she was feeling the benefits of treating herself more like the goddess she was.

The party was hosted by Simone's parents, since they had ample space in their modern Victorian mansion in Mount Royal. Simone's father, Harold Cormier, was the CEO of a successful oil and gas company and their beautiful home was a reminder of the luxury in which Simone had grown up.

The party was held in the ballroom, where large tables were set up with beautiful catered desserts, gourmet appetizers, and sparkling signature champagne cocktails. The ballroom was decorated with large flowers arrangements in fall shades of soft peach, cream, orange, and burgundy. The space was bright and expansive, the Cormiers being used to hosting large parties.

A giant sign had been custom made, congratulating Anika and Tom on their engagement. Their guest list consisted of many of Anika and Tom's relatives, family friends, and coworkers.

When Louise gazed upon the lovely flowers and beautifully arranged food, she felt like they had made the right decision. It would have been impossible to fit all seventy-five guests in her tiny house. The conservatory was a large room attached to the ballroom composed of mostly windows, where the Cormiers had arranged overstuffed chairs and sofas in various seating arrangements for people to lounge comfortably as they indulged themselves. Potted topiaries covered in twinkling lights dotted the spaces around the room, adding to the romantic ambience of the evening.

The place was full of people; Louise recognized some and was introduced to many new ones. At first, the knot in her chest had weighed heavily on her, but gradually, Louise had forced herself to play the role of co-hostess. She looked around for Simone, since she had been running around helping the caterers set up and making sure the place was perfect for Anika and Tom.

"Louise!" Anika called from the other end of the ballroom. Louise's gaze fixed upon her dear friend, and she walked to meet her where she was standing with a couple that looked very familiar.

"Kelly and Eleanor, nice to see you," Louise said, shaking their hands.

Louise recognized the couple as Tom's aunt and uncle, also her and Georgie's neighbors from down the street. They lived in a comfortable house in the section of Garrison Woods that had larger homes with greater square footage. Louise took some time to visit with their neighbors, talking excitedly about the upcoming destination wedding. Eleanor seemed rather frazzled in appearance while Kelly seemed clean cut and wearing a modern dark grey suit to cover his large six-foot frame. Kelly walked away to go chat with some of his business connections, leaving Louise and Eleanor together alone with Anika.

"There he goes again," said Eleanor, as though she forgot Louise was with her. "I feel like we never get any time together these days." Louise cleared her throat.

"So, Eleanor, this trip will be fun. Will you be bringing the kids?" Louise asked, changing the subject. Making conversation was not one of her talents, so the words came out in a nervous jumble. Luckily, Eleanor didn't seem to notice.

"Yes, I believe we will. Kelly is always so busy at work, I imagine I would be bored and lonely if it was just the two of us. I'll bring the nanny though, just so it feels more like a vacation. I can't imagine taking care of the kids all by myself. They're so demanding at this age."

Louise speculated with Eleanor as to the location of the wedding and what they would wear depending on the chosen location.

"I basically need a complete makeover before the wedding, I swear," Eleanor said, indicating herself to Louise. "I mean, look at me. I'm a mess. Between the kids, my volunteering, and the amount of time I spend at the club, I barely have time for myself. I'm sure I need Botox refresher at least!" Eleanor giggled, though her face belied the level of enthusiasm or energy she had.

Louise laughed uncomfortably with Eleanor, shrugged and looked awkwardly at her drink. Louise felt a kinship with Eleanor, with them both needing to take the time to care for themselves. Louise understood needing that boost. She looked around, trying to come up with a reason to extricate herself from the conversation without sounding rude.

The crowd buzzed with wedding destination rumors. Anika and Tom had remained very quiet about the destination, telling everyone they would have to wait to make plans.

Louise downed her champagne cocktail and announced that she would be going to get a refill. It was unusual for her to spend this much time in such a big crowd, and she was starting to feel a little exposed. She sidled up to a waitress with a tray of drinks and grabbed one, then walked alone to the conservatory, where there were fewer people, and the atmosphere was noticeably quieter. She stared out the window at the stunningly manicured gardens, perfectly designed to look pretty in every season. The hydrangeas were puffy shades of golden brown and cream, with leaves that had turned burgundy in the fall. The trees and bushes were proudly displaying their foliage.

Louise found a sense of calm staring out the window and enjoyed letting out a few deep breaths to ground herself. She felt a soft touch around her waist and a warm whispered voice she recognized in her ear.

"Hey," Gregory said softly in her ear.

Louise turned around, making an effort to hide her happiness, so as not to reveal her excitement too much.

"Hey," she replied in a neutral voice. Louise kept an awkward distance between them, which belied the longing that she felt to touch him.

"How are you?" he asked, trying to act casual, putting his hands in his pockets.

"I'm good. How have you been? Any news on the case?" Louise felt safe picking this topic of discussion, since they both had a vested interest in the case.

"I'm still waiting on some things. People always expect investigation results to come in quickly, but it's more like a slow trickle of evidence. Why are you over here all by yourself? Seems like the party is over there." He tilted his head in the direction of the ballroom, where people were talking, drinking and enjoying themselves.

"I'm not good at this kind of thing anymore. I used to be, but parties make me…nervous. I feel exposed, you know? I am more comfortable being at home."

"Well, this is a good way to dip your toes in the water," Gregory said, indicating the party.

"Yeah, I'm slowly getting accustomed, but I need to take a step back once in a while," she replied. "To catch my breath."

Gregory nodded, closing the space between them ever so slightly. Louise could feel he was trying to keep his hands away, even though they were drawn to each other. The energy radiating from his body created a throbbing in her own. Regardless of the power of their attachment, she wasn't ready to make it public before they had named it. He hadn't wanted to kiss her because of his case. Would he hold off on dating her because of it? Louise chewed her lip, thinking that perhaps Detective Band was laying the groundwork for his next escape.

"I'm happy to stand here while you catch your breath." Louise gave him a shy smile as he stood next to her, and they both looked out the large expanse of windows.

"Can I just add that this party is amazing? You and Simone did an incredible job planning it. You say you're not good at this kind of thing, but your hard work speaks for itself," Gregory said.

Louise smiled, looking around and feeling a measure of pride. She had ordered the flowers, chosen the group of classical musicians, and picked out the decorations. Simone had handled arranging the drinks and catering. Anika had peppered the entire planning experience with her own opinions and wants. It all came together well. She was proud.

They both perked up and looked up to the stage area where the musicians were interrupted while playing a suite by Bach, by the sound of tinkling glasses. Simone's parents came up on the stage to speak. Louise and Gregory made their way back to the ballroom and stood on the outside edge of the crowd. Harold Cormier's voice boomed over the crowd.

"I'd like to thank you all for coming to our house. We are so happy to host the engagement party for this wonderful woman we have known since she was in grade school playing in pigtails with our little Simone. Thank you to everyone who has come. We love you, Anika, and we have loved getting to know you, Tom. Let's toast to congratulate these two."

Everyone raised a glass and took a sip of their drinks as Anika and Tom made their way to the small stage. They hugged Simone's parents, and Anika grabbed the microphone.

Gregory seemed to have lost a battle within, since Louise felt the warmth of his hand trace its way behind her, leaving a trail of tingles and resting on her hip. Another guzzle of champagne made its way down her throat as she tried to suppress her instinct to wrap herself around him. Act casual. This is fine. Don't look into it too much.

"Thank you all so much for coming to our little engagement soirée. Harold and Dolly, thank you for always being there for me and my family. We love having you in our lives. Thank you to my best friends, Simone and Louise for planning this wonderful party for us. Simone and Louise come up here!" Anika looked for them in the crowd, clapping eagerly for them.

Louise reluctantly parted from Gregory and walked up to the stage, blushing red and not loving being the center of attention. She waved at the crowd and hugged Anika and Tom. The crowd cheered and clapped for them, and Anika started tapping her large engagement ring on her champagne glass to bring everyone's attention back to her.

"I know everyone has been speculating and we want to put you all out of your misery!" Anika said, as the guests took a few moments to quiet down to lingering murmurs. "Tom and I would like to announce our wedding destination. I hope everyone is ready because we are celebrating our nuptials in…." Anika looked at Tom and they smiled lovingly at each other before announcing together: "Oahu!"

The crowd roared, and everyone happily shared their experiences or their hopes for the trip to Hawaii. Louise, overwhelmed by the noise and enthusiasm of the crowd, slinked away back to the conservatory for a moment of peace. She looked around for Gregory and spotted him watching her on the edge of the crowd of people. As though drawn by invisible wires, they moved toward each other.

"Isn't it exciting, can you believe I'm going to Hawaii? Do you think you'll be going too? I know you and Tom are good friends."

"Yeah, we've known each other for a long time. I've always had fun with him and Roger when we went out looking for trouble, though his days of being a wingman might be over now, I guess."

Louise smacked him playfully in the chest.

"He can still be a married wingman, I think," she considered.

Gregory shrugged. "I have a feeling I'll be going to the wedding, especially if it means watching you strut around in a sexy bathing suit." He closed the space between them.

Louise felt a surge of longing inside. A longing to do something so very normal, like a vacation with a boyfriend. Her body responded so dramatically to his nearness that it startled her. Louise batted him playfully on the chest, her hand lingering where it landed. He would make someone a great boyfriend.

"I'm not going on vacation with you, we haven't even had a date yet, you weirdo. I'm fulfilling the very serious role of bridesmaid and will have a lot of important responsibility."

Gregory chuckled and gazed at her lovingly. "Well, I guess I'll have to rectify that situation then."

"You had better," she said. "I'm going to head out. I think it's time I made my French exit." Gregory's hand snaked up her back, and he pulled her to him.

"I promised the guys we would go for drinks after the party. But hey, remember you promised me a date. Soon," he whispered in her ear, lingering a moment. Goosebumps covered her entire body, and she shivered. She reluctantly pulled away from his embrace.

Her hand grazed his as she quietly slipped out of the ballroom. She needed to escape before Gregory could see the desperate longing for that date in her eyes. It was essential that she play it cool and keep her emotions under control. There was no sense in getting excited about something that was bound to end anyway.

19

GREGORY WALKED WITH SOMETHING of a skip in his step, then sobered, remembering where he was heading. Every encounter with Louise made him dizzy with desire and Gregory was alarmed at the power she had to completely distract him. His employment required him to keep a cool head, examine scenes and files with an unflappable focus and discerning eye.

Every time Louise entered a room, all he wanted to do was make that attractive blush bloom on her cheeks and dig into that beautiful brain to learn what made her tick. That, and press her against a wall and kiss her until they were both panting and breathless. She needed to catch her breath? He wanted to catch her breath, and her moans and her sighs. All of them.

Gregory shook his head. This problem was getting out of hand. He had to focus. He walked up to the towering building of the chief medical examiner.

Today was autopsy day, and he was keen to know what new information would be revealed. The coroner who had been assigned to the case was his personal favorite, the detail oriented and mouthy Doreen Heather.

"Sleeping Beauty wasn't asleep, she was drugged," explained Doreen. "Drugged, then asphyxiated. We've got telltale signs of strangulation, marks on the neck, petechial hemorrhaging, and all that jazz. You'll see it in my detailed report. The killer used the makeup to cover up many of the bruising and signs of struggle. I could tell it was freshly applied postmortem."

Gregory gazed at the victim on a stainless-steel table under the glaring surgical spotlight. "What kind of drug did he use?" he inquired, eager to know more.

"She tested positive for high levels of GHB, meaning she would have been conked out and he could asphyxiate her without any struggle. He definitely enjoyed himself before she died, signs of sexual assault were clear, and we were able to get a few traces of DNA from hairs on her body, which I've sent away for testing."

The discovery of GHB in her system made the lack of signs of a struggle make sense. GHB could be used in its liquid or powder form. It had little or no flavor and could easily be masked by a beverage such as the wine Angela had been drinking.

Doreen sighed. "Bottom line is, she did not have an easy death, and I'm hoping I've collected something good enough to catch this guy. I haven't seen an autopsy like this in a long time. This feels like someone who enjoyed torturing his victim and if not stopped, he will likely seek out another. I got a bad feeling about it."

Gregory asked where her clothing had gone.

"I sent them away for testing. You'll get her clothes back when they've gone over it with a fine-toothed comb."

Gregory spent quite a bit of time with the victim, hoping she was at peace now. He felt her sense of violation personally. Someone had invaded her space and her life and taken something that did not belong to him. It sickened Gregory to think how innocent Angela had been, just a normal woman trying to go on a date and make a connection. She did not deserve this.

Gregory eagerly waited for the results to come back from the various evidence that was being tested. His gut told him the red slip dress Angela had been wearing was not a coincidence. There were too many similarities with Louise's case for him to feel any sense of comfort. He put his hands in his pockets and started to say goodbye to Doreen, reminding her to send him any results that came in as soon as possible. She gave him a side-eye as she tapped his arm.

"Aren't you forgetting something?" Doreen asked with a smirk, enjoying the dumbfounded look on Gregory's face.

"You're going to owe me five beers, Greg. And you bet your ass I'm going to collect," Doreen said and chuckled as she waved him off.

Gregory told her to name the time and place, and he would be there.

Next on his list was to spend some time looking over every inch of his crime scene one more time, knowing it would be released back to the victim's family the next day. One more moment alone with the place could reveal more of its secrets now that all the crew was gone. The scene was a silent place where he could think and put the puzzle pieces together, but only if they fit. His gloves and booties on, he walked in, trying to retrace what Angela would have gone through that night. He opened the door as she would have and walked into the apartment.

On his right, he could see a bowl where she kept her keys, which made sense. Gregory imagined she wasn't alone when she came in the apartment, so he looked around for a place to hang coats, as the nights were very chilly in Calgary at this time of year. He went in her closet, looking for any missed clues. Any relevant evidence would have been taken away with the initial search, so he made a mental note to look at the contents of her coat pockets in the evidence locker.

Gregory checked the floor of the closet for shoes. She had worn pretty heels that night maybe, as he saw them as being the most recently worn pair of shoes. She was very tidy and organized. He walked into the kitchen, checked the counter where the glasses had stood. He went to her cupboards to get a glass of wine, looking in and turned around. The killer would have been sitting on one of the bar stools, waiting for a glass. He would have been lulling her into a false sense of security with his looks and his charm. The killer's account had been deleted, and they were waiting for forensic analysis of the site to try to connect the account to a computer. The neighbors had not noticed any noises or odd sounds that night. She walked into his trap like a lamb to the slaughter.

Gregory considered what Doreen's haunting words meant. Could they be looking at a serial killer? He had studied serial killer patterns and knew that becoming a murderer was a gradual process. While he waited for DNA comparisons to come through, he had examined the commonalities between this case and few others in the area. A crime of this magnitude had not occurred before, though several crimes, such as break-ins, rapes, and attacks like the one Louise had survived had happened in the last few years.

Gregory wondered if he should stake out the place for a while, maybe watch the house, in case the perpetrator made an appearance. Serial killers were known to visit the sites of their crimes to relive the experience. Out of curiosity, Gregory turned off the lights in the apartment and headed to the large picture window in the living room, which was at the front of the building. He carefully peeked through the window, using only a sliver created when he pushed aside the cream curtains, and looked outside.

At first glance, he saw nothing, scanning the street and looking mainly to the right. It was a dark cloudy night, with little or no light provided by the moon to help illuminate his exploration. He switched sides to see out of the other side of the window, again making only a tiny sliver of space through which to look. South Calgary was a very hilly neighborhood with lots of old trees and old houses mixed with new infills, all casting an irregular pattern of shadows.

Gregory could see nothing, though he took more time on this side to adjust to the darkness and look beyond the pools of light created by the streetlamps. There, beneath a bush, he could barely see a pair of dark sneakers poking out, as though someone was hiding behind it, using the shadows and branches as cover.

How odd, he thought to himself as he slowly backed away from the window, trying not to cause a ripple in the curtains. He moved away quietly from the windows and carefully made his way to the apartment door. Even if his eyes had been mistaken, he was going to check it out.

On impulse, he called Marty on the radio to let him know he was investigating a suspicious perp seen near the South Calgary crime scene, giving few details beyond that as he ran from the apartment down the stairs to the main doors of the building.

He exited out the side door and made his way quietly to the other side of the building which would be the closest to the peeping individual. Gregory pulled his gun out and pointed it in front of him, raising it to the person in the bushes yelling at him to show him or herself. The person was startled and ran into the yard of the house he was standing before and let himself in the gate, shutting it behind him. Gregory ran to follow him and through the gate, then again though the back gate to the alley. The alley was quite steep and went down on one side and up the other.

Gregory looked both ways, trying to ascertain where the person had run with no success. Regardless of who that person was, he or she knew this neighborhood very well and had prowled here before, since they would be easy to spot running up or down the hill, though not if they had hidden in another yard. Gregory swore softly to himself, furious that he may have just let his killer slip though his fingers.

He walked over to his patrol car, he opened the door and got in, surveying the area a few times by circling the block and the alley with his brights on. After heading to his desk at the major crimes office, he wrote some notes on the encounter and checked his emails before ending his shift for the evening.

As he scrolled though his messages, he noticed an email with its subject line in bold: WE HAVE A MATCH. He clicked the email open as fast as he could and scanned the message. They had matched the attacker's DNA from Louise's crime scene to the DNA found at Angela's murder scene. Gregory read the email again, each word a punch to the gut.

Though he had no way of proving that the person he had chased earlier was the murderer, the fact that they had matching DNA on two different cases caused a chill to run down Gregory's spine. The stakes had been raised. Louise was in immediate danger from the Marda Loop murderer.

It was made clear now that her assailant had intended to kill her. Lucky for them he was interrupted. She was the killer's unfinished business, which put her at greater risk if he found her on one of his neighborhood prowls. Gregory left his department in a rush, planning on warning Louise that she needed to be extremely careful. He sent her a text asking her if she had time to meet up.

"Hey, are you busy right now?" he texted, using his car Bluetooth to send the message. He didn't even care if she answered. He needed to see her, make sure she was okay. If this killer thought he was going to get his hands on this particular mark, he was sorely mistaken.

20

A MESSAGE PINGED ON LOUISE'S PHONE as the drama unfolded before her on the screen. Was one of the girls going to walk off, leaving *The Bachelor* crying in her wake? Louise's eyes barely glanced at the screen, not wanting to miss a moment.

Gregory: Hey. Are you busy right now?

Louise assessed her level of activity, watching *The Bachelor* and finishing a package of Oreos on the sofa in full sweats. She reluctantly paused the episode.

Louise: Um, no I guess not

Gregory: Can I drop by?

Her heart began to palpitate almost instantly, filling Louise's chest with sudden excitement. She looked down at the cookie crumbs in the lap of her sweatpants and cringed. She was not ready to meet up.

Louise: Yeah, what's going on?

Gregory: It's about the case, I'll be at your place in fifteen minutes.

Crestfallen, Louise had to accept that he wasn't coming because he missed her and was desperate to spend more time in her presence. She made an effort, just in case, and ran upstairs to change into her favorite dark skinny jeans and a white tee shirt with sparkle ball earrings, a little mascara, and some lipstick.

As much as fashion tried to push her in the direction of getting rid of her skinny jeans and moving on to modern wide leg jeans, she could not understand how this fashion was supposed to work on a short, curvy girl. It just wasn't flattering on her body. She was team skinny jeans for life. She brushed her hair into a low bun with a middle part, added a little hair spray to smooth out the flyaways, and instantly felt cute and sexy.

Louise reminded herself that she wasn't going to throw herself at him, regardless of how hot he made her. He was going to have to work for her love. She wanted to challenge his self-control a bit, given that he was always acting like Detective Band with her, so strict, in his perfect uniform and with his perfect hair part. Louise wanted to test the limits of his control.

His car pulled up to her home and Louise looked at him through the open door, leaning against the doorjamb. He ambled up the walkway, his eyes flaring as he took in her outfit from head to toe. Her body reacted physically to his scrutiny, and she broke the silence to remove herself from under the heat of his gaze.

"Hey," she said, trying to sound casual and not too excited. Louise shivered as Gregory's gaze travelled up her body, taking in her appearance, and leaving her completely unsettled. She willed her heart to stop racing.

People looked at her all the time.

Why did it feel like he could touch her with a simple glance?

"Hey," he replied breathily, swallowing and rubbing the back of his head. "You look nice. I was just going to chat with you here but get in the car, let's go somewhere." He opened the car door for her, and she went in. Louise put on her seatbelt as he started up the car again. He was listening to some interesting electronic music that she surprisingly liked. The music matched the mood, the night and the tension floating between them.

"Cool music, who is it?" she asked.

"Oh, just a local guy, Underground Wires. I just went to his show, and it was pretty cool."

"I've never heard of him. To be honest, I hate instrumental music, but this is tolerable." She gave him a crooked smile and looked out the window.

"Thanks, I dig it."

Gregory seemed to take that as a compliment as he drove them somewhere to hang out. He decided on The Mash, a nearby place with good beer and pizza. Gregory hadn't eaten supper yet and told Louise he was famished. They parked in the underground parking lot, took an elevator to the main street then walked into The Mash.

Scanning the room, they selected a sturdy wooden table with thick wooden chairs. The restaurant had dark forest-green walls and lovely repurposed antiques and art on the wall. The paintings had a playful quality, because they were old paintings that had been refreshed with funny modern additions painted onto each image. There was a huge neon pink sign on the wall that read "Slice, Slice Baby".

"This place is cool. I've never been," Louise said. Enjoying the aroma of fresh dough mixed with the slight tang of beer in the air. She perused the menu, considering an old standby, pepperoni pizza. It never disappointed.

"What do you think you want to order?" Gregory inquired, his eyes scanning the menu briefly, and deciding with a speed that told Louise he had been here before.

"I don't know… what do you like?"

"The dill pickle pizza sounds weird, but I'm addicted right now," he confessed.

Louise considered.

Pepperoni pizza was a comfort zone move.

And she was done with the comfort zone.

It was a lonely place.

"Sounds great. I'm sure it tastes amazing."

Gregory ordered a couple beers and a dill pickle pizza for them to share. "Are you sure you're okay with the dill pickle? I like weird pizzas, and I didn't think the Grim Reaper pizza was a good choice for tonight."

"Uh yeah, totally inappropriate. Dill pickle sounds achievable, but super spicy pizza? No way."

Gregory's eyes widened in appreciation.

Louise was still wary of the pizza selection but kept an open mind, since her new self would definitely be more adventurous and outgoing.

When the beers arrived, Gregory took a big gulp before speaking. "I needed to see you tonight because I've got some good news and bad news," he began.

Louise braced herself. Oh boy, she thought. She gazed at her hands on the table and prepared herself.

When she looked up at him, he decided she was ready and continued, "There's been a break in your case." An intake of breath was Louise's only possible reaction, as her body started to tremble from within.

"What does that mean?" Gregory sighed, not giving her the most optimistic feeling.

"We've been able to find a match for the perp DNA evidence in your case. Only, it's not with a person, like a specific suspect. It's with another case."

Louise put a finger up as though to pause the conversation and took another big gulp of her beer.

It was something.

She had to be happy it was something.

So why was this familiar fear blossoming in her chest, stealing her appetite?

She nodded for him to continue.

"Your attacker's DNA matches the murderer's DNA we found at the scene in South Calgary. That means the same guy that murdered my victim was the one that attacked you two years ago, and I'm guessing maybe a few others in the last few years." Gregory stopped talking to take another drink of his beer and to give Louise time to absorb the information.

She placed her arms on the table and rested her face in her hands.

"That is so freaky. I don't really know how the hell I'm going to deal with this?" she swallowed, looking away. Gregory kept his worried eyes trained on her.

"I mean, I'm pleased we have made a connection that gives my case a new breath of life, but this means my attacker is not only still here, but he's also prowling." Gregory nodded, aware of all the terrifying implications.

"Not only is he still hunting in my neighborhood, but now he's killing?" Louise rested her head in her palms, willing her tears to stay in her eyes. Gregory reached a hand to caress the side of her arm. The feel of his thumb swiping along her forearm stilled her racing heart.

She suddenly didn't feel so alone.

"I'm so tired of being scared. What do I do with this information? Do I move or something?" she asked desperate for someone to wake her from this nightmare.

The pizza came, and they took a break to eat. Louise attempted to slow down the wave of fresh fear inducing thoughts that were running at breakneck speed through her head.

She chewed the pizza thoughtfully.

Dill pickle pizza was weird.

But still pretty delicious.

"It's good. You were right," she said. Gregory blushed and seemed almost... delighted that she enjoyed the slice.

Louise shook her head, dismissing the thought. The reality was, she could barely taste the pizza.

And pepperoni would probably have tasted better.

They ordered two more drinks and pushed aside their plates. Gregory grabbed Louise's hands in his.

"Look, I've got a lot of skin in this game," Gregory said, his voice calm and steady. "I can't leave this guy out there to kill someone else or...or to come after you. It's just not gonna happen."

Louise straightened her spine and looked at him. Her hands formed into fists on the table.

"I've been working so hard to get my life back to some semblance of normal. If I stop now, it's like I'm letting this guy win. He's a predator and I'm his prey. I get that, but if he hasn't found me yet, maybe I can still be safe for a while. I'll keep my pepper spray on me when I go out. I'll take more precautions. Maybe I'll get a guard dog and a home alarm."

Gregory ran one of his hands down the length of her arm to soothe her, then he grabbed her tightly balled hands and kissed them.

"I just can't quit," she said.

"I care about what happens to you. Those are all great ideas; they'll at least give me a bit more peace of mind. Cosette would object to the dog, I'm sure," he said gently to relieve the tension, as he must have seen the despair etched on her face. It was all too much to bear. An unexpected laugh bubbled up in her chest, thinking of how insulted Cosette would be if she brought home a guard dog.

"You know what? Let's get out of here," he said, coming off his chair and grabbing her jacket for her.

"I'd like that."

Louise walked to the bathroom to freshen up her lipstick and came back to join him at the bar where he was paying. She wondered where Gregory would take her next. Even though he had delivered some unexpected news tonight, she was enjoying his company. Her gut told her she was where she needed to be.

Gregory would always help chase the monsters away.

That was his job.

She leaned with her back against the bar, putting her elbows up on it, and stood next to him while she waited. Gregory had purchased a few beers to go, and the bartender went to the back to grab them.

"Hey, I thought we would go Dutch. I'm a modern woman, you know. I can pay my own way," she teased, giving him what she hoped was a captivating smile.

Could she be captivating?

She shrugged and went with it.

One mustn't forget that while she was scared, she was also

craving everything this man had to offer. Her body trilled when he walked around to place his hands on either side of her and closed the distance between them.

"Maybe we can work something out," he said, as he brushed his lips against hers and ran his tongue along the seam of her mouth.

She pulled back. "Hmm, that's a bit shady. You want me to pay for my pizza with kisses? Not very progressive, Detective Band. Kind of problematic." Her chuckle became a small gasp as the evidence of his growing desire grazed her leg. He nuzzled her neck for a moment, both inhaling each other's essence deeply and pressing her gently against the bar. Then Gregory pulled away abruptly from Louise as the bartender came back. He rubbed his lips to cover the smear of red lipstick left on them. Desire pooled in her lower belly and her mouth tingled in memory of their brief kiss.

Gregory grabbed the beers then pulled her with him as they walked into the courtyard behind the restaurant that led to the apartments on the upper levels of the same building as The Mash. He scanned his fob to enter the building's residential entrance.

"Where are we going? Wait, do you live here?" she asked.

"Yeah," he replied. "I'm just renting here until I figure out where I want to plant my roots. It's a great neighborhood, as you know." He opened interior door for her, and they walked to the elevator.

"It's cool to see this building from the inside. This is kind of exciting," Louise said as she held on to his hand for dear life. She felt on the edge of a precipice, and she had no desire to keep from jumping off the cliff. Gregory would be there to catch her.

21

They took the elevator to the fifth floor and walked through the pristine white, almost sterile, feeling hallway. Everything was white, crisp, and modern, except the soft grey carpet with a geometric pattern.

Louise could barely focus on her surroundings, feeling so nervous and reckless to be just following Gregory blindly. They entered unit 505, a sparsely furnished yet comfortable apartment. It was apparent that Gregory had spent little time furnishing the place. He had a table and four chairs, a TV sitting on what seemed like a shabby antique piece of furniture, and a sofa. He dropped his keys on the counter and placed the beer in the refrigerator.

Leaning against the fridge, he turned and gazed at her, raking her body with his hungry stare.

"So, do you want to have a drink, sit on the sofa, and talk or something?"

She walked up to him and wrapped her arms around his torso. With a quiet shake of her head, she lifted up on her tiptoes and kissed him. She couldn't wait anymore.

"Later," she said.

Louise didn't know what possessed her, besides a yearning to feel the connection with Gregory again. A desire to feel his safety and love winding its way around her, even for just a moment.

He led her to the bedroom in silence and they stood by the bed for a moment, kissing as he unbuttoned her pants and slid his hands into them to caress her skin. As he moved his hands to the front of her, she felt a painful flame of desire, as though she would die if they didn't consummate their relationship this time. She had been in only a handful of relationships since they stopped seeing each other, and after her attack, she was basically a barren desert, where plants only survive if you water them yourself. She wanted no one to touch or come near, her only comfort a blanket of isolation and fear. The loneliness was cold and frigid. She caught a glimpse of the warmth radiating from Gregory and was drawn to it, like a moth to a flame. Out of sheer nerves, she placed her hands on his, stopping them, and looked up at him.

"It's been a long time," she said. "I want this, but I'm a bit nervous."

He smiled at her with reassurance. "Don't worry, Lou. I'll take care of you. I get it. We can stop if anything makes you uncomfortable. I'll only be happy if you're happy," he said.

She looked up at him, knowing he meant every word he said. His affection wrapped itself irresistibly around her, pushing away her walls effortlessly. She was addicted to the rush of warmth and light that entered her when she let him in. Her eyes misted from the sheer elation she felt at having someone standing in the dark with her.

"Take care of me, Gregory," she said, running her hands through his hair and bringing his head down to kiss her. He continued exploring her pants and found her throbbing clitoris, aching to be touched.

Her moisture spread easily, showing how ready she was for him.

"Babe, you are drenched," he said as he put a finger inside her, and she gave a small gasp of pleasure. He made a tortured sound in response.

"I don't want to alarm you, but I'll probably lose my mind if I don't have you tonight."

"Well, we can't have that, can we?" She tipped her head back in response to his lips near her ear.

He pulled his hands out of her pants and sat her gently on the edge of the bed. Jeans and lacy panties dropped to the floor, forgotten, and Gregory began to run his hands slowly up her legs. She blushed at thinking how shameless she was, greedily wanting him to take care of her.

Gregory kissed a path along her inner thigh, causing an involuntary shiver throughout her body. His finger dipped inside her and rubbed the outside of her heated center until she begged for him to end the torture. He brought his finger inside her and she moaned as he placed his mouth above his finger and kissed her sweet bud. He licked and moved his finger back and forth until she thought she would lose her mind if she didn't touch him.

She sat up and pulled him to her, helping him take his shirt off and reveling in the softness and warmth of his skin. She kissed his chest, inhaling the scent of him and then began unbuttoning his jeans ever so slowly, taking extra time to rub her hand on his erection through his boxer briefs.

"You better stop that, little vixen. You're going to make me blow my wad in my pants and I haven't done that since high school," he threatened.

He finished taking off his jeans and her shirt, untied her bra and finally got his hands on her breasts, which were throbbing and begging for attention. They slid between the sheets, only his underwear between them and he lay on his side, bringing his mouth to her aching nipples. Her body flushed with heat as he suckled on her one nipple, and slid his finger back inside her once again, then another. She whimpered helplessly as he stroked her relentlessly until he felt her bear down and come on his fingers. Gregory took his underwear off, desperate for his own completion. He quickly put on a condom and paused, just outside of her body.

"Are you ready for me? If you say no, I might perish, but I understand," he said, his breath panting heavily as he held himself above her. "You're in control here, Louise."

"I hardly feel in control, I'm gasping for you. Stop making me wait."

She kissed him as he brought himself into her honeyed sweetness and groaned.

"Oh my God, you feel like heaven," he moaned as he slowly pulled himself out, then pushed back inside to fill her again.

Had their sex always felt this good?

No, it was better.

She sighed and continued to kiss him, surprised at the familiar tension building up within her once again. Louise was amazed at how it felt like they had never been apart, like they were made to fit together. The feel of him throbbing inside her and stretching her once again filled her with delicious satisfaction.

"You are so fucking hot," he hissed as he seemed to savor their joining. "I'm waiting for you to come. This is pure torture," Gregory said as he continued to piston her relentlessly. He reached a hand between them and began to stroke her slippery clitoris, giving her the stimulation she needed to push her over the edge. Her release came with a soft grunt, and she pushed up against him, bearing down on his cock, which elicited a moan from Gregory. He came with alarming speed, unable to contain his desire anymore.

After a moment catching their breath, Gregory rolled off her.

"Wow. Just wow. I didn't know how much I needed that. That was incredible," he said, his chest rising and falling as his breathing returned to normal.

Louise giggled and cuddled closer to his body heat, resting her head on his shoulder. His heart raced as quickly as hers. He went to the bathroom to get a warm cloth to wash off the last traces of their love, then scooted back between the sheets and into her arms.

"It was magical," she said with a sleepy sigh. Louise felt so safe in his arms it made her feel drowsy. As her eyelids fluttered, Gregory's gaze remained on her, watching her doze, and she giggled.

"Stop, Gregory, I can't sleep with you watching me."

"Can't a guy be entranced by your perfection and loveliness? You have the sweetest pink lips, the softest hair, and such a pretty blush in your cheeks."

Louise smiled and buried her face in the pillow, feeling shy under his scrutiny. He saw in her a beauty that she never had. She felt his gaze until she fell asleep, feeling content knowing that whatever had to be done, he would keep her safe.

When they awakened at dawn, Louise took a moment to examine the profile of his face in the glow of the city lights from outside his window. He looked adorable, his dark eyelashes resting on his symmetrical cheeks. He had a boyish charm when he slept, with his hair mussed carelessly and his brow free of the cares he must carry with him every day.

"Can I open my eyes now or are you still looking?" he said softly, his mouth curving into a grin.

"I'm good. I was not staring, by the way," Louise retorted, sitting up in the bed and searching for a light. She noticed one sitting on his dresser and walked over to turn it on.

"Why don't you have a light on your nightstand? Don't you read in bed?"

"I don't know. I read in the living room, I guess. I got that one from my mum and didn't really think to go out and buy another," he said with a chuckle. The light from the lamp revealed a turntable on one end of the dresser, as well as a box of records sitting beside it.

"I guess that makes sense. Hey, are you a music nerd? You don't have bedside lamps, but you have a record player on your dresser?" Louise's eyes traveled playfully back to him with a teasing glint.

She slipped her underwear back on. After lifting various clothing items, she found her shirt on the ground as well and blushed at the haphazard way they had tossed their clothing everywhere.

"Why are you rushing off?" Gregory asked as he rose from the bed and helped her gather her clothing by tossing it on the bed near her. "You don't have to leave."

"I do. I don't want Georgie getting any crazy ideas," Louise said, noticing her hair in the mirror and frowning as she noticed it had come out and was ponytail kink crazy. She grabbed at her hair to bring it back under control and searched the room for her elastic.

"Wait, leave it. I like it messy," Gregory said as he brought his hands into her hair and pressed a kiss on her lips. "I have something to show you, you can't leave yet." Warmth bloomed in her chest, chasing the shadows that seemed to have established themselves there.

Louise gave him a tilted head look and smirked. "Okay, what

do you have to show me?" she asked, quirking a brow.

Gregory walked around to the side of his dresser and scrounged around in the antique butter box filled with records. He found the one he was searching for and brought it up to show her.

"Cool, I like that band," she said, as she watched him pull the black record from its sleeve and place it on the turntable.

"Hang on," Gregory said as he selected a particular song and placed the needle on the record, then turned to wrap his arms around her, placing his hands directly on her bottom, which was peeking out from beneath her t-shirt. The music filled the room, and he began to sway her.

Louise giggled. "Are we dancing in our underwear right now?"

"Yeah."

"You're so funny," she said and shook her head, then kissed him, spreading the last traces of her lip gloss on his lips. His hands traveled silkily up her back. He pulled back with a sigh.

"Our last slow dance was interrupted, if you recall, and I couldn't get that song out of my head. I blame you, really," he said as she rested her head on his chest. His hand traced the outline of her head, running his hands achingly slowly through her hair.

"You're right, it's only fair," she said, her head nestling into his shoulder where it belonged.

Gregory managed to convince her to dance that entire side of the album, before Louise could see the sky starting to turn orange with the rising of the sun.

"This is so lovely, but I have to go. I don't want Georgie to worry," Louise said.

Gregory reluctantly allowed her to leave, acknowledging that he wanted to stay on Georgie's good side.

They searched for the rest of their clothing strewn about the room and Gregory drove Louise home. She would be in bed before her mother woke up. After giving him a quick kiss, Louise ran quietly to her room, throwing herself on her bed and wrapping her arms around herself in disbelief that she could be so lucky. She had only had a few lovers besides Gregory. No one else could compare. Their connection was so powerful, she worried that no one would ever make her feel the way he did.

She cherished the lingering warmth of his love as she dozed until her alarm rang at six. Louise truly felt it was a new day. The pinks, oranges, and purples of the morning sky shone brighter. Even her coffee tasted better, and her warm bagel somehow seemed like the best she had ever had. Perhaps it was because she couldn't stop smiling as she crammed it in her mouth. Was she a new person? No. But it was a new world, and she was finding her place in it.

22

Louise was finding it difficult to focus on her work since her night with Gregory. She struggled with conflicting feelings of happiness and disbelief that she was doing the right thing for herself. It was really important for rebuilding her life that she did not create situations that would make her too vulnerable and set her back on her journey to repair what had been broken.

Her powerful response to Gregory had surprised her, making her wonder if the passion was fueled by the end of her sexual dry spell, or if it was the wonderful man himself that was inspiring her to feel those feelings again. It was overwhelming for her to think of being in love, dating, being normal when she had spent so much time hiding and avoiding life.

When she arrived home after work, she called Simone to see if she'd be available to go for a drink, since her mother was away for canasta night and Louise felt restless. Simone met her at the local wine bar in Marda Loop. The server helped them select some wines for them to try to each settled on a glass she enjoyed.

"So, are you going to tell me what is going on? You look like a mixture of constipation and nausea, and it is not sexy," Simone asked.

Louise swallowed, knowing she had to come clean about her situation with Gregory in order to feel less stressed about it.

"Gregory and I ended up meeting for beer and pizza the other night, and I haven't been well since," she replied.

"Did something bad happen? Tell me!" Simone insisted.

Louise shook her head.

"Nothing bad. We have amazing chemistry, and he brought me back to his apartment, and we had the most incredible sex. I am freaking out because, do I like him? What if the same thing happens that did before? I felt like after my attack I would never be able to be with a man again, yet somehow, he makes me feel so good and so safe," she replied, sighing longingly. "Simone, tell me why I feel like I've screwed something up? I'm an adult. I can do this, right?" Louise sighed heavily and played with her wineglass. Simone considered for a moment.

"Well, you've kind of closed yourself off from all people and for what? To protect yourself from some person that attacked you three years ago? Not all people are bad, Louise," Simone said. "You want to be careful, I get that, but you can't let this bad person control your life forever. You deserve to be happy."

Simone reached across the table to take Louise's hand. "That being said, if you're trying to keep from being hurt by Gregory again, the way he left things in university, that makes sense too. But a girl's gotta live," Simone said. "And let's face it, a girl has gotta get some."

Louise looked to the side, feeling the truth of Simone's words as they sank in. She wanted to live again so badly. To abandon her fears and enjoy life.

"You needed to be shaken up," Simone said with a wave. "Time to start enjoying your life again. Drink! Have sex! Laugh! Look hot! Who cares if things are messy? I mean, look at me. I'm a serial dater, which is not everyone's cup of tea, but it is so much fun!"

Louise smiled and looked at her friend, who somehow knew exactly what she needed to hear. "Thanks. I needed a custom Simone pep talk; they always get to the point."

Simone nodded in agreement; a no nonsense look of pride on her face.

"How's school going?" Louise asked.

Simone sighed. "Work and school are both really busy. My bar exam seems to be coming faster than I can cope. I'm just trying to stay focused. It's hard to have fun and be adulting at the same time, you know?" Simone pinched her shirt at the shoulders as she raised them boastfully. "Becoming a hot shit lawyer is no small feat." Louise snorted in her wine glass. No one could do confidence like Simone. There was a lot she could learn from her friend.

"I guess if you don't have all your shit together, that must mean I'm normal?" Louise asked playfully.

Simone laughed. "Honey, ain't no way you are normal. Normal is way too basic. We are two girls trying to build a life here and things are getting a bit spicier than you can handle. You'll survive. The more spice the better, I say."

Louise and Simone tried to map out what she should do next, giving Louise a little hope that maybe she was building something special with Gregory. Louise was more inclined to play it cool and let Gregory make all the moves. Simone encouraged Louise to chase after what she wanted. A few more glasses of wine later, it was decided that Louise would stay open to starting a relationship with Gregory, rather than running away like she was naturally inclined to do.

Easier said than done.

Simone also encouraged Louise to download a few dating apps and start a profile, so that she wouldn't just be putting all her eggs in one basket with Gregory. Louise hesitated at the idea. They shared an Uber that dropped them both off at their respective homes, and Louise climbed up to her bedroom with a smile on her face. She was open to learning about the different dating apps, though in her heart, she knew she would find it hard to kiss anyone besides Gregory.

She smiled at herself in the mirror as she washed her face. It would remain her little secret that a certain detective held all her eggs in his basket. She wasn't even sure she would be telling him anytime soon.

23

GREGORY REMAINED in a bit of a daze for a few days after his night with Louise. He marveled at how he went from wanting to keep her safe and warn her about the danger she was facing, to having the steamiest night of his life. He had no idea that reconnecting with Louise would highlight with painful clarity something that he had been missing in his life.

Now he contended with the reality of having started something he couldn't finish, while simultaneously creating a need he could no longer live without. His primary goal was to be a good person in his everyday life and Gregory questioned whether what he had done was right or if he had set Louise up for being hurt. Though he wouldn't consider himself a bad guy, or a player, he wouldn't say he was looking for a relationship when Louise quietly drifted into his life. It was like he lost complete control and could not help himself when he was in her presence. She was the ultimate culmination of his sexual fantasies all in one place. Her luscious curves, her silky soft skin, her bright hazel eyes, he hardened at the mere memory of her in his bed. Their romance just happened, each unable to resist the pull that existed between them.

He looked down at his nails, seeing that he was once again chewing them all the way down. Not a good sign. He was stressing about how he could continue to see Louise and work on her case. A conflict of interest was coming on and he did not like what would have to be done to correct it.

His phone buzzed in his pocket as he sat in his car outside of Angela Duffet's former apartment, doing what had now become a favorite use of his free time: staking out her place to see if her killer would show up again. Unfortunately, stakeouts gave him a lot of time to be alone with his thoughts and with his bag of stakeout jellybeans. He chewed a glob of them thoughtfully as he watched Angela's home. He ignored the phone and replayed his time with Louise in his head.

First, they reconnected through an interview about her case. Nothing wrong there, just following protocol and interviewing a witness. Then he happened to see her at the Wild Rose bar. He sighed. Oh yes, she had looked positively gorgeous that night. He had been around gorgeous women before and barely noticed. Louise didn't even try to get his attention, yet he could not keep his eyes off her.

What else? Oh yes, they danced together, and she fit so perfectly in his arms. Like she belonged there. He had danced with women at that same exact bar many times before. Why did this feel so different? He was haunted by the warmth of her skin, the sweetness of her breath, the softness of her kiss, and the look in her eyes that told him how much she needed him.

He banged his head on the steering wheel, trying to knock some sense into himself. What was wrong with him? What was wrong with him? His phone buzzed in his pocket again and he looked at the screen, seeing it was Roger looking for him. He answered his friend, and they agreed to meet for dinner at a Mexican place they both enjoyed later that evening.

Gregory drove home and decided to sweat out his angst with a good long run before getting into the shower. His feet kept him well away from Louise's house, to avoid another blissful loss of control like the other night. Out of habit, he passed by Angela's apartment, as though an obsessed predator looking of his prey. He needed to get his head on straight and work out what he was going to do. His priority had to be the cases waiting to be solved. People were relying on him to be successful, including his victim, Angela Duffet.

After his run, he showered and changed into jeans, a plain grey t-shirt and a navy sweatshirt on top. He combed his hair and put his dark brown rimmed glasses on, took a moment to assess his look in the mirror and deemed it acceptable.

An Uber dropped him off at Native Tongues restaurant to meet Roger and could see his friend already sat at a table with a beer in front of him.

"How's it going? What did you order to drink?" Gregory asked.

Roger chuckled, saying, "I ordered a beer and some shots for us. It's a double shot kind of day."

Gregory paused to ponder the menu and order himself a cerveza. "So, why the double shot day?" He put down the menu.

Roger sighed and replied "I feel like I'm just batting zero when it comes to women. I'm a hot mess is all, nothing new. We all know whose fault that is. Are there negative health consequences to going too long without sex? I feel like there might be," Roger said and put his hand on his chest as though checking to see that his heart was still beating.

Gregory rolled his eyes and shook his head in exasperation. "You'll be fine. Maybe give those dating apps a break. Those people are only looking for casual hook ups. I don't think you need that right now. You need to get your shit together," Gregory said. "Besides, I don't remember you and Bianca being that hot and heavy. You've gone without it before."

Roger's eyes widened and his mouth gaped open, but he agreed. "Perhaps that is precisely why I'm on those apps, right? I'm a good-looking guy, girls like me. I just need to figure out how to close the deal without looking like an asshat."

Roger looked at Gregory jokingly and asked him how he went so long without sex. Gregory blushed, not really wanting to answer, but knowing his friend would not be satisfied if he balked at the question.

"I really focus on work and that keeps me so tired and busy that I haven't really thought about sex or women or anything. It's been a few years since I dated anyone."

Roger's mouth frowned and shook his head in concern.

Gregory put up a finger to stop him from commenting. "Hang on, I am happy to announce that at this time, I am no longer living in a sexual desert." Gregory felt a surge of excitement in his body, as though announcing his connection to Louise filled him with pride. He tempered his reaction, not wanting to seem too eager.

Rogers eyes grew big in disbelief. "What? I don't believe it, with who?" His hand smacked his forehead, and his jaw opened in shock…or was it delight?

Gregory put his face in his hands and cringed at the idea of discussing these personal details about his sex life. He didn't want to sound like he was bragging, but his best friend, would never let it go if he wasn't truthful.

"Well, I met this sweet girl for pizza the other night and we had a good time, and we went back to my place, and we continued that good time."

Roger chuckled, unable to contain his mirth as he looked at Gregory. "Look at you, you're blushing!" he said, pointing his finger accusingly at Gregory. "You sexy bastard, tell me who!"

Gregory groaned in discomfort, not wanting to share anymore details. They paused to drink their shots, and Gregory welcomed the feeling of the tequila as it burned down his throat. They chased it with the sweet tartness of the lime they popped into their mouths and sucked immediately after. Gregory shivered.

"She's someone I dated in the past, lost touch with, and recently ran into again. It's probably not going to work out, so I don't really want to make a big deal about it."

The waiter came by, and they ordered two more beers and some fresh guacamole with tortilla chips.

"Listen, pal, I'm sure your lady appreciates your discretion, but I'm going to figure it out."

"Fine, go ahead and try."

"Okay, she's someone you dated previously, well that's easy, because women rarely want to date you. Or rather, you don't really make time for them. That's only a few girls…" Roger tapped his finger on his mouth with a theatrical hum. "She's someone you recently reconnected with." He tapped his mouth again with a louder hum, then made a knowing face. "Easy. It's Louise. You came on the date to make things a little more relaxed with Simone and somehow you ended up getting action and I'm over here dying of sexual deprivation.

Not fair. You are paying for my drinks tonight." Roger slapped the table dramatically.

Gregory laughed, his shoulders sagging in acceptance. Fair enough.

They took a few bites of their chips and guacamole and washed it down with the refreshing Mexican pilsner. Roger clearly decided it was time to spill his own secret about their group date at the Wild Rose Saloon.

"You want to hear how that night ended for me? I ended up chatting with Simone and crying about Bianca with my head in her lap like a baby. What a winner. I need to figure out how to avoid crying on dates, I guess," Roger said, hiding his face in mock shame.

Gregory cringed and chuckled, shaking his head. "Why were you crying?"

"I don't know, we got talking about the divorce, and I guess she somehow touched a sore spot. I have no idea. Maybe I had too much beer." He shrugged with a sad sigh. "I swear, in my normal life, I have charisma and charm. When I'm on a date? It goes out the window completely!"

Roger swore him to secrecy about his moment of weakness and Gregory made him promise to keep his lips sealed about Louise. They sealed the deal with a few tacos and a lot more Mexican beer. Gregory shared his concerns about his relationship being a conflict of interest, since Louise would qualify as being a witness or a victim, depending on which case he was working on.

"So, you see, I'm in the worst dilemma, because I'm hot for this girl, yet if I keep going out with her, I'm compromising a case that I worked hard to get. If I mess up this case, who knows how long it will be before I get handed another important one?" Gregory said.

Roger pondered the dilemma. "That's a tough one. You haven't connected with anyone in so long, which makes Louise special. On the other hand, there are a lot of girls out there for you to choose from. Typically, a guy puts on that uniform and women throw themselves at you, right? Maybe Louise isn't the only option? I don't think a woman is worth your career, but that's just me."

Both men shrugged and decided they wouldn't be solving all their problems on this night. Gregory had lots to think about before making his next move. They also agreed that there must be something wrong with both of them, since maintaining a healthy relationship was clearly not in the cards in either of their futures.

24

LOUISE WAS GLAD TO HAVE SOME TIME ALONE to think about the things that had changed in her life recently. Her feet were standing on a precipice, with a vision of her perfect future laying before her and many obstacles standing in her way that she was going to remove. If she could.

When she had first set out on her mission of creating a new life for herself, free of the pall of fear and torment her attacker had placed upon her life, she had done so thinking he was in her past. She planned on moving on and resurrecting the life she had and the person she once was.

Her goals were simple:

Find an apartment.

Keep killing it at work.

Get back to the activities she previously enjoyed.

Nowhere on her list was falling in lust with an irresistible officer, or having her attacker become a murderer that was prowling the streets of Marda Loop.

The chaos made her wonder how she was going to create a nice and neat put together life, when things kept blowing up in her path. How on earth had she gone from being an almost nun with vows of celibacy to being a lustful creature that wanted to climb Gregory Band and drive him wild with desire? Her original life plan was simple and low stress. Having a man or a relationship had not factored into the equation. She wasn't confident about her ability to be in a healthy relationship yet. She felt too raw, too fragile, too protective of her heart and her body. Second, how was she supposed to build a life knowing her attacker could be stalking her still? How was she supposed to escape the fear when it kept following her and gaining strength faster than she was?

Would it be wise to start living on her own, knowing he could be out there waiting for the perfect moment to strike? How would she be able to focus on the important building blocks she was laying out for her future, when she was a horny basket case?

Around ten p.m., she finished looking at her latest episode of *The Bachelor* when she saw a message from Gregory pop up on her phone.

"Can I call you?" he messaged.

Louise groaned. "Okay," she typed in response.

She picked up as soon as he saw his name in bold on her phone screen.

"Hey, what's up?" she started.

"I don't want this to seem like a booty call, but can I come see you? I've got some interesting news for you. It's about the case," he said.

"Okay, as long as you're not making booty call habits with me. I'm not that kind of girl. I'm still recovering from last time," she replied with a giggle as blush suffused her cheeks.

Gregory knocked as she was still on the phone, so she hung

up and opened the door. He pushed into the door closed it quickly behind him, not wanting anyone to see where she lived, possibly being overly protective. One final cautionary glance through the living room window seemed to reassure him that he was not being followed or watched. He began to lower the curtain.

"This should be closed for the next little while. Can't have anyone peeping through your windows," he said, acting very much like a man used to having people obey his authority. Louise crossed her arms and quirked a brow at him.

Glancing down at her arms reminded her she was in her sofa uniform, very comfy and cat friendly, but also very unattractive. Gregory scanned her from top to bottom, as though he was exercising a certain level of restraint and control.

"Are you Gregory right now, or Detective Band? I need to know how to behave," she questioned playfully.

Gregory sighed and grabbed her by the hips, pulling her close to him. "Hang on," he said as he gave her a soft kiss on the lips. He lingered for a moment, as though debating kissing her longer, but in the end, he pulled away.

"Ok, now I'm Detective Band. Let's have a seat in the kitchen. I've got an interesting update on our case in South Calgary, which might affect you if things line up nicely. I can't give you much information, as you know, but what I can tell you is we have picked up a guy we like as a suspect for this South Calgary murder," he explained, his eyes scanning her face for a reaction.

"That's good, right?" she ventured, a glimmer of hope bathing her insides with lightness. Maybe it was all over.

"He ticks all the boxes: Ex-boyfriend, messy break up, you get the idea. He says he's innocent and I won't jump to conclusions before we have proof, but we've sent away for DNA testing and our fingers are crossed."

Louise thought for a moment, absorbing the information. "Does he seem like a multiple offender type? What makes you think he came after me?"

His confidence flagged, which gave Louise pause.

Gregory explained that DNA testing would be crucial. It would take a few weeks to confirm, so Louise still had reason to be cautious.

"He confessed to visiting and watching our victim's house after she had died. I picked him up after staking out the place for a few days. He's definitely got a creepy vibe, though I'm still not sure if it's a creepy ex-boyfriend vibe or a creepy serial killer vibe."

Louise considered the information, still wondering if her next moves would be wise given this new information. "I've been hoping I could move on with my life, maybe get my own apartment. This makes me feel like I have to wait. Do you think I'm in immediate danger?"

Gregory slowly exhaled, reaching his hand across the table to touch her arm. "I don't think you're out of the woods, but this lead is promising. Where were you thinking of moving? Not to another city, right?"

Louise explained that she had looked at some places and had not decided yet. She was not convinced that he needed to know what all her next moves were. It's not like he was her boyfriend.

"Why are you so interested? I believe this has nothing to do with your case, Detective Band," she asked, challenging.

Gregory smiled and pressed his hands on the table as he stood up.

"You're right, I'm sure you'll tell me when you're ready."

He came up in front of her, using her hand to pull her out of her chair.

"We're friends, right? I care about what happens to you. I like to think there might be more pizza nights in my future. I'm suddenly in love with pizza," he said, placing his arms around her as he moved his face closer to hers. She inhaled the scent of lime and cedarwood and found it purely intoxicating.

"You like pizza, huh? Well, I like pizza too. We could have another pizza night I guess... You might just have to convince me."

He pressed his lips to hers, relishing the sweet taste of her. His tongue joined hers as they deepened their kiss. He kissed her down the side of her face and neck, pausing in the crook of her neck to inhale her scent.

"Mmm, it's so hard to resist you, you feel so good in my arms," he moaned, bringing his lips back to hers. She felt the curl of desire rising inside, creating an insatiable hunger. She pulled away reluctantly.

"My mum will be home soon from dinner with her friends. She's not usually out this late. I'd hate for her to walk in on something. I don't want her to get any ideas. She has a wild imagination," Louise said. Gregory groaned and pressed his forehead to hers.

"Yeah, I have to get back to work. You are going to drive me mad," Gregory said as he stepped back reluctantly, his hand clutching hers until the last possible moment. The flutters in her chest told her that even though she thought she was on the fence about a relationship with Gregory, her body had no doubts. His proximity had a dizzying effect on her, and she would have to reign in her passions if she was to give herself time to think and make the best decisions for her future. Gregory had yet to declare himself or give her any hint that he was interested in anything serious.

For the sake of her sanity, she had to guard her heart.

Pizza nights could lead them into dangerous territory.

Louise couldn't believe the end of October had already arrived, and she was dusting off her cat ears for her annual Halloween neighborhood walk. She was a little bummed that her mother had canceled since she was not feeling well. Georgie ended up happily staying home and handing out candies to all the trick-or-treaters coming to the door.

Louise was putting on her black puffer coat, since it was the most complimentary to her kitty ears and the evenings had a cold bite to them. As she finished getting ready, she looked down at her phone, seeing two missed calls from Simone, who also enjoyed partaking in the neighborhood walk with her. Louise called her back only to find out she had to cancel because her car battery was not working, and she needed to wait for the AMA guy to come give her a boost.

Disappointed, Louise was tempted to just stay home and cuddle on the sofa with Georgie watching a movie, when she decided to be bold and send a message to Gregory.

"Hey, are you working tonight?" she asked.

"Nah, just on a self-inflicted stakeout, what's up?" he replied.

"Want to come walk the neighborhood with me? Maybe patrol

the streets to maintain trick-or-treater safety? I was going to go walk the streets and visit a few neighbors with Simone and she had to cancel," Louise said.

Gregory was silent as he considered, and she hoped he would accept the invitation, since it would be reassuring having him there protecting her. Besides, patrolling the streets of Marda Loop was definitely something he could feel good about doing. No shady romantic dealings there. Keeping the citizens of his community safe on a busy night of mischief.

"Ok, I'll walk over and meet you," he said.

When Gregory arrived, Louise met him on the doorstep, eager to see him, yet oddly shy. They had not yet defined the nature of their relationship, so she wasn't at the comfort level required to throw her arms around him and kiss him in front of other people like she wanted. She felt the nervous flutter in her stomach as he approached and a giant smile paint itself on her face.

"Thanks for coming," she said.

"It's my pleasure," he said. "I love walking down the street with a beautiful woman on my arm." He bent his arm, creating a space for her to insert her own arm and walk beside him.

Louise flushed at his comment, feeling lucky to be spending time with such a dashing police officer. She was grateful for this comforting touch, since being out at night usually made her nervous. With the brightly lit Halloween decorations all around, the festive feeling of children and parents walking and chatting joyously, she felt energized.

Gregory turned to her and smiled. "I like your kitty ears, they're very cute."

Louise smiled up at him and cuddled his arm, happy to be walking through the neighborhood and seeing how all the extreme

Halloween fans had decorated their homes. Creepy sounds could be heard playing from giant speakers, colored spotlights all around, creating an atmospheric interplay between the light and the darkness. They walked by neighbors' homes and enjoyed the famous "witches brew" that one house always handed out, a delicious concoction of Baileys and hot chocolate that was just for the adults.

Louise had the chance to catch up with another neighbor who was handing out beers and welcoming people to chat and warm up in their garage. It was a wonderful night that reminded her of how much she enjoyed being part of her community and all the great people that surrounded them.

They entered a crowded side street which was so busy it felt almost like a street festival. The houses were covered with lights, giant skeletons towering over tombstones on their lawns. They laughed at the hanging skulls and scary ghosts and admired the variety of blow-up Halloween decorations that seemed quite over the top.

"Hey, thanks for inviting me to this, this is pretty cool. I've never seen a place so lit up for Halloween."

She looked up at him and smiled, her gaze then traveled around to try to capture all the action that was going on around them. Her gaze traveled and stopped suddenly, fixated on a person dressed like a pilot in a leather jacket with wool trim and a hat with goggles on his head. She recognized a familiar outline and stared at him slightly longer than was appropriate.

Riveted, she could not take her eyes off him and when the man turned, she nearly fainted with the shock that slammed into her body. It was him. Even though her memories from that night were a blur, she felt she could recognize the profile of his face. He was walking with a group of people, laughing, and someone walked in front of

Louise, blocking her sight of him.

Gregory had noticed her sudden fixation and stared at her. "What is it?"

"He's over there. I think I see him," she whispered in shock.

Louise felt the suffocating choke of her voice as it worked to come out. Her heart began to thud in her chest, and she felt the beginnings of panic-induced electricity spreading to her fingertips. The uncontrollable shake began, her body pushing her to run for cover.

"Where? How do you know? I thought you didn't see him," Gregory questioned, taking her by the arms to bring her back to his attention. He followed her gaze. "Where is he?"

"The pilot," she whispered, struck dumb by her fear.

Gregory turned, pushing through the crowd and looking for him while dragging Louise behind him by the hand.

"Tell me in which direction he moves," he said as they looked around desperately for the pilot.

She scanned the crowd, her awareness back and spurning her on to find her attacker. She saw him as he turned down a side path where townhome residents were handing out candies and children were moving around them at different speeds. They had to be careful to not run into the little ones running excitedly from one house to the other.

They followed the pilot down a brightly lit pathway, coming out onto another street. It was a busier street with more car traffic, and fewer trick-or-treaters. They could see further around them, since there were very few people around them. The pilot was nowhere to be seen. Gregory turned desperately to Louise.

"Do you see him anywhere?" he asked.

She shook her head in response, almost disbelieving she had seen anything at all. "Do you think I imagined it?" she asked Gregory with trepidation, shame creeping in slowly.

"Of course not. It makes me feel sick that he could be out there, so close to you. We have to be more careful," he suggested. "Come on, I'll take you home."

Louise was overcome with a sense of doubt. She had barely seen her attacker that night. Why did she get the impression that she had seen him?

"Wait, maybe I did imagine it. Like a hallucination, you know, because we've been talking about the case so much. Could be just that," she considered.

Gregory looked at her, unconvinced. "Is that really what your gut is telling you? I saw your face. There is no mistaking that. It's not a stretch to think he could be out there, possibly hunting for his next victim," he said, hoping to validate her instincts. "Besides, you went through a trauma, there's no telling what memories are buried inside your mind, trickling out over time."

They walked back slowly, taking a winding, indirect path to avoid having anyone follow them. Louise could not be sure if it was her attacker, since she only knew brief glimpses of him. She just felt so convinced she had seen him. She forced Gregory to stop when they went through a fenced pathway that ran between two houses near the cottage.

"I need a minute. I need to chill before I see Georgie," Louise said, pausing Gregory. She leaned over, placing her hands on her knees and taking a few deep breaths. "She's either going to be worried about me or mad because I'm letting my attacker get to me."

She huffed as Gregory came to rub her back gently, bringing her a warm comfort that slowed her heartbeat. Her eyes closed as she enjoyed the simple touch, something she was not yet accustomed to, yet knew instinctively she had been missing. Pushing up on her thighs, she straightened herself and leaned against the tall white fence closing her eyes.

"Okay, I think I'm okay now," she said blinking to dry up the tears that threatened. She passed a finger beneath each eye, to catch anything that might have been attempting to escape.

"Take as long as you need," Gregory said, wrapping his arms around her and placing her head against his shoulder.

Louise inhaled the scent of cold air on his cheeks mixed with the delightful tang of his deodorant. She felt she could fall asleep here, nestled in the strength of his arms. "I just want to feel safe, if just for a moment. Why does that seem so impossible?" Louise wrapped her arms around his waist.

"You're safe with me. I'll take care of you," he whispered into her ear.

"I want to feel safe with me," she said, her lip trembled, and her face scrunched, as though trying to retract the moisture that was slipping for her eyes.

"You will be," he said, his hand moving in a circular motion on her back. "We just have to catch him. We're gonna catch him."

Gregory lifted her face to gaze into his determined eyes and she felt the power within him reigniting her own inner strength. She almost believed his ambitious words and a small smile curved her lips. She could only nod in response, feeling the strength of his will dominate her fear and doubt.

"You're right," she croaked, clearing her throat.

"Damn right, I'm right," Gregory said. "No one's going to lay a hand on my girl."

His lips came upon hers as though to mark his ownership and

Louise was happy to submit to his possession for a moment, anything to take away the sick feeling of despair clawing at her chest. It was a dream to imagine being his girl, to one day be sheltered by his love and protection. She pulled away, convinced their relationship had shifted, gone to a level it had never gone before.

Perhaps it was too soon, too much to hope for already, but a whisper of something filled her chest, pushing away the darkness and making her feel like all was not lost. They walked back to Cambrai Cottage hand in hand, with Gregory scanning the area to ensure no one was watching the residence. The silence in the living room suggested Georgie had gone up to read in bed, so the couple shared one more quiet kiss, Gregory's hands lingering on either side of her face.

"Take care, okay? Set your house alarm when I leave. Don't go out alone and pay attention to your surroundings. I'm going to go catch a few hours of sleep and then get back to work. Getting this case solved is the only way I'm going to know you're safe," he said.

Louise watched him walk away, feeling bereft of his comforting presence. She checked all the locks and windows, scanning the house's perimeter through the windows to ensure no one was indeed watching. Had she let her guard down too soon and had taken on too much too fast?

Thoughts of kissing Gregory made her shake her head in denial. If she had stayed home and done nothing, she would still be afraid. Now she got to be afraid, and hopeful. And giddy.

Gregory's girl.

There was no going back for her now. Louise reached for her bat beside the bed, needing the feeling of security it provided. She cuddled her baseball bat in bed once again, wishing it was a certain detective instead.

26

THE MORNING NEWS SEEMED BLEAK, announcing a winter storm warning was in effect for the area, a typical development at this time of the year. Calgary had predictably unpredictable weather and quite often, citizens could enjoy beautiful summer weather late into September and October.

However, there was a chance of a blizzard any time after between September and May. Given that the month of October had just ended, Louise shrugged and accepted it, knowing it was not a huge surprise.

Louise ate her buttered bagel and coffee, dreading her next encounter with the winter closet. Every year she thought it would get easier, but to her dismay it was not so. She tried on her long winter jacket and realized this one was too tight. It would have to do, since the storm was on its way, though shopping was once again in her future. After her attack, she had hit pause on the natural progression of her life.

At one time, she had been fit and active, taking more time to be outside or go to fitness classes like Pilates and yoga in the past. She had dieted a lot to better fit within societal expectations for a woman in her twenties. Louise would be the last to say that she had loved and appreciated her body back then, since it seems to be a woman's curse to never truly be happy with their bodies. The younger version of herself spent too much time dieting, restricting food, and punishing herself with exercise. After having her life nearly end, she had spent time recovering from that trauma, while learning to appreciate that she had been given a second chance at life.

Two years later, she was feeling like she had lived for a reason beyond looking perfect like the influencers on social media. She was ready to climb out of her hole and become human again. The time she had spent going out with friends and Gregory, reminded her of the human connections that had once made her life so wonderful. Yes, she weighed more than she ever had, which meant she needed a new wardrobe beyond the black tunics, dresses and leggings she often wore to hide her body, but she was living. She was breathing. She was existing.

Louise researched the classes she used to attend and planned on getting back to reestablish those previous connections. She missed the time spent with friends at yoga, or in her running groups, not the constant desire that she wasn't good enough. She knew that getting back to her classes would fill some of the emptiness that remained inside her as she looked to rebuild her life.

Having been so close to death reminded her that her life was worth living, and her hole, though it was so safe and cozy, was becoming a jail from which she was ready to break free. Her goal was no longer to be who she once was. Louise was ready to become the woman that life had forged into being. That woman was currently a size twelve and needed a new jacket. She loved carbs and beer and knew that life could be snatched from you anytime, so you had better enjoy yourself.

Louise had arranged to take the morning off work to go down to the police station to see the person Gregory had identified as a possible suspect. DNA evidence was crucial to identify the perpetrator, and a witness would make the case against any suspect stronger. She dreaded going because this would make one of two things official. She might lay eyes on the man who had violated her in her home, shattering her life and snatching her peace. Conversely, she might identify the suspect as not her attacker, which would mean there was still a predator roaming the streets.

She had a serious case of déjà vu when she pulled up to the police station, although she was very excited to see Gregory this time. He met her at the door and kept a professional distance as they walked through the hallways of the station. This time, rather than going down the interview rooms, Louise was led down a different hall to a room where she walked in front of a large window looking into another beige-colored room.

Gregory gazed at her, checking to see if she was ready. Louise nodded, then he walked through another door to give the signal to someone outside the room. Five clean cut men entered the room, crushing Louise's hope inside her chest almost instantly. Gregory came back into the room, his eyes filled with questions.

"They can't see me, right?" Louise asked nervously.

"No, they can't. Now they are going to say a line I picked out from your witness testimony. Brace yourself, this part can be hard."

Each man took his turn. Her breath stilled in her chest as she listened with apprehension.

"I've waited so long to be with you," each spoke when their time came.

Louise heard each man in turn, using all the strength she could muster to hold back the tears welling up in her eyes. She knew she had to be strong. This was not over by a long shot.

Her face must have communicated to Gregory that she was getting upset, because he walked into a side room and asked for the men to be taken away. He then came in and wrapped his arms around her. Since no one was around, she was grateful he permitted himself that breach in protocol.

"I'm sorry. I know that was so hard. I need you to tell me," he said, pulling back and looking at her in the eyes as a few tears trickled down her cheeks. She wiped them with her shirtsleeve.

"Did you see him? Was one of those men your attacker? Think carefully and try to remember," he questioned, his eyes boring into hers. Louise closed her eyes, tears coming down in earnest as she felt herself deflate and want to curl up into a ball on the sofa at home. Go back into her hiding place. She shook her head.

"He's not here. I may not be a super reliable witness, but they didn't sound like him or look like what I saw of my attacker." She pressed her head once again into his chest, trying to find comfort in his arms. He gave her another squeeze and let her go.

"Let me take you home in your car. Marty can pick me up from your place."

Louise nodded and allowed herself to be led back to her car. They stopped for a moment as Gregory told Marty to follow them in his own vehicle.

When Louise arrived home, she ran into the cottage, shutting and locking the door quickly behind her and letting out a giant sob she had unknowingly been holding. She went up to her bedroom, resentful of the fact that she would be trapped here for longer than she thought. She curled up into a ball on her bed and allowed the tears to flow.

Louise knew she wasn't moving out; she couldn't imagine starting over on her own now. She cried tears of mourning for the life she had just barely begun.

Georgie came in, knowing without asking that Louise was going through it. Louise had informed her that morning of her trip to the police station. In her motherly way, she patted Louise's back as she cried. Louise mourned the idea of starting over, feeling she would be forever encased in these walls of fear.

"How do I go on with my life while he's still out there?" she wailed. "How, Mum? When I know he could be watching me, hunting me, just like he did those other girls?"

"You don't have to do anything you're not ready for, honey," Georgie said. "Maybe you're trying to do too much too fast."

Louise knew she needed to give her heart time to catch up with all this change. Her body physically needed more processing time. She trembled, allowing the depth of the fear and anxiety wash through her. She knew if she decided not to move out, it would be okay. Georgie's cottage would always provide her with a soft place to land.

27

THE BLACK AND WHITE CALGARY POLICE CAR drove carefully along, managing through the snow-covered and icy streets after the previous night's snowstorm. Marty and Gregory had traveled to re-interview some neighbors about the Marda Loop murder case, hoping they could shake out some new tidbits of information. Gregory sat in silence, pondering what his next move would be regarding this case, since he had already hit a dead end.

The DNA results comparing the ex-boyfriend to Louise's case would most likely not be a match for both cases. She didn't single him out in the lineup, though she clearly had some memory of what her attacker looked like, since she thought she had seen him on Halloween night. He would continue to keep the ex-boyfriend on his radar until he confirmed the results.

"So," Marty began, giving Gregory the impression he was going to start an awkward conversation. "I know you want to stay on this case, but what are you gonna do about her? That's going to be a problem if Antonio finds out."

Gregory's eyes widened as he considered the question before replying. "Well, to be honest, I'm not sure what to do about anything. I've known her since we were in university, it's hard to not have a relationship with her. We're friends."

Marty harrumphed, his brow furrowing in disbelief. "Listen, don't be an idiot, you can't be making goo-goo eyes at a witness in a case. It just isn't done. You guys are way more than friends. Having a relationship with a witness would compromise any court case down the line. Think about it."

Gregory clenched his fist, launching into a frustrated silence fraught with misery as he gazed out the window.

I'm going to have to deal with this situation sooner rather than later.

Even though he knew this already, having Marty say it out loud somehow made it worse. His guts were all tied up in knots, thinking of how badly he was screwing up his first big case.

When they arrived at the police station, he went back to his desk to analyze his notes and collect any new information that may have come in while he had been with Louise. The tech group had completed their analysis of Angela Duffet's telephone and discovered some important texts with a new person. The good news was the texts came from a contact on a dating app. The bad news was they came from a burner phone and could not be traced.

The man Angela had connected with had sent her some steamy texts. They had been out together a few times before she invited him to her apartment for a glass of wine. In the last series of texts, the suspect had insisted on going to her apartment rather than going out and used whatever means of persuasion needed to get there. Gregory suspected these texts to be coming from her killer, who had set up a meeting on the night she was killed. He would investigate where the phone was purchased in hopes of seeing the suspect on camera.

Only a positive DNA match would give him a definite suspect so he continued to look for more clues that would shed light on his case. He needed more suspects to test.

In the back of his mind, he mulled over what he was going to do about Louise. He couldn't imagine such a beautiful, sweet, breath-of-fresh-air woman could cause such havoc. When they decided to enjoy each other so thoroughly, neither had imagined they would get to this point, where difficult choices had to be made. His heart was hurting, which he didn't understand.

In the past, he had never had any issue putting his career first, love life second. If he was honest, love wasn't even a player in his life until Louise. He buried his head in his hands, hoping to stem the pain that was roiling within him. He could not compromise this case in any way. It would risk having a dangerous predator set free because of his involvement with a witness.

The idea of breaking things off with Louise when they were feeling so right was completely gutting. How would he protect her if he couldn't be always in her orbit? He meant to keep her close during this case so that she could share her thoughts with him and ideally, assist him in cracking both cases.

If he broke things off with her, she would hate him, and he wouldn't be able to keep her safe. That's all he ever wanted: to keep her safe. To keep the citizens of his city safe. Maybe he had gotten way too close, but he convinced himself it was all in the name of providing protection.

28

THE NIGHT WRAPPED AROUND HIM like the walls of a deep freezer. Everything was covered in a thick coating of solid frozen snow and ice. The storm, as expected, had been epic and the citizens of Calgary were hunkering down for a lingering cold spell.

Gregory shivered in his long black parka, thankful for its warm embrace, which helped fend off the chill outside. It could not help with the chill emanating from his heart on this night. He felt like the worst piece of garbage walking to Louise's house, knowing he was going to have to end things. After an exchange of messages, he had established that she was available for a talk, so he walked over to her house.

Georgie was out for canasta night, so he appreciated that they would have some privacy. It had been such a blessing to watch Louise find her inner strength and transform into the empowered woman that resided within her. Working on her own case and getting back out into the world seemed to almost agree with her at times. Other times it was a struggle, given that the Marda Loop murderer was once again making his presence known in the area.

Regardless of what was happening with her case, she was work-ing on rebuilding her life and claiming her space in the world from which she had hidden for so long. It had taken her time to open up and trust someone. As a recipient of that precious trust, Gregory dreaded the moment when he would be breaking it and possibly setting her back in her recovery. He sighed deeply, resenting the rise of steam from his breath in his glasses making it impossible to see what was in front of him. Luckily, he knew the neighborhood well and could tell where he was, otherwise it would be very disorientating.

He couldn't believe she had chosen to share such special moments with him, given that he did not consider himself worthy of her. Now he was planning on revealing himself as the villain and setting her up for heartache. Though they hadn't been together very long, she had come to mean a lot to him. He wanted to see her happy, glowing like she did after they made love at his apartment or when they danced at the Wild Rose Saloon. He wanted her to feel free, unencumbered.

Ugh, he thought, would this mean she would start dating other guys? Sharing those bedroom moments with someone else? His blood boiled at the thought. His hands curled into fists inside his heavy mittens. She was not his possession, and he knew once he set her free, she would be able to move on with someone who could give her all of himself.

Gregory couldn't fathom making her wait, loving in secret, while he finished up with a case, a trial, all while keeping their relationship hidden from his work. It made him feel dirty. Dating the victim or witness on a case was not forbidden, but it would definitely raise some eyebrows and Gregory would be horrified if it compromised the case against the Marda Loop murderer one day. So long as he was working on this case, most likely the biggest case of his career, he needed to be hands off with Louise. His heart squeezed painfully. Either way, he was damned.

He stood a moment staring at the red door of the Cambrai Cottage, gathering his strength and trying to stave off the awful feeling in his gut that he was making a huge mistake.

Louise opened the door with a joyful expression on her face. She threw her arms around Gregory and gave him a big hug, then softly kissed him on the lips. The warmth of her could be felt all the way down to the tips of his toes. Just what he needed to fend off the chill of the unforgiving winter. He held on for dear life, knowing she wouldn't want to be in his arms anymore once he said what he came to say.

"I'm so glad you came; I was all alone, and I missed you." She pointed to the coffee table in the living room. "Look, I took out a bottle of wine. Have a drink with me?" she asked.

He nodded, defeated. "A drink sounds great," he said as he took off his coat and placed it on the arm of the sofa. He was devastated by the sweetness of the scene.

He could see Cosette nestled in the blanket, right next to the spot where Louise had vacated. Louise had set out two wine glasses on the coffee table and opened a box of chocolates. The deep ruby colored wine was poured into the glasses, a perfect warm up for a frigid night. She went to her spot next to the cat and patted the sofa cushion next to her. He came and sat next to her, and she wrapped her arms around him again. With her head on his chest, she looked up at him expectantly.

"So, what did you need to tell me?" she asked.

Gregory cleared his throat and reached over to the coffee table and grabbed his glass, taking a large gulp. Louise must have sensed his discomfort and had a sip of her wine too, suddenly feeling suspicious that something was off. Gregory was not giving off romantic evening vibes. He knew he was giving off an I-have-to-tell-you-something-you-won't-like vibe. They were momentarily distracted by Cosette, who nudged Gregory rather aggressively, begging for attention. Gregory patted her absently on the head and was rewarded with more aggressive head butts and some drool.

Louise seemed to grow more and more tense as she watched him. "What is it, Gregory?"

Gregory could tell she already had her guard up. Louise was too smart. He let out a large sigh and took a moment to get his words out correctly. There wasn't an easy way to crush someone's hopes and smush out the flame of their passion.

"Tell me," she said. Her hand rubbed his, and Louise looked like she was ready to throw up. Her demeanor had changed from happy to fearful in mere seconds.

Gregory cleared his throat, not wanting to torture her any longer than necessary. "Listen, I've really treasured our time together, but I've come up to a bit of a roadblock. I — we can't do this anymore," he said pain etching itself on his face. Louise pulled back as though she had been slapped in the face.

"What? Why?" she queried.

The way her eyes widened in surprise was a punch to the gut. Her eyebrows came together in confusion. Gregory could tell the moment the spark left her eyes, and she looked away. Her look told him he had not only hurt her, but he had also done what she had expected. Which was worse.

"This is the biggest case I've ever had in my career, and I cannot afford anything to go wrong. The stakes are too high. Too many lives are at risk if I screw up, including yours," Gregory replied, the words tasting like poison in his mouth.

He watched her face transform from worried to crushed. He hated causing her this pain, though he knew he was doing the right thing. Solving this case had to come first. An incredulous look painted itself on her face.

"I am getting a real sense of déjà vu right now, Gregory. I thought maybe you had changed," she said, anger clearly displayed on her face. Louise rolled her eyes. "I am such an idiot. Of course, this is happening again. Let me guess — you can't date me because…you're worried about your career right now?"

Gregory hesitated and looked away shamefully, taking another drink of his wine. Her negative thoughts toward herself seemed to light a fire in him.

"No, hang on a minute. You're not the idiot here, I am. I started something shouldn't have. You did nothing wrong; you are so…so perfect."

"Not perfect enough for you, clearly," she said between tightly drawn lips.

"Louise, please, you have to understand. I can't have you waiting while I work on this complex case, then go through the trial process. It could take months or years. It wouldn't be fair. And the optics aren't great, people are already starting to ask questions."

Gregory could see Louise bringing her legs up to her chest and wrapping her arms around them. She looked away from him, unable to make eye contact.

"This case has to be my priority right now. Lives are at risk. If

I'm caught dating a witness, well, it could compromise my investigation, or the trial. It's too risky," he said and reached for her shoulder,
wanting to reassure her in some pathetic way, but she shifted out of
his reach. Gregory sighed, knowing it was probably best if she was
mad at him. Better than thinking of her being heartbroken. Louise
sat in silence, unable to make eye contact with him.

"It's been amazing getting to know you again, but the timing just
isn't right," Gregory said, trying to hide the chagrin he was feeling
inside. "I hope you can forgive me one day." Louise rested her face
in her knees, silence stretching taut between them, with only the
hum of the refrigerator being heard between them. Louise looked
up, her eyes damp with unshed tears. Of course she wouldn't cry in
front of him, she was so used to putting up a brave front.

"Are you sure? I really like you. It seems a bit premature to end
it before things they even get started. I don't get it."

"It's for the best."

"You said I was your girl," Louise said, a pleading look in her eyes.

She looked at him like he was a lifeguard holding a buoy and
she was drowning. Louise was waiting for someone to help pull her
out of the turbulent waters. Against his instincts, he shook his head,
denying her the salvation she needed. They both needed.

"I can't change the situation. I was living in a fantasy," he replied,
"it's best to stop it now, before we, you know, develop actual feelings
for each other."

Louise exhaled loudly. Her mouth flattened and a mask of
indifference came on her face. "Right. I should have learned from
the past. I won't make that mistake again," Louise said as she stood
up, Gregory followed.

He placed his hands on her arms, a resigned look on his face.

"I can't tell you how much this kills me. I don't want to hurt you, I only wanted to make you happy, and now I have robbed you of joy. I hope you'll be able to forgive me one day," Gregory said, choking on the finality of their conversation. It felt too devastatingly final.

Louise looked away.

"Just go away, Gregory. Leave me alone. I'll take care of myself. I'll protect myself," she said, walking him to the door.

"I don't want to leave it like this. I truly care about you, Louise. When you're ready, I would feel privileged to count myself among your friends," Gregory suggested, bracing himself for a rebuttal. He suspected his statement wouldn't be well received, but he had to say it. He meant every word.

"I don't fuck my friends, Gregory. And I certainly don't dance in my underwear with my friends either," she replied tartly with a stiff wave. "Bye, Gregory, have a nice life. Don't call me, unless it's about the case."

He hung his head in shame as the red door closed in his face with an unsettling finality. He leaned his back against the door, pausing to collect himself as he pulled on the warm hood of his jacket and braced himself against the blustery cold. He needed to regroup. He needed to focus. There would be time to fix things with Louise later, if she could ever look at him again.

29

SHE HOPED SHE NEVER LAID EYES ON that handsome devil again. Louise didn't even think he knew what he had just thrown away tonight. They could have had something really nice, really special. He had no idea.

Louise plopped back down on the sofa, grabbing her glass of wine and swallowing her bitterness with a hint of pinot noir as she watched him arrange his jacket, then pause for an annoyingly long period of time and walk away. Louise reached for Cosette, hoping a few rubs and a few soft purrs might calm the rage burning inside her.

But then she remembered.

The betrayal.

"How could you let him pet you, Cosette? You're supposed to be on my side."

The cat yawned in response, seeming very satisfied with her actions. It was hard to stay mad at Cosette as the furball curled up beside her once more. Louise would direct her anger where it was deserved.

She gave a miserable sigh, devastated by the knowledge that he was the only person she could have ever trusted to touch her again, to make her laugh, to make her shudder with pleasure. It was impossible to fathom trying her relationship building experiment with anyone else. Whatever.

"Fuck that guy," she said to the empty room as she turned on *The Bachelor*. She would opt for enjoying the romantic progressions of other peoples' relationships. The contestant's misery was a great comfort, a reminder that there were more dysfunctional relationships out there. She would stay far away from any kind of relationship. She would not engage, she thought with a deep sigh. Much safer and much less painful for her heart.

Louise buried herself in her work after the romance that never was with Gregory. It provided a challenging distraction from thinking about the handsome detective or wallowing in misery at home. She was determined to stop indulging in her isolation whenever things got difficult. Work had picked up as everyone tried to finish up projects before taking time off for the holidays. She had been assigned a few cases to collaborate on and relished having to bury herself in books to gather information for the partners in her firm. It was a welcome distraction from thinking about her love life, something she had completely lost control over somehow. Her mind, heart, and body were constantly battling for supremacy, and she felt like a bystander eagerly waiting to see which part of her would dominate.

Time had not healed the wound. Even a few weeks after the break with Gregory had occurred, Louise hardly made any progress getting over the guy. Louise questioned if it could be defined as a breakup, since they had only enjoyed a fleeting whisper of a love affair. It was over in a blink of an eye. So why was she still thinking about him?

She attempted to exorcise Gregory's presence from her life. She blocked his number, then unblocked it, because if there was news on the case, she wanted to know. She deleted their text stream, which definitely felt permanent, and she labeled his contact name as a three red flag emojis, so she would be able to gird herself against his charms in the future.

Louise would never fall for it again, she told herself. She was worth more than a hot sex hookup and a quick goodbye. Regardless of how intense the connection and how irresistible the chemistry, she needed a man who would fight for her, a man who would stick around. A man who would take her heart and keep it safe.

Gregory had been good for her in some ways. He reminded her that within her chest, a beautiful heart was beating and was ready for something deeper than just a connection with her family, her friends, and her cat.

It longed for something just for herself, a love to be shared with someone and a future to which she could look forward. He reminded her that she was more than a shell. Within her was a sensual woman with powerful lust that had now been activated to an alarming degree. If Simone had reminded her she was a hottie, Gregory had awoken the sensual being living inside of her. She was not just a trauma survivor; she was a whole woman, with powerful desires, a heart ripe for love and longing for a connection.

Her next attempt at a relationship would be with someone who was ready. She wouldn't give so much of herself so quickly next time. Her walls would only come down once she knew it was perfect. She would only reveal her heart if she was certain he was ready to show up for her and stay.

Unlike stupid Gregory.

For a detective, the man certainly had a hard time seeing a good thing when it was standing right in front of him. Stopping things before they got too involved made sense in theory, but he was a fool to think she wasn't too involved. She had heedlessly jumped into the waters of his love and now she was drowning in them. She snorted, thinking of his wrong assumption that he had ended things before they went too far. Boy, had she ever gone too far. She turned back to the reports she had been researching and sighed. Her work never let her down. It was always there, a welcome distraction from the pain of taking charge and living her life.

* * *

As Louise sat enjoying her coffee with Georgie later that week, she was dismayed to hear on the news that another body had been discovered nearby. The death was deemed suspicious. She felt her skin responding to the information, the familiar creep of gooseflesh covering her body. Whoever was killing women in her neighborhood was now working at a faster pace. Her heart began to speed up its rhythmic beat in her chest. As she listened to the attractive light brown-haired morning anchor describe the details that were known about the case, she shivered. She rubbed her arms to bring warmth into her body, a chill suddenly overtaking her. Her thoughts raced, wondering what was happening at the police station. Were they turning over every rock? Would they finally be able to find that missing clue that would lead them to the killer? Would she ever feel safe again?

"Relax," Georgie said, reaching across the table and taking her hand. "Gregory hasn't called you so I'm sure it's not something you need to worry about. We can't go around jumping at things we think we see in the shadows. It's no way to live."

She nodded at Georgie, feeling pensive. Gregory would contact her if there was any news that pertained to her case. She found it hard to believe that he would avoid talking to her. He was an officer first, before anything else in his life.

She scanned the news reports online to see if she could find any more details about the case. The most recent death had occurred in Altadore, a few blocks away from her home. Autopsy results would reveal whether the death was suspicious. She was desperate for information and would have to wait. More developments would be revealed on the news.

Though her patience would be tested, she would have to wait for information like everyone else. She no longer had a connection to information like she did before and she sure as heck wouldn't be begging for any from Gregory.

The case was forcing her to have something she was very short on lately.

Patience.

30

Detective Band had a sinking feeling as he once again entered a scene which made the hair stand up on the back of his neck. The air in the townhouse still felt like someone had just left the room. The feeling was electric. Sickening. Everything was so fresh, so posed to look just right. The deceased influencer had been reported missing to police by her own followers, given that they were used to her frequent posts and became concerned when her feed went dark.

Delaney Savoy was a gorgeous woman, her sooty black lashes resting upon her perfectly made-up bronze skin. She had been posed much like the victim in Gregory's other case. She appeared to be sleeping peacefully in a pink nightgown with black lace trim, on her back, posed with one arm up resting beside her face and the other sitting on the sheet and blanket, which had been folded over to look like a perfectly made bed. Her hair was laid out, long silky straight red hair spread out on the pillow around her. She looked so peaceful, sleeping like a princess in the fairy tales. If only a kiss could wake her. Gregory shook his head and sighed in resignation.

"She looks posed like a perfect sleeping princess," Gregory said, feeling a squeeze around his heart. "How could anyone do this?" he said aloud. He would never get used to seeing what these horrible people would do to innocent victims.

"No one is going to be able to revive this one with a kiss though," Doreen made that very clear when they arrived on the scene. She was doing a preliminary examination to establish time and cause of death.

"Marty, are you seeing some creepy similarities with this one?" Gregory asked, hoping he was mistaken, and this case was completely unrelated.

"It's unsettling for sure. I'm going to have to investigate more about what's going on over here in this corner. It's like this guy set up a fairy tale garden or something. What is this round light thing? He's changing up his MO and I'm not getting it."

Gregory chuckled, reveling in having some knowledge for once that, Marty did not have. "Actually Marty, that's an influencer background. She probably shoots some of her videos with this as her background, see?"

Gregory had taken time to check out the social media profile on his way to the scene. Her bedroom had a wall covered in pink and white puffs of roses and feathers. At the bottom, there was a line of lush looking fake grass, which gave a secret garden vibe. She had a white spherical pendant light covered in feathers hanging over a stuffed antique bench. Everything was perfectly laid out in the corner of her bedroom like a movie set.

Gregory pointed to all the aesthetic props jumbled on a shelf, which would be out of the viewer's sight lines. "These would be her props, for photos and flat lays and all that stuff. I've seen them a bit on Instagram. Pretty fancy. This circle thingy here?" Gregory looked at Marty through the circular standing light.

"It gives you a perfect complexion and lighting when you are taking videos. So, you always look like your skin is dewy and glowing. This here is where you put your phone or camera," Gregory explained.

Marty whistled, clearly impressed by the wealth of new knowledge he was acquiring. "Well, she kept things looking pretty perfect, even in death," he noted.

Gregory made notes about the scene, having the crew bag anything that seemed important, and even some things that didn't. His killer always picked attractive women. Gregory noticed the change in gown color, though after having looked at the influencer's closet, he perceived that almost every item in her closet was varying shades of pink.

"Marty, did we find any drinks lying around, any wine glasses by chance?" Gregory asked with a sense of foreboding as he walked through the bedrooms and back down the stairs to the kitchen. There, sitting on an immaculate counter were two glasses of wine, one with fuchsia lipstick marks on the rim and one perfectly clean.

Gregory told a nearby tech to photograph and bag the glasses, making sure they tested for traces of the date rape drug. The results left no mystery for Gregory, his gut told him one glass would test positive.

He mentally calculated how far this townhouse was from Louise's place. Only a few blocks. Despite the difficulty he had breaking things off with Louise, he was reassured that he had done the right thing. This case had to come first. The stakes were high and more innocent women would be targeted if the Marda Loop murderer wasn't stopped. All his energy had to focused on saving lives and catching the killer. He pushed away his concern for Louise's safety, he had a job to do. He couldn't focus on his scene and think about Louise. It was his job to find out who was killing these women, to ensure the sicko never got his hands on the one that got away.

31

Louise gazed at the snow falling outside her window as it danced on the light wind and slowly drifted to the ground. It was a perfect winter day, not too cold and frigid. Though she had actively avoided being outdoors or doing anything lately, it was still possible for her to enjoy the breathtaking beauty of the Calgary winter. When the snow fell quietly into soft, thick mounds, not yet soiled by the passing cars and accumulation of salt, gravel, and mud. She gripped her cup of tea with milk and sugar. It was the perfect color and sweetness, just as her mother had taught her to prepare, when they had enjoyed daily teatime after school.

She was bored with all her usual shows that were recorded and sitting ignored on her PVR. She felt cheated, knowing she had taken steps to re-introduce herself to the world and start living again, and had then quietly withdrawn when it all felt like it was too much. Louise was mildly disgusted by her lack of resilience, though it was possible to take a few steps forward and then a few steps back, as she had discussed with her therapist. Progress was the goal. It didn't mean she had completely given up her plan. She had just faced a setback. Time to dust herself off and get back up again.

She gazed sightlessly outside the window, transfixed by the delicate movement of the flakes as they made their way to earth.

"Another day on the sofa, eh?" Georgie said, breaking her concentration.

Louise glowered at her mother, wishing she could be more understanding. "It's hard to know what to do with myself, Mum. It's not safe to go out until that guy is off the streets, if you ask me," Louise said.

Georgie harrumphed in response. "Are you telling me some unknown person is keeping you trapped in the house? Sounds more like an excuse to me. Go do something, be safe. Call Simone, see if she's busy. You can't stay here all day. It's too beautiful out."

Louise gave her mother an angry side-eye, growing quite weary of people telling her how to better live her life.

Georgie went out to pick up some groceries, reminding her as she opened the door that she would be out with her friends that night for dinner. The chill from outside momentarily filled the living room, forcing Louise to bury herself deeper in the blankets. Louise finished her tea sitting on the sofa and turned on one of her shows to have some noise in the room while she lay as a useless pile on the sofa for a few hours. Laziness was what she felt she needed, so she decided to go with her feelings. She lay on her side with Cosette curled up under one arm and dozed as she enjoyed two solid hours of *The Bachelor*.

The show was very comforting, and she fell asleep somewhere between the first group date and the episode's rose ceremony. When she awoke, it was late afternoon, and she felt a tiny desire to leave her house. To do something. She couldn't let herself backslide to the place she was before. Louise didn't want to be alone anymore. Her fingers typed a quick message to Simone, and she invited herself out with her friends.

Simone and Anika were meeting up to go skating at the gorgeous outdoor rink in Stanley Park. Though she had initially declined to join them, Louise abruptly changed her mind and tossed the blankets to the side. It had been years since she had laced up her skates and she was looking forward to basking in a night of wholesome nostalgia, while enjoying some movement, since she had spent almost the entire day on the sofa.

She put on some thick, fleece lined black leggings and an oversized cream-colored knit sweater. She wore her new navy puffer coat, which fit her like a dream and would keep her warm and cozy. She opted to keep her hair simple and put it in a low bun, since it would be stuffed under a warm oatmeal colored tuque. Her hair would most likely be messy and sweaty beneath the hat, so there was no point in excessive styling. She added her white sparkle ball earrings and a touch of sparkly pink lip gloss to make it look like she had tried.

While it was still light out, she went to the garage to find her skates hanging in a bag on the wall. Before hitting the outdoor rink, she brought her skates to the local hockey shop to get sharpened. She sat on the bench and waited while the guy working at the till took her skates to the back to get sharpened. As she sat patiently and messed around on her phone, Louise looked up and spotted Roger walking in, a man on a mission.

"Hey, Roger," she said, waving in his direction.

"Oh, hey, Lou. What are you doing here?" he inquired.

Louise explained that she was on her way to go skating in Stanley Park.

"Oh yeah? How romantic. I used to go there with my wife. Are you going there with someone or on your own?" he asked, with a flat mouth quirked up on one side.

Louise got the impression he was trying to converse normally while avoiding thoughts of his ex-wife. Louise felt a bit grumpy too and thought he might need a friend.

"I'm meeting up with Simone and Anika. How are things with the divorce? You look kind of sad today. It can't be easy."

If possible, Roger's face took on a more darkened gaze. He became slightly furious and bitter every time he spoke about his wife. Roger was unable to hide emotions when he spoke of his ex-wife.

"Well, we're basically divorced. I'm still waiting for the paperwork to go through and all that. She continues to torture me, but she's turned evil, so I shouldn't be surprised. Part of me still loves her and wants to go to therapy to see if we could fix things. Then she tells me she's dating someone else, and she's moved on."

Louise gasped. "If she's got a boyfriend already, you're wasting your time."

"Yeah, if I'm honest, I think they were dating when we were still married. So, what's the point, really? I don't know. I'm just here picking up my new hockey equipment."

Louise nodded in understanding, her eyes widened as he spoke so venomously about a woman which he simultaneous loved and hated. "Hockey helps me get my rage out."

"Well, hang in there. Love is complicated," Louise said, cringing. She knew all about unrequited love.

"Speaking of complicated love, I feel bad about you and Gregory. Seemed like something was going to start there for a minute."

"Yeah, it was a minute. Time for me to move on too, I guess."

Roger nodded, handing his ticket to the clerk, who then went to the back of the store to get his order. Roger turned to face Louise, a look of sympathy on his face.

"I don't really know what happened there. He seemed happy," Roger said and shrugged. "But he's got his own things going on, I guess."

Louise dismissed the conversation with a wave of her hand. She wasn't interested in discussing Gregory's issues. It was too soon.

"I'm off dating for a bit. It's too much work."

"Yeah, I feel like I give off a repellent vibe to women. Not feeling very charismatic these days." Roger looked down at his shoes, indulging in a quick pity party before Louise's eyes.

"I feel ya there."

"I used to be charming, before all the divorce nastiness took over my life."

"Well, you'll get it back. You just need a fresh start when all this is over."

"Thanks, Louise."

Louise looked up as the clerk came back to the front counter with her skates in his hands. She stood up to go pay and tapped her credit card.

"Well, it was good seeing you. I'm here for a beer and a chat whenever you need it," she added. "Just no dating."

Roger smiled, chuckling at her comment, and waved her off from the bench.

Louise sat for a moment in her car, wondering what Roger had meant by his comments about Gregory. Was he unhappy since they have severed ties? Good.

At least she wasn't the only one feeling like a hot heap of garbage since they stopped seeing each other. She smiled to herself, comforted by the thought of Gregory suffering for the loss of her. Louise shook her head, dispersing the thoughts of him. Even if Gregory had a major epiphany, she would not be waiting around to witness it.

32

THE SKATING RINK AT TWILIGHT was a beautiful place to be, Louise observed as she walked up to it. The sky was quickly darkening, and the twinkling string lights illuminated the expansive perimeter of the rink, hung upon the branches of the surrounding pine trees. There were two designated sections to the rink. One had nets and was more for kids and adults to work on their hockey drills or enjoy an informal game. The other section was shaped like a figure eight and was dedicated to casual skating.

She was overcome with the joy of her memories of skating as a child and as a young adult. Skating was a happy activity for her, associated with hot chocolate and holding hands with her dad, or being pulled in a sled behind him when she was a little girl. As a teenager this rink had been a gathering spot for them, a great place for boys and girls to hang out and have a good time, sharing a lot of laughs and at times, some teenager romance drama. Louise hadn't been to this rink since her attack, and she was suddenly angry with herself for forgetting how much she enjoyed skating.

She met up with Simone and Anika under the glow of the twinkling lights by the fire pits. They skated around a few loops until the cold had reddened their cheeks and turned their hands into icicles. Simone and Anika had planned to go to a nearby pub after skating to warm up with a beer. Louise felt like calling it a night after skating, so she told them to go have fun and went to have a few more rounds around the rink before going home.

Though her friends protested her staying at the rink alone, she assured them that she would be safe with all these people around and she planned to take an Uber home when the time came to leave. Simone and Anika agreed to the plan on the condition that she texted them when she left and when she got home, so they would know she had arrived safely.

The chilly evening and the shimmer of lights in the night created a lovely warm ambience around her. The families and big guys playing hockey increased her confidence that no one could hurt her while she was there, the rink was safe. She took a break on an empty bench by one of the five fire pits that were sprinkled around the rink to warm herself up and considered getting a drink at the cute yellow hot chocolate truck parked near the rink.

Looking around at the families and couples enjoying the ice, she reasoned that this would be a wonderful place to visit with a lover, as Roger had mentioned he had done, once upon a time. She sighed longingly, hoping that one day she'd be able to share this with someone special.

Behind her, she could hear the crunch of boots on the snow, more skaters arriving and putting on their skates on and laughing. She closed her eyes and blocked out the sound as she breathed in the cold air, the crackling fire and the sweet scent of spilled hot chocolate on snow. It is good to be here, she thought as a smile curved on her lips. She jumped as a low voice floated suddenly in her ear.

"Come here often?" Louise startled and turned to see Gregory standing there in full uniform, arms crossed and slightly indignant. She placed a hand on her chest to still her heart beating out of her chest.

"How dare you scare me like that! You are such an ass!" She smacked him on the chest as he laughed.

"Okay, okay, I'm sorry. Perhaps it was poor judgment of the situation, but it's too late now. It was certainly funny to see your face," he said still chuckling.

Louise was torn between being angry and laughing because he had startled her so much. She shook her head and wagged a finger at him. "You are a brat, and to think an officer of the law could harass an innocent citizen like that. Terrible," she chastised. "What are you doing here? I thought we weren't doing, you know, this anymore," she said as she pointed to him then herself as if to indicate the two of them.

"Just because we're not dating, doesn't mean I don't worry about you. I was tired of staring at my computer screen and trying to make evidence jump out at me from my files and decided to do a wellness check on you."

Louise rolled her eyes as he put his hands on his hips in an authoritative way. "It's a beautiful night, and it's nice to get a breath of fresh air. No big deal."

Louise looked at him, still wary of being in his presence. "Um, so you're checking up on me now? I have people in my life to do that, I don't need you to be my keeper," she said, shaking her head at him, trying to prod a reaction out of him that was anything other than his happy, composed demeanor.

"You're probably right." Gregory scanned the rink, taking in their surroundings with a suspicious eye. "Everything looks good here, no crimes happening at the moment. How are you getting home?"

Louise rolled her eyes and stared at him indignantly. "I can take care of myself. I was going to have a nice hot chocolate and enjoy the bonfires, then take myself home."

Gregory's mouth flattened, seeming convinced that she was being evasive. "Okay, but how are you getting home?" he asked once again.

"Gregory, thanks for being such a *good friend*, but my plans are none of your business," she responded tartly.

His gaze scanned her face as he placed his hands on her shoulders. "Tell me."

Louise huffed and told him she planned on calling an Uber.

"Let's go have a hot chocolate and I will take you home," he said, getting down on his knees and untying her skates as she sat down once again.

"Don't. I can do that. I just need my boots," she said, indicating her boots were over by another bench.

Gregory got up and went to fetch them for her, which embarrassed her, as she began unlacing her skates. Surely that was why she could feel a blush creeping up her cheeks.

"Allow me," he said, getting back on his knees and grabbing the laces out of her hands, letting his fingers graze hers as he began to undo the laces.

She was overwhelmed by the sensuality of his hands being so close to her body. She had to remind herself to breathe as her chest tightened uncomfortably. Since when was untying skates such an erotic movement that caused her entire body to warm with suppressed desire? She could feel the blush traveling all the way up her body, filling her with warmth and turning her face pink. This was not good. When she reminded herself to breathe, she filled her mouth with air and let it slowly trickle out in an attempt to quieten the beating of her heart.

Once she had her boots on, Louise tossed her skates over her shoulder, and they walked up to the food truck selling hot chocolate and treats for skaters. Gregory nodded at the various people around the rink that recognized him from his neighborhood patrols. Before working in major crimes, he had been patrolling the streets, and directing traffic. Marda Loop was like a small town in the city and he had worked in the community since his career had started, so it was not surprising when he was recognized. She was dismayed when he got her hot chocolate, given that she prided herself on maintaining her independence and wasn't used to a man taking care of her.

"You don't have to pay for me. This isn't a date. I can pay for myself," she said.

He smiled at her, saying he had no problem getting his *friend* a hot chocolate. The food truck owner recognized him and gave him the two hot chocolates on the house. They walked to the fire pit and talked while enjoying their drinks.

"So, what is going on with the Marda Loop murderer? I hear there has been another victim. Are you getting any closer to finding him? I've been really jumpy and kind of isolating at home again, which is so frustrating. Even though I survived the attack, it still feels like my attacker is forever controlling me," she said.

Gregory seemed to understand her frustration. "I'm working on some new leads with this case, but I'm convinced it is linked to your case and my other victim's. Only the killer's DNA results can tell us for sure. No one is safe while this guy is roaming the streets. Which is why when Roger told me you were skating at night, I got worried. You shouldn't be out here alone," he said, taking on a more serious tone.

Louise smiled at him. "Ah, so that is how you found out, you sneaky devil. Don't forget I sleep with a baseball bat, and we have a security alarm. I can press a button, and police will be sent to my house. My attacker doesn't know who he's messing with. He caught me off guard the first time. He won't get so lucky again."

Gregory raised his eyebrows, impressed. "How about I drive you home? Surely you can see the sense in getting a ride with a guy who's packing heat. I know you're into that," he said with a wink at her playfully, trying to lighten the tone of the conversation.

She accepted at last and picked up her skates. They walked over to the squad car, and she hopped in next to him. Gregory drove to her home, where the light was on outside, but the house was dark, given that Georgie was still out with her friends.

As she stepped out of the car, she stopped dead in her tracks, frozen, looking at the large picture window next to the bright red door of Cambrai Cottage. A steady path of footprints could be seen, made in the fresh snow beneath the window of the home. The footsteps made a path that went to the side of the house, then continued until they could no longer be seen. She searched her memory for a time when she would have walked there, but the snow had fallen so recently and up until then, their small patch of grass in the front yard had remained covered in a pristine layer of thick, undisturbed snow.

Gregory came out of the car. Louise wondered why she felt frozen in place, her fear exploding like a heavy bag of sand hitting her in the chest.

"Louise, what is it? Why aren't you going in?" Gregory asked as he walked up behind her, putting his hands on her shoulder and following her gaze to the front of her house.

"The footsteps in the snow," she managed to get out shakily, "they weren't there before."

Gregory seemed to understand that she was so frozen in fear she wasn't quite ready to move. He physically turned her to look at him. "What are you saying? Do you think someone made those tracks in the snow? Could you or your mother have made those, maybe?"

Louise shook her head. "No, I was looking out the window this afternoon and it was pristine and perfect. Not a mark on the surface. No one walks there. Everyone uses the path I shoveled there. It looks like someone was peeping in my window, then went around to the backyard," Louise explained. "That's where the footsteps disappear."

Gregory agreed and went into his patrol car to radio his partner to come out and check the scene with him. Time was precious and more snow would be falling throughout the night, though the flurries had paused for the afternoon. He said he would check out the prints and get a team out to photograph the tracks as soon as possible.

"Look, I don't want to leave you here. Why don't I bring you to my place and you can chill there while I check out the house? We know this guy is good at breaking and entering, and I'll have a good look around and inside the house before I can let you and Georgie come back here," Gregory said.

Louise looked at him, still unsure what the best course of action would be. Her mouth could do no more than gape at him. She swallowed thickly, her thoughts spinning in her head. She tried to remember if she had set the alarm or if Georgie had come home before going out? The alarm would be screaming if anyone had gone into the house, but only *if* someone had set it before leaving. She rubbed her forehead in hopes of bringing her memories to the surface from within the turmoil of thoughts.

"Okay, so I'll call Georgie?" she asked, too numb to make decisions.

"Call your mom, tell her to stay where she is while you hang out at my place. I'll come up and let you know what I find," Gregory replied.

He seemed energized by the fear that was pouring out of her eyes. The knight was coming out, and she felt his need to protect her from the realities of the danger she was in. Deep down, she knew. The Marda Loop murderer was a predator, and she was his prey. He was staking out the house she was living in. He had found her at last.

"What does it mean, now that he has found me?" she asked, her eyes shiny with unshed tears. She blinked to contain them, knowing she had to gather her courage at this moment.

Gregory shrugged, though they both knew there was no way of knowing until the crew investigated. Louise's hand trembled as she opened the door to the patrol car and sat, locking the door as she gazed back upon what had once been her safe haven. The place where her attacker had never found her, never penetrated. Until now.

Gregory walked her up to his apartment, seeming satisfied that she would be protected by several secure entry points.

"Lock the door behind me. I'll come to you later," he said. "Make yourself comfortable."

Louise gave Gregory her house keys and her alarm code to help him search the home for any intruders. Gregory left Louise and headed back to the scene, where Marty was supervising the evidence collection in his stead. She closed the door behind him and turned the bolt, hearing it hit home. She released a breath she didn't know she had been holding that entire time.

Dropping her coat on the chair in his dining room, she walked over to the sliding doors overlooking the neighborhood and wondered if she would see her attacker out there hunting for her. Her body shook as she continued to process the intense fear that made its way through her. She wondered where he was hiding amongst the sparkling, colorful Christmas lights of Marda Loop glistening under the blanket of snow. Everything seemed so festive, yet somehow, her attacker had made the holiday scene sinister, for those streets and alleys were possibly sheltering a killer.

Louise made herself a cup of tea and sat on the sofa, desperately trying to warm up and watch a show. It was easy to locate the chamomile tea bags, since Gregory had very little food in his kitchen cabinets. She found herself too distracted by her thoughts and wondered if Gregory would mind if she went to sleep.

It was late, and she had no idea how long he would be investigating in and around her house. She walked into Gregory's bedroom and gazed longingly at the bed. The memories of their night together flooded her, and she felt a warmth suffuse her entire body. They had enjoyed a magical night together in that bed. She was impressed by the fact that his bed was made. His bed, like the part in his hair, showed the discipline that he lived with every day. She pulled back the thick navy blankets and the crisp white top sheet, feeling a little guilty messing up such a nice bed, but there was no other option. She took off her clothing, and looked around for something to wear, since she was still wearing her skating clothing, and it was too warm and tight to sleep in.

Gregory had left a sweatshirt on a chair that seemed like a convenient choice as sleepwear. She put it on, enjoying the scent he had left in the shirt a little too much. The smell of his deodorant, mixed with the intoxicating essence that was just…Gregory. She sighed longingly and closed her eyes, breathing in deeply. The sweatshirt made her instantly feel so safe and comfortable. The sheets surrounded her with thoughts of him. It was impossible to ignore the effect he had on her, she felt so good and had slept so well when he was there, even if it was just the scent that permeated his soft cotton sheets.

Being in such an intimate place, where Gregory laid his head every night overwhelmed her senses. It broke her heart, feeling the depth of her attachment to him, and yet still hurting from the wound he created in her chest when he cut her off so abruptly. Louise squeezed her eyes shut to keep from thinking anymore. She was so tired from the events of the night and needed to close her eyes and forget for a few hours.

33

GREGORY ENTERED HIS APARTMENT around two in the morning and felt pure nervous exhaustion come over him. He was familiar with this feeling after a particularly grueling day. When he worked on his previous cases, he was often rewarded with a sense of accomplishment when he completed the task, caught the criminal, closed the file. This case gave him none of that. He felt like Hansel, looking through the forest and following crumbs, but never actually finding his way home. He was on a path which kept leading him nowhere.

Each day he didn't solve this case, he imagined his killer was choosing someone new, fantasizing and stalking a new prey, making plans. This killer made Gregory feel like an incompetent idiot. He was so angry. So many clues but no satisfying solution. His guts were a ball of turmoil, considering how close this person had been to Louise, had she been sitting on her sofa and watching television, as she often liked to do in the safety of her home. The knowledge of the imminent danger she was in made him sick to his stomach. He wanted to wrap her in bubble wrap and keep everyone away from her until the killer was found.

He looked around the living room, expecting to see Louise. A stab of fear slashed through the pit of his stomach when he saw that she wasn't there. Once he checked his bedroom, all thoughts of his case vanished. She was curled up in his blankets, fast asleep. He remembered she had trouble sleeping and felt bad waking her, so he sat on the sofa in the living room. It would be best if he let her sleep.

The look of peaceful tranquility on her face belied the ordeal she had been through and the fear that stalked her every move. He couldn't even imagine waking her. He lay on his side, propping his head with a pillow and tried to sleep on the stiff sofa cushions. The flurry of thoughts and worries about his case returned with a vengeance. He turned on the sofa, punching the pillow to soften it and lay facing the back of the sofa. If he closed his eyes, he could picture her on his bed, low ponytail spread across her shoulders, soft brown lashes resting on her cheeks.

Was she dreaming?

His hand pressed on the back of the sofa, and he closed his eyes, as though he could feel her through the layers of fabric, drywall, and wood that separated them.

His eyes opened with a start.

Maybe she's having a nightmare.

What if she's afraid?

He shook his head to clear the worries out and squeezed his pillow. A few deep breaths and he closed his eyes again.

Time to be serious about sleeping.

The thought of only a mere wall separating him from Louise made falling asleep a challenge. She made a soft sound in her sleep and his eyes abruptly popped open again. He needed to check on her.

I'm sure she wouldn't mind if I watched her sleep.

Just for a little while.

Just to help myself calm down, no other reason.

After any development in the case, no matter how small, he always felt wired. He walked into the dark bedroom and sat on the floor, next to the wall, watching her sleep. His bedroom was dimly lit by the light coming in from the streetlamps outside. He could see her features as she rested peacefully. He couldn't put a name to the flush of warmth that touched him deep inside as he watched her softly breathing with eyes closed. His chest felt like it was bursting with the emotion he was too afraid to identify. The ache only got stronger as he approached. Her sweetness overpowered him, and he would rather drown in it than tear himself away. He burned with a primitive desire to protect what was his, and right then he knew. She was his. She would be his alone.

If only he could dig himself out of the pit he had dug for himself. He winced, rubbing his fingers between his eyes to ease the tension there.

"Gregory?" she mumbled from the bed. "What are you doing?"

He stood up suddenly, embarrassed, glad for the darkness in the room so she wouldn't see him turning beet-red from head to foot. He was mortified.

"Oh my God, I'm sorry. I was having trouble sleeping, and I found you looking so peaceful. I will leave. It is so creepy to just watch you sleep like that." He began to back out of the room. "Just go back to sleep. I'll go on the sofa. Again, I'm sorry," he said. He leaned against the wall in the hallway, his hand on his forehead, as he silently cursed himself.

She sat up in the bed and called out to him. "Gregory. Wait.

Come here. I need you."

Gregory's eyes widened with the knowledge that he should definitely not go back in there. She was too vulnerable. He was completely powerless against anything she asked of him. With a resigned sigh, he made his way to the bed and gathered her up in his arms. She felt warm and smelled sweetly of sleep. He fought the urge to bury his head in the sweet space between her head and shoulder. Just one inhale of her intoxicating perfume of red roses and cozy comfort, whatever that was, it was magical.

"I don't know what to do anymore, Greg. I just want to live. Why can't he just leave me alone?" she asked, her gaze discouraged.

Gregory shushed her, wanting to make her feel safe and protected.

"He's not going to get you. I won't let him. I'll protect you with my life."

Louise looked at him and, even though the room was somber, he could see the confusion on her face. "Why, Gregory? Why would you protect me with your life? You don't want to be with me, but you would die for me? I don't get it," she said, with muted sadness in her voice.

Gregory frowned, aware that he didn't really make sense. He brushed the hair softly out of her face, unable to resist touching her skin.

"I always take care of my friends," he said, knowing it would only deepen her frustration. He was unable to think clearly while she was in his arms. The seductive blanket of darkness, the allure of her mouth, the softness of her gathered in his arms was too much. He could feel Louise holding her breath, as though waiting for his kiss.

He desperately wanted to kiss her.

And there was no way he was going to kiss her.

He had drawn a line, and he would not cross it.

Even if it destroyed him.

"Gregory, take care of me. Please. I need you tonight. I need comfort," she pleaded. His body stilled with the effort to control himself, when every fiber of his body was telling him to take what was being offered.

He pulled away from her, his brain, heart, and body fighting for supremacy. Gregory groaned in frustration. "I don't want to play games with you. I'll just break your heart. I respect you too much to use you," he said reluctantly. He was made of iron.

His resistance would not falter.

She reached a hand to touch his cheek, and he shuddered.

Oh boy. He was going to falter.

As their warm breaths mingled, he could feel electricity emitting from her touch, lighting him on fire with absolutely zero effort. He was so aroused that it was physically painful for him to tear himself away. She grabbed his collar, bringing him back toward her.

"Comfort me, Gregory. As a friend," the words kissed his lips, sending desire careening throughout his body. His body was a raging inferno of lust burning out of control, and she was going to get what she wanted, despite his better judgment.

Gregory considered for a moment, only a moment, because there was no way he could refuse her twice. The pull of her body to him was just too strong. He pushed back the blankets, feeling that she was dressed in a sweatshirt, which he recognized as one of his own. The thought of her wearing his clothing made him unbearably hard and he could barely breathe from wanting her. He pulled off his pants and crawled into bed with her, leaving on his shirt as though to offer her protection from him. He was here to offer comfort, as much as she needed for as long as she needed. He kissed her sleepy mouth, and she opened it up to him. She slid her hands under his shirt, unable to resist touching the heat of his skin.

"You feel so good," she said, unable to suppress her enjoyment of the feel of his skin on her wandering hands. "You make me feel so safe, Gregory."

He moved his hands so that he could also have a turn feeling the searing heat of her body warm from sleep. She wasn't wearing a bra, which stole his breath, he found it so incredibly arousing. Gently sliding his hands up her sweater, he caressed her breasts, finding her nipples already hard and wanting. He pushed up her shirt, eager to get his mouth on her, to kiss and suckle her until she whimpered. She took one of his hands and pushed it down to her underwear.

"Please," she begged.

His hand went eagerly across her plump mound and down into the pool of warm wetness that welcomed him. She reached her hand down into his underwear as he entered her with his finger. She was not wasting any time driving him crazy. He marveled at how good it was to touch her again and have her silky hand on his hard length.

She would be the death of him.

If their love was an addiction, Gregory would die for a fix. The feel of being in her hand, the burning of his arousal made him hunger for the feel of being inside her again.

If only he could be so lucky.

She stroked him gently. Her finger rubbing a pearl of moisture on his tip and sending a burning frenzy of lust crashing through him. She was clearly trying to render him as helpless, and it was working. She brought her mouth to his, moaning as he pressed another finger inside her.

His kisses devoured her like he was a starving man and this was his first meal. He stroked her relentlessly as she let out little cries of pleasure. His thumb rubbed circles around her clitoris until he felt her head go back. Her release came, and she cried out loudly against his mouth. He groaned.

"You're so goddamn hot. I'm going to burst if I don't have you," he said.

He reached over into his bedside table, hunting desperately for a condom and rolled onto his back to put one on. She climbed on top of him as he put it on, and he was undone.

"Louise, you're my fantasy," he confessed as his eyes rolled back in his head, and he sucked in his breath as she rubbed the tip of his cock with her slippery passage.

He placed his hands on her bottom as she lowered herself onto him. She kissed him as she began to bring herself up and down the length of him, clearly savoring the feeling of being in control. He stopped her, as though warning her that he would be lost if she continued.

"I need a minute, you feel way too good," he warned.

"What's the matter, Gregory? Feeling a little bit out of control? I know you want me," she said, as she kissed a path on his chest and his head tilted back with a groan.

"You know I want you," he repeated in a haze.

She pulled him up to her and kissed him deeply as she sat with him inside her. He brought his hands back to her breasts and stroked them, squeezing and rubbing her nipples until he felt those familiar twinges from her on his cock. She began moving on him again, unable to cease until they both came hard.

He savored the sweetness of being inside her, knowing in the morning, they would have to go on with their lives as though nothing had happened. He would go back to his case, and she would go back to her life without him.

For tonight, he would enjoy the warmth of having her in his arms and the feel of her heartbeat beneath his hand. She was a sweet siren that kept calling him back to crash into her. He was a goner, and she didn't even know it. He buried his face in her hair trying to inhale as much of her as he could as she fell asleep. It would have to satisfy him until he found a way to make things right. To solve the case. To make her his again. He was Gregory Band, and he was a man who worked for what he wanted and always achieved his goals. This would be no different.

34

LOUISE AWOKE THE NEXT DAY nestled next to Gregory, feeling like she had attained pure heaven last night. Again.

Which was a problem.

She had endeavored to move on from this person, in the most efficient way possible, even if it meant not dealing with her feelings for Gregory.

He had once again left her hanging, her heart in shambles, yet here she was, warm and cozy next to this man who clearly needed space and time to figure out what he wanted. She begrudgingly admitted she had no doubt what she wanted, but every time she tried to entertain the thought of a relationship with Gregory, he threw impossible obstacles in their path. Louise longed for something simpler. She wanted a love she could rely on, without having to battle with his career or his priorities. People successfully balanced a career and a personal life every day. Why couldn't Gregory?

Her stubborn heart was finding it hard to let go of him, even though her mind knew it would be the best path forward for her.

Perhaps it was good they had been able to have one more night. One blissful night to say goodbye, to have the closure to end the chapter of their relationship. If only her heart would obey her mind and let him go.

Louise rolled over and sighed, grateful it was Sunday. She had an entire day ahead of her to get it together. First, she needed to escape Gregory's warm bed and act like none of this had happened. She gathered her clothing after climbing out of bed and attempted to get dressed quietly and quickly.

Perhaps if she didn't wake him, it would be easier to leave.

Gregory seemed to sense her exiting the bed and his eyes opened to look upon her. "Are you trying to sneak out without saying goodbye?" he asked.

Louise rolled her eyes, frustrated.

"Yes, Gregory. You know why. I shouldn't even be here. You wanted space, I'm giving you that space. Thanks for last night."

She focused on locating her clothes and found her underwear between the sheets and couldn't help the heated blush that spread across her cheeks. She shook her head at her weakness.

"Back to reality, I guess. This," she said as she pointed between them, "won't work if we're always sneaking around. I need a man who wants to be with me. A real boyfriend. No halfway stuff."

Gregory groaned and stuffed his face back into his pillow. "I know. I have to leave you alone, I just…Nothing." He shook his head and ran a hand through his hair. "No excuse. I get it. I get it. I don't want to play games with you." He turned back to face her, sitting up in bed, watching her get dressed.

"You can go home. My crew is all wrapped up. I made sure of that last night. We didn't get a ton of evidence, but I managed to get a boot print, which might be helpful later. I've asked for a watch to be placed on your house for the next little while, given that we have reason to believe you might be in danger," Gregory added as he spotted one of her socks lying on the floor and grabbed it, handing it to her. "If you see someone watching in a patrol car outside your house, just wave. It's one of my guys."

She nodded with a tight smile as she headed to the bathroom. Using his brush to give her hair some semblance of style, then she rinsed her mouth to help with the terrible taste lingering there.

"Can I give you a ride?" he offered, his eyes filled with concern.

"No, Gregory, I need a minute before seeing Georgie," she said and rubbed her eyes. "I'll meet up with her and we can enter the house together. I won't be alone."

"I can follow you in my car if you want to be alone," he suggested, clearly not approving of her leaving by herself. She shook her head.

"I'm going to have breakfast downstairs. I won't be alone," she gathered her purse to her chest and exited without a backward glance.

She couldn't look in his eyes anymore.

It was devastating.

The breakfast place, Diner Deluxe was on the main floor of the building. She went in, liking the idea of taking herself out for a warm breakfast, to regroup and collect her thoughts. She ordered fluffy pancakes, bacon, and coffee, then grabbed her phone out of her pocket to call her mum. Georgie had slept at Myrna's last night. Louise explained to her that the house would be monitored, and it was safe to go back. They arranged a time to meet there so that neither of them would have to be there alone. Overcome with a sense of sadness, she knew she could no longer rely on Gregory to be a comfort during this difficult time. It was just too much temptation.

She blushed as she recalled the night before.

"I know you want me," she said.

"You know I want you."

She shivered as her body warmed and she felt a heat simmering between her legs at the mere thought of their passion. Of course he wanted her. His body had confirmed it last night. Regardless of what he was working through, Louise had no doubt anymore. Gregory had highlighted a lack in her life, and she longed for a relationship with someone that she could count on. Though her body burned with a powerful lust for the handsome detective, she could not bear the thought of a future forever doubting his commitment to her. She was selfish and wanted a man she didn't have to convince to be with her.

Gregory had run away from her the first time he felt the strength of their connection, when they dated in university. He was running away again now, and her heart could not take the pain. It was time to move on to someone who was ready for love. She wasn't sure if what she felt for Gregory was love, she hadn't dared to open that door for him. In that, he had been correct. It was best to break things off before that was a possibility — even if she felt like she was tearing off her own limbs in the process.

After finishing her breakfast, Louise tried to enjoy the beautiful sunny November day by walking to the grocery store and picking up a few essentials for dinner. She envisioned hunkering down at home for a little while, waiting for all this excitement to blow over and for her heart to mend.

They would reset the home alarm code, and she would always be accompanied when she left her house, unless she was going to work. Her body thrummed with nervous, jumpy energy as she pushed away thoughts that would make her spiral and get lost in a cloud of panic. The race was on; the police had to catch up with the Marda Loop murderer before he caught up with her.

35

Louise sought the comfort of her routine as the next weeks passed uneventfully. She went to work where she felt safe surrounded by people there and started going back to her weekly yoga class with Simone and Anika. This simple yet fun outing made her feel normal again. Almost. Going to yoga and spending time in quiet relaxation and meditation helped her sleep better and keep some of her anxiety in check. She still spent many evenings on the sofa keeping an eye on the patrol cars switching shifts outside her home and another eye on the last few episodes of *The Bachelor*. She loved the tears and the drama, especially when they were not her own.

As Louise expected, Simone was incensed when she found out about her latest night with Gregory. Louise felt fortified by her friend reminding her that though the detective was delicious, he could not have his cake and eat it too. Simone had pressed her to join the dating game again but given that there was a homicidal monster roaming the streets of Marda Loop and no one was safe, she considered carefully. Although Simone's view toward relationships was starting to make a lot of sense — have fun and meet new guys, without getting your heart engaged. There was a layer of safety in taking the casual approach.

Daytime coffee dates seemed like a harmless and sensible way for her to achieve what she wanted, which was to stand on her own two feet again, to live on her own and to find a love that was hers alone. Disappointed as she was that Gregory could not give her the love she had sought; she was grateful to him for awakening that hunger inside. A hunger that left her wanting to be satiated. Louise wanted to be an actress in her own story, not an observer. After years of being numb, she was ready to take her heart off life support and let it start beating again.

* * *

Georgie suddenly burst into the house with her hands full of bags. Louise stood up to grab them from her mother's hands and took them into the kitchen, observing that they were full of new Christmas decorations, gift wrap, and other treasures as she dug through them.

"I thought it would be fun to get in a festive mood! You've been so glum lately, and it's time to get out of the dumps. Let's decorate today! I'll put the kettle on for some tea," Georgie said as she filled the kettle and pressed the button to start it.

Louise decided to indulge her mother and emulate feelings of cheer she was not feeling. She went down to the basement to dig up the boxes of old decorations and bring out their favorite blankets and pillows to freshen up the living room. Louise flipped through the channels until she found the Christmas movie channel and put it on to inspire her. Georgie loved watching festive movies about love, regardless of how cheesy they were, because they instilled a feeling of love and hope.

Against her own will, Louise began to feel excited about the holidays. She draped beautiful greenery on the staircase intertwined with garlands that matched the ones they would be putting on the Christmas tree. They enjoyed digging up their old decorations, which included antique glass balls of many colors, as well as some whimsical ones they had collected over the years.

It did not take them too long to give the home a warm and cozy holiday makeover. When they finished putting all the boxes away in the basement, they were both too tired to cook, so Louise ordered a deluxe pizza from Inglewood Pizza and opened a bottle of red chianti for them to share. When Louise went to pay the delivery driver, she peeked outside to see the reassuring presence of a squad car; the driver sitting and watching the home.

"I'm happy to say we still have a police officer outside watching the house, in case we need them. Thankfully, we haven't needed them yet," Louise said. She took a sip of her wine and placed a hot pizza slice on each of the two plates on the table.

"Well, I feel it might be overreacting a little. I've always felt safe in my home, especially now that you're here and we have the alarm. It's been weeks now since any incident," Georgie said.

Louise nodded slowly and frowned. "That's nice and all, Mum, but it's good to be careful when there's an actual killer out there," she said. "Gregory told me to be careful."

Georgie shook her head, a small frown on her face. "Well, you take careful to the next level. We need to live our lives. You're happier when you see your friends, and Gregory," Georgie said with a challenging look.

Louise shrugged in response to her mother's comments, knowing she had been happy in Gregory's arms, there was no denying it.

"I'm sure a certain detective had something to do with the skip in your step and the smile on your face. I wonder why you two weren't able to work things out," Georgie observed, making Louise blush uncomfortably.

"There's nothing to work out with him. He's not interested in having a girlfriend and I want someone who is going to stick around. Don't despair, Mum, I will get back out there," Louise said.

Georgie looked at her, raising her eyebrows in disbelief.

"Really, Mum. Simone told me all about these dating apps where I could look up cute guys and chat with them. Maybe I'll go on a date or something," Louise added.

Georgie lit up at the thought. "Maybe you'll have someone for the holidays, wouldn't that be nice? You're a gorgeous girl and you need to get out there. You need a reason to get dressed up. Take off those awful sweaters. Put on a dress and some lipstick."

Louise hid her face in the blanket she had wrapped herself in and laughed, delighted that her mother was still irritated by her sweaters.

"Ugh, I will, Mum. Maybe you should get on the app and meet someone too? We're both single, remember? We could double date, eh?" Louise said as she winked suggestively and laughed.

Georgie brushed her off, saying she didn't want to take care of a man at her age. She just wanted to have fun doing what she wanted with her time.

"Remember, Louise, at my age, you're either someone's nurse or someone's purse," she said, which made Louise chuckle. It was probably true, but Louise wasn't convinced, since Georgie was such a romantic.

After dinner, they returned to the sofa to finish watching their movie and drinking their bottle of wine. It felt good to be doing something that did not include moping around the house, or maybe that was just the delicious effects of the wine. Louise didn't care. She had a renewed desire to take charge of her life and stop hiding in her house like the hermit her mother thought she was becoming. She glanced again at the patrol car sitting across the street watching their house and wondered if Gregory was in there. She smirked, hoping he saw how much fun she was having without him.

36

LOUISE WAS LUCKY TO BE WORKING DOWNTOWN, as everything seemed cleaner and brighter as a soft coat of white snow draped itself upon all the buildings, gardens, and streets. Downtown Calgary positively sparkled around the holidays. Lights were strung all along Stephen Avenue and the Calgary Tower changed colors based on the holiday they were honoring at the time, be it red and green for Christmas or blue and white for Hanukkah.

Louise was in the office, wrapping up for the holidays, when a few new files showed up on her desk, dropped off by Mr. Braithwaite's assistant. She endeavored to complete as much work as possible before signing off for her vacation days. She had some new legal resources that had to be reviewed to see if they could be added to their library, then catalogued if they were useful. It fell in her realm of responsibilities to always keep the information in the library current, to facilitate efficient and accurate research. She loved Fridays because she typically went out for lunch with Anika and Simone, which gave her a chance to catch up with what was going in their lives. Things had been busy in their work and personal lives that month, which meant they didn't get to see each other as often. They met at their usual table at La Cucina and ordered salads and pasta from the waiter, as well as a large bottle of sparkling water.

"So, Anika, how's the Lorimer file going? I'm glad I dodged it, since I was assigned all the new materials to review and catalog," Louise asked.

"Ugh, it's a bit of a slog, but I'm enjoying the challenge. Mr. McCarthy feels confident we can be successful if we get all our ducks in a row," Anika answered. "That reminds me, we'll have to chat after lunch. I need your thoughts on a few items."

The waiter brought them their glasses and filled them with sparkling water. Louise took a sip and nodded. Simone, seemingly unimpressed with the topic of conversation, decided to chime in with a fresh topic.

"Enough about work. Anika, you have to spill finally. Where are we going for the wedding? Have you guys picked a hotel? I'm dying to know!" she said, her amber-colored eyes glowing with excitement.

Anika's dark brown eyes lit up with the subject. "Well, we've decided on the island of Oahu and we're still deciding between a few hotels including the Four Seasons and the Royal Hawaiian. Both hotels are gorgeous, but the locations are so different, so we have to think about it a bit. What do you ladies think?" Anika asked, eager for their input.

They pulled out their phones and started looking up both hotels.

Louise spoke up first. "Both hotels look gorgeous! You need to pick which one will look better in your wedding photos. It's all about making the bride look amazing, right? The Royal Hawaiian is so pink and beautiful. The Four Seasons is so classy and elegant. We are going to have such an amazing time, I can't wait!" she said.

"Hey, I know I haven't sent out invites yet, but do you think you ladies will be bringing a plus one?" Anika asked with a playful smirk. She tossed her chin length hair over her shoulder and raised her eyebrows, knowing she was putting them on the spot. Louise and Simone looked at each other with a conspiratorial gaze.

"I don't think so," Louise said, looking back down at her plate and avoiding eye contact. "I'm not seeing anyone right now. Besides, I want to focus on you. Your wedding must be perfect."

Anika brought a hand to her heart and gave Louise a grateful smile.

"Maybe?" Simone replied, an awkward smile on her face. "I'll have to get back to you on that. Worst-case scenario, Louise and I go as each other's dates and meet cute guys during the wedding festivities. You've got some cute cousins coming, right?"

"Oh my gosh, I've got so many cousins, not all dating age, but still. Indian weddings are always huge, it's an expectation! Tom's got some cute groomsmen, too. We'll set something up, I'm sure," Anika said, trying to think of which guys would suit her friends the best. "Yes, I'll give it some thought and let you know the details on our guys. I'll try to make sure we get some hotties on the guest list for sure!"

"We can make a list!" Louise said excitedly, clapping her hands.

Louise looked down and checked her phone, realizing their lunch hour was almost over. They agreed to continue going over the details of the guest list as well as the hotel choices the next time they met up. They all had a glow about them, excited to be part of such a luxurious and exciting wedding. Anika would make the most beautiful bride, with her classic beauty and timeless taste. Louise and Simone would do everything in their power to make the bride's journey to wedded bliss go smoothly.

37

AFTER FINISHING UP AT THE LAW FIRM, Louise was content to settle in for the evening with her box of Oreos, a cup of tea, and Cosette when the phone rang.

"What are you wearing? Wait, let me guess. Sweats. No bra."

Louise rolled her eyes, knowing exactly where Simone was going with this. "First of all, you sound like a perv asking me questions like that on the phone, and second, I'm at home, wearing cat friendly clothing, so sue me," Louise said.

Simone giggled, knowing she nailed her description of Louise's attire exactly. "Well, I've planned our night out and it's going to be fabulous, so you better go shower and do your hair. We are getting our nails done and we are going out. Gotta get started on finding our plus one for the wedding, am I right?" Simone said.

Louise cringed at the idea of trying to pick up guys. She was so shy and not confident enough to try to pick up strangers. Simone had a talent for it, and she always had the gentlemen hanging on her every word.

"Alright, I'll be your wing woman, but don't you dare try to leave me with a guy like last time," Louise replied reluctantly.

Simone groaned on the other end of the phone. "Gregory? He's not just any guy, he's our friend, but yes, yes, it's understood. I will not abandon you this time. Let's go get our nails done, then we'll go out."

When they sat at the nail salon, it felt like such a treat to make their toes and fingers look so beautiful. Louise decided she would treat herself more often as she gazed at the glossy red nails that would match her lipstick. She resented the amount of people that commented on her lax appearance at home.

During her self-imposed isolation, she had taught herself to live without a lot of things that brought her joy in the name of safety. She had avoided people and social interactions, which also meant she had given up the activities she often did to take care of herself. For her, there seemed no point. Who would she dress up cute or do her hair for?

Louise enjoyed treating herself with a bit of extra love. She needed to give herself more time to look good for her, and no one else. Though she would never admit to her mother and Simone that they were right, she would not be looking back when it came to reaping the benefits of self-care.

They went back to Louise's house to finish getting ready, which felt like when they were university students getting ready to go out. Laughing and giggling about the gossip they had heard at work, swapping stories about the pain in the ass younger articling students that always thought they knew everything, Simone excluded.

It felt like old times in a way that Louise enjoyed so much. By the time they were ready, the two women in the mirror looked hot, Louise admitted, as they gazed at their reflection after some touch-up hairstyling, makeup, and a good push-up bra.

Louise wore a body-hugging black dress and pointy-toed black booties. She looked very cute indeed. Red lips and simple gold jewelry completed her look, and she thought she might actually be a good wing woman for Simone tonight. Simone knocked it out of the park, wearing a deep V-neck gold sequin dress that gathered at the waist, accentuating her curves. She had tied up her long blond hair in a severe top knot and lined her light brown eyes with black winged eyeliner, which gave her a more severe, sophisticated look.

Louise drooled at the patent hot pink heels she wore. "Sick heels."

"I know, right?"

They took an Uber to Major Tom, a restaurant located in a high-rise building, which afforded them stunning views of the city at night. They sat at the bar on black leather stools and ordered some pretty lavender-colored cocktails garnished with baby's breath.

Major Tom was a midcentury modern sixties inspired steakhouse with a *Mad Men* vibe. Tables were lined along floor to ceiling windows, treating guests to a stunning view of downtown Calgary. The restaurant was so high up, it felt like you could almost reach out and touch the bright red cylindrical top of the Calgary Tower. They enjoyed a couple cocktails, sitting up on comfortable leather bar stools and chatting with the bartender while seated at the green-grey marble bar. Louise's mouth watered as she perused the elaborate menu and selected her food along with a bottle of wine for them to share.

"So, what's your life plan now? I feel like you were on the up and up and now it's back to square one?" Simone asked.

Louise sighed, sad to feel like a project for so many people. "Well, after Gregory, I was down in the dumps for a bit, but I'm coming out of it. I really liked being with someone again, even if it wasn't for that long. I was annoyed that Gregory and I couldn't make it work. He just gets me so hot, and I like him so much…" Louise said, looking away and taking a sip of her cocktail.

She paused, then smiled again, willing herself to be more upbeat. "Do not fret, Simone, I am moving on! Give me all your dating tips. I have zero skills," Louise said.

Simone thought for a moment, trying to pick the best advice she could muster, since she had so much expertise on dating.

"Well, listen, the first thing you gotta know is stop looking for a forever guy! You've got time for that later. You need to start looking for Mr. Right Now. You know what I mean? Practice makes perfect," Simone joked, nudging Louise with her elbow.

Louise nodded, feeling like she was learning so much from the master dating goddess. "How do I find Mr. Right Now, though?" she asked.

Simone paused to think. "Do we have any hot guys at work that could have potential? Nah, I don't think so. Most are too old or too cocky. And most of the articling students are too young or pricks. Okay, so let's go out and look for some fresh hotties. The guys around the bar are cute, but it looks like they're coupled up. I'm thinking we go femme fatale mode and hit up a few bars on Stephen Avenue," Simone suggested.

"Oooh," Louise said, "yeah, let's have some more cocktails."

Their order came to the table, roast chicken for Louise and a rack of lamb for Simone. It was delicious, as expected, but the ladies were now on a mission. After dinner they walked a few blocks, since it was not unbearably cold, to The Belvedere on Stephen Avenue.

They took a moment to enjoy the lights that were strung along the avenue, from one side of the street to the other from the tops of the buildings. A few light snowflakes were falling from the sky, adding a festive charm to the dark night. The Belvedere was a narrow cocktail bar situated in an old sandstone building. The walls were lined with mirrors to visually expand the space and the old grey stone floors paid homage to the history of the building. The lighting was dim and intimate, allowing for people to enjoy a sense of privacy even when surrounded by other tables.

They sat in two comfortable black leather club chairs and looked at the menu sitting on the small Carrera marble table. They ordered two chocolate martinis and Louise tried to turn on guy hunting mode, scanning the place for any single looking guys. There were none, and they were surrounded by a decidedly older crowd.

"Do you find the people here look a lot older than us? Maybe we picked the wrong night to come here," Louise noticed after checking out the other tables.

"Okay, so this place wasn't the best one for picking up guys. I mean, do people even go to the bar to pick up guys anymore? I get way more luck at the Wild Rose. Sorry, Lou. Next time we're going western. Worked for you last time, right?" Simone asked playfully. "Unless you're into one of those age gap romances," she added, "which can also be a lot of fun."

Louise shook her head, scrunching up her face.

"Not to worry. This gives us time to regroup and discuss strategy. What apps are you using for meeting guys online?" Simone asked.

Louise hid her face, embarrassed that she hadn't checked out any yet. "I don't have a profile anywhere yet. It was hard to figure out which ones were good and which ones were just for casual hookups."

They worked together on downloading a few apps, and Louise was most intrigued by the Meet Cute app. They wrote a rather flattering bio for Louise that made her seem much more interesting and open than she was in reality.

"Ugh, this is so cringy. How do I write this and not seem like a cat lady?" she asked.

"How about we don't bring up the cat, save that for if things get serious. Cosette doesn't want a bunch of strange guys trying to become friends with her," Simone replied.

Simone used her expertise on sexy angles to take an attractive picture of Louise looking super cool with her martini and they uploaded it. After finishing uploading, they finished her profile, and she was ready to start swiping.

"The guys are going to go mad once they see the tight dress and the red lips. You are so hot!" Louise blushed and waved away the compliment.

They practiced reading a few guys' descriptions and swiping a few times, which Louise found quite entertaining. Simone swiped right on a few more guys while Louise went to the bathroom to freshen up. Louise was outraged, but very forgiving, since she knew Simone's bar was very high for potential candidates.

After ordering pear and peach martinis, they started discussing the upcoming wedding and what they would wear. Since they needed a bridesmaid dress color that would suit their pale coloring, as well as the darker brown skin tone of Anika's sister, Daphne, they found some pretty gowns in light pinks and light blue, which could be good options for the three of them. They were so glad that Anika had decided to have a destination wedding next summer, yet they bemoaned going broke for such a pricey destination.

"We'll have to see which hotel she picks, because we can't have a pink dress at a pink hotel, right? We would blend in with the building too much," Louise said, sipping her peach martini and enjoying the sweet fruity summery flavors, which contrasted with the chilly, snowy environment outside. It reminded Louise that spring and summer were right around the corner, and brighter days were ahead with the wedding celebrations and holiday in Hawaii. Simone was positively drooling over the possibility of a vacation fling.

"Imagine, we could be sipping cocktails in the pool, checking out hot guys with gorgeous tans. It'll be heaven!" Simone mused dreamily, picturing the gorgeous men waiting for them in Oahu.

"I'm more excited for cocktails by the beach and piping hot malasadas," Louise said, since she had already started writing down some places where she would be going for food and drinks on the island.

They took an Uber home after finishing their drinks and agreed that Louise would continue reading through more profiles and swiping right when she got home. Louise was nervous, not sure what she would do if she had a match, but Simone reassured her she would continue to coach her through it when the time came. Time to get back on the horse and continue building the life she had always wanted.

38

THE NEXT FEW DAYS, Louise filled up her free time swiping right on all the guys she thought were cute or had good profiles. It was more fun than she had expected. Simone had explained that she would need to give it a few days before actually getting some matches. She found it strange reading the men's profiles. They seemed to all look alike, tall, blond or light brown hair, and handsome. Perhaps she was only looking at the ones that were her type. Many of them had features that reminded her of Gregory. Well, that ship had sailed and with each swipe she felt herself getting more and more settled with the idea of moving on.

Louise had come to regret the fear which had prevented her from putting the money down to rent the Marda Point apartment. She had never gotten in touch with Myrna about renting it after the viewing, which Louise now lamented. Myrna's place was most likely rented out by now, since it had been a month or so since she had seen it, and it was a really cute apartment in a stellar location in Marda Loop.

Louise resolved to check out a few more apartments in the area and finish what she had started. Even though her life had taken a bit of a detour, her goals hadn't changed and neither had her will to achieve them. Since it was hard to envision dating guys while living with Georgie, it was time to get her own place. Louise hummed a song to herself while preparing dinner, overcome by a sensation of hope and lightheartedness. She warmed up some prepared soup and fresh bread from a local shop. She heard a ping from her phone and noticed that her app had a match. She opened it up excitedly to check her messages.

"Hey, I'm Brandon. I guess we're a match," he messaged.

"Hey, Brandon, I'm Louise. Nice to meet you! First time chatting on the app." Louise could see his picture was a bit blurry, blame it on a poor quality or dirty camera lens, but she thought he seemed nice, and his location wasn't too far away, which would be convenient for meeting up.

"So, what are you up to tonight?" he asked.

"I'm just making some soup. Real exciting," she replied.

"Soup can be exciting. Is it spicy?" he asked.

"No, it's hamburger soup. Not spicy."

"Okay, so, yeah, your soup isn't exciting. I'll give you that," he said, making Louise chuckle. She sent him a giggling face emoji.

They continued to chat as the soup warmed on the stove. Louise sliced the bread and set it on the table. She also pulled out two large bowls and opened a bottle of red wine, deciding to have a glass while waiting for Georgie to come home after her hike with her friends.

Louise messaged Simone about the match, and she was very insistent that Louise set up a meeting with the guy. They both agreed that it needed to be somewhere safe, close, and during daylight hours.

Louise stood in the living room with her glass of wine contemplating taking this leap when she spotted the police car sitting a few houses down, watching her house.

Hmm, she wondered, what would Gregory think if she went out on a date with someone else? Would he be jealous? Would he realize he had made a huge mistake? Well, that would be too bad. She was done waiting around for him to decide he was ready to be in a relationship. She continued to chat with Brandon, hesitating only briefly when he asked her to meet him for a drink at a local coffee shop. She wasn't sure if she was more excited about the coffee and treats or meeting a new guy. Time would tell, but this girl had made a match and was moving on.

Nervous as she was, Louise set up a date her favorite coffee shop with Brandon the following Wednesday. Louise thought this was a fantastic place to meet up, since it was in the heart of Marda Loop, and she had many places to walk to or hide if things got dodgy. She had gotten a good impression of Brandon, and he seemed to be easy to talk to and friendly. She mused that even if the date didn't go well, it was good to practice "getting back in the game" of dating and push herself to meet new people in the neighborhood. Practice makes perfect.

39

When Louise set off for work that day, she realized she was once again feeling that spark of hope within her chest. She even scraped her windshield with a newfound enthusiasm. Louise was confident that she was on the right path and so deliriously happy to be moving on with her life in such a positive direction. She would plan on looking at apartments in the new year and looked forward to booking that phenomenal wedding trip with her best friends to Hawaii.

After hearing she was going on a date the following day, Simone and Anika popped by Louise's place after work and had a look at her closet to pick out an outfit for the date. Upon going through her closet carefully, both friends looked at Louise with regretful expressions.

"Bad news, Lou," Simone said, "we looked in your closet and it's Shakespearean. It's so tragic. I know you picked up a couple of new things lately, but we need you to look hot for this date. If not for you, for Gregory. He needs to know what he is missing. Let's go to the mall. I love having a project. It's so invigorating."

Anika nodded enthusiastically in agreement. Louise frowned, resenting being called a project, but she agreed to go shopping. They browsed the shops for cute tops to go with jeans. She settled on a blue-and-white striped tee and some cute sparkly earrings as one possible outfit. Simone also forced Louise to buy a beautiful navy mini dress that made her legs look amazing. Louise and Anika were not surprised when Simone came away from their shopping trip with more things for herself than for Louise.

"I still think the top you chose was very safe, but it makes sense to have a classic and cool look for a coffee date," Simone said. "I would also consider the dress we chose; it is stunning on you. You don't want to look too fancy and fussy. That's probably why I end up going on so many first dates, not so many second ones," Simone added.

They stopped for a bite to eat in the food court and chatted about first date strategy, which Simone seemed to know a lot about.

"If he talks too much about his cat or his mother, get out of there. If he has weird habits like biting his nails or making crude jokes, get out of there. If he lives with his mother — red flag."

Louise looked up with an offended look on her face. "Now hang on, I live with my mother and that's just fine."

Simone and Anika looked at each other, then back at Louise for a moment, thoughtful, with smirks on their faces.

"Right, well, you won't be doing that for long. We have a plan, right? You are definitely moving out of your mother's house soon. Otherwise, red flag!" Anika said, laughing.

Simone nodded in agreement and patted Louise on the shoulder in a teasing manner.

They continued walking until they ended up at the bathing suit store in the mall. Louise was overcome with joy and anxiety at seeing all the colorful swimsuits available. She was reminded of how awful it felt to go bathing suit shopping in the past. Once she decided to stop dieting, it gave her a different perspective on her body. She knew she could rock most, if not all, those swimsuits on her curvy physique. She had a certain appreciation for her body and her life that could only come from almost losing it. Simone, Anika, and Louise touched fabrics and looked at coverups and other possible swim accessories. Louise asked the saleslady for some recommendations and found a couple suits that hugged her curves and made her look and feel really sexy.

"Wait, how did we end up here? Aren't we shopping for a dating wardrobe?" Simone asked, "Also, why does this feel like a workout?"

"I think we're really looking forward to this destination wedding coming in May and are getting a head start on shopping for it. Can you believe we're going to Hawaii? It's so exciting, I've never been! I feel like I haven't been anywhere different for ages," Louise replied, panting in her dressing room. "Also, it's a workout getting those bathing suits on and off for sure! I'm so sweaty."

Simone managed to acquire an adorable brightly colored tropical bikini. Anika selected a low-cut V-neck one piece, something a little more risqué for her honeymoon. Louise got a blue-and-white striped two-piece set with a bow to the side of the top and high-rise bottoms that were adorable and flattering. They agreed that even if their trip was ages away, they would enjoy buying cute swimsuits and clothing for the trip in the months leading up to it. Even if Louise's date was a dud, she wouldn't regret the time it gave her with her friends in preparation.

40

AT THE PACE HE WAS WORKING, Greg would need a miracle to solve this bizarre case. Two deceased victims, possibly more assault victims who would be connected later, including Louise. Gregory sighed loudly at the thought of Louise. He had such a strong desire to get justice for these victims, yet none of his clues were providing him with the clarity he needed.

Locations were similar, young women at home, dating app connections, both deceased victims had been seduced into a false sense of security and lured to their deaths. A drink of wine with a hit of GHB, and they were his. Both victims were posed in an eerily similar way and appeared to be sleeping peacefully when they were found. The killer was clever, wore gloves to commit the crime, and left virtually no DNA on the scene, save for the minuscule scraps they had been able to use to connect the scenes.

Gregory had explored the location of any sex offenders in the area with no success, since the offenders' DNA was already in his database and there had been no matches to these current crimes. The scenes told him this guy was good-looking, most likely charming, since the victims seemed to feel safe around him. The killer was extremely neat and tidy, almost obsessively, which made it difficult to find much evidence.

The attack on Louise gave the impression that he had gotten better with each of his attacks, harder to trace. Gregory knew he was looking for a handsome guy that just blended into the crowd, did not stand out in any way, and wouldn't be considered a threat to his victims.

Even though he was trying to stay away, he wanted to check-in with Louise, to make sure she was safe and maybe bug her to see if she had come up with any new memories or information. There was a lot of pressure to solve this case, given the nature of the danger to the citizens of Marda Loop, as well as the increase in activity by the perpetrator.

Gregory messaged Louise, knowing at this time of day she would be at work. He hoped she would answer, since she had made him feel like such a villain the last time they were together. He almost didn't deserve to see her, though this knowledge did not dissuade him. If he didn't do everything in his power to solve her case, then breaking up with her would be for nothing.

Louise: "I'm at work. What is it, Detective?"

Gregory sensed a slight tension in her tone when she referred to his job title and chose to ignore it. It wasn't fair to assume a tone when reading a text, yet here he was.

The way she wrote "Detective".

Why would she say it like that?

Did she sound angry?

Of course she was angry.

Gregory frowned, typing his response despite his misgivings.

Gregory: "I need to touch base with you about the case."

Louise: "Want to meet me downtown at my building?"

She shared her building location pin with him. They decided she would take an extra-long lunch to meet with him at one in the afternoon.

Gregory ended the text conversation with a skip in his step, knowing it was silly for him to be excited to see her, especially when their meeting was for professional reasons. Why his heart skipped a beat as she exited the elevator to meet him in the lobby of her building, he would not explore, for it would only lead to disappointment.

She looked breathtaking dressed up for work, with a snug black pencil skirt and a white dress shirt. She wore a gold heart locket around her neck and matching gold ball studs in her ears. Her long light brown hair was styled in a soft curl, which made him ache to touch it. He knew exactly how those silky curls felt when rubbed between his fingers. His chest seized at the memory. He marveled at how she was alive, yet she haunted him.

"Hey. What's going on? What do you need to tell me? I'm dying to know if you have any updates on the case," she said inquisitively as if attempting not to sound too excited.

He cleared his throat. "Well, this is sensitive information. Is there somewhere quieter we can go and chat?" he asked.

Louise thought for a moment and asked him to follow her. They took the elevator to the third floor where there was a lovely indoor garden with trees and tropical plants surrounded by benches, tables and chairs for people to eat their lunch. People tended to hang out there during their lunch breaks, often purchasing meals in the food court of the connected building network.

The gardens were packed at noon, then desolate by one in the afternoon. They picked a bench overlooking the street through large floor to ceiling windows. Trees surrounding them and the trickling sound of a water feature provided a wall of privacy from people walking through the gardens.

"There is another victim to add to our list. You've really got to be careful. Our suspect is getting more comfortable and ramping up the pace of his killings. Until we find a DNA match to a suspect, we are in a race to avoid him getting his hands on any more victims," Gregory said, a look of concern on his face. "We've increased patrols in Marda Loop and we're looking over all the old case files and testing a selection of new people just to rule out more suspects. I just hope he doesn't change his hunting ground before we can catch him."

Louise's brows came together in worry as she looked at him. He could almost see the thoughts buzzing around in her head as she processed the new information.

"I heard there was another victim in Marda, but I was hoping it wasn't connected. That is terrible news. It feels like this monster is almost too clever to be stopped. I wish I remembered more. My memories from that night are just so foggy," Louise sighed, her shoulders curling in, as though she wanted to make herself smaller. The fear that hung around her shoulders like a cloak must be so heavy for her to bear alone.

Gregory wished he could lift that burden from her shoulders and carry it for her.

"Just be really careful. We are getting close but have not found him yet. I care about you and want you to be safe," he cautioned, not wanting to stoke the fear any more than he already had.

Louise rolled her eyes and smirked. "Watch it, Gregory. You

keep talking like that and I might get the wrong idea."

He was doing it again, but he couldn't fight the urge inside him to cover her in bubble wrap and keep her safe.

If he gave her the impression that she was his to care for, so be it.

He grabbed her hand. "You've come to mean a great deal to me, and I value our friendship. I would do anything to keep you safe," he said.

He wished there was another way to prove it.

Louise lowered her eyes, looking at their hands, then pulled hers away as though she had also felt the intense sensation that coursed through his body every time they touched. She tucked both her hands under her arms, wrapping them around her midsection.

She felt it.

Gregory took it as a good sign.

But he needed to focus.

"I get it, Gregory, but I'm not going to stop living. I will do everything to keep myself safe. I am my keeper," she said, placing a hand on her chest.

"You," she continued, "do your job for the citizens of this city. I will take care of myself. I protected myself before you came back into my life and I will continue to do so," she said with conviction.

Gregory nodded in understanding.

He could respect her wishes.

To a point.

"And guess what? I'm going on a date this afternoon."

"Louise, you can't."

"Relax, I'll be surrounded by people. I always take precautions, so I'll be okay, you don't need to worry," she said, looking up at him challengingly as she said those final words, daring him to say anything.

"This killer meets girls through a dating app. It's too dangerous." Gregory's hands curled into tight fists in his lap.

Great.

Cancel all plans.

He was going to stalk Louise all afternoon.

"I'll be at Distilled. It's just a cup of coffee. I'm not going home with anyone."

"Fine, I can come with you and sit at a table. I can act totally casual; you won't even know I'm there." Louise sighed, her head shaking.

"Logan can keep an eye on me. Don't you dare show up."

His lips made an involuntary pfft sound.

Logan.

That chump couldn't protect a cup of coffee from a sugar pack.

"Who are you dating?" he asked through clenched teeth. "Is it someone I know? I don't like it, Louise, it's too risky."

"That information is out of your jurisdiction, Detective."

"Louise…" He gritted his teeth, attempting to restrain his level of fear.

And Louise smiled.

She smiled?

Right. Louise was pleased at his reaction. Her main goal had been to upset him with her dating. Her arrow had hit its mark. "Listen, Gregory, you can't tell me you don't want to date me AND prevent me from dating other people. That's a bit confusing, don't you think?" She twirled her hair, giving him a teasing smile that provoked an involuntary twinge in his groin.

He opened his mouth, then closed it, setting his mouth in a hard line and narrowing his gaze, knowing she was right. Inside him the kettle was boiling over.

He was so mad.

"Okay, well, take all the necessary precautions and make sure you are letting everyone know where you are. Ugh, I do not like this," he said, frowning. He hated sounding like a disapproving parent, but he could barely keep his frustration in check.

Resigned to the situation, he stood up, ready to leave.

The sooner he got back to work, the sooner she would be safe.

He reminded her to keep in contact if she remembered anything else and to take care. She reminded him that she was a big girl standing on her own two feet.

He wondered if she could see the steam coming out of his ears.

Though Gregory had made to leave, he followed Louise to her elevator and saw her safely back up to her office. She would always be safe under his watch. He cursed under his breath as he exited the building, as the knot in his chest returned and plagued him evermore.

Louise was his girl, and despite the fact that she was angry with him now, he would have to do everything in his power to make her realize it. Gregory was terrified that the situation he had created would put Louise in more danger than ever. He growled and kicked the ground, oblivious of those around him watching in busy downtown Calgary. He was so confident he was doing the right thing, yet he didn't feel any comfort from that knowledge. All he felt was an absurd desire to insert himself in her dates and make them awkward.

Keep those guys from asking for a second date.

But then, what would he achieve?

Louise would be even angrier with him than she already was.

He wasn't in a position to prostrate himself at her feet. Yet. Louise dating another man was just plain wrong. And dangerous.

Gregory was powerless to stop it. Well, maybe there was one way to stop it, but it would require him to make a bold move. Change directions. He stuffed his hands in his pocket and sighed. Regardless of which path he chose, he was doomed. Truly doomed.

41

THE WEATHER WARMED UP, as it sometimes did in Calgary during chinook weather conditions. They were enjoying a streak of warm and sunny days, with temperatures melting the piles of snow that had accumulated and giving everyone the necessary vitamin D they had been missing.

Louise opted to wear a navy dress with a large bow at the collar and her tan-colored pea coat, along with her beloved tan heeled booties. Simone would be proud of her outfit, she thought.

Since the weather was pleasant, she was able to skip the leggings and opt for skin-colored tights to keep her legs warm. Though she hadn't abandoned her black wardrobe one hundred percent, she was glad she had taken the time to visit some shops with Simone and give her closet a much-needed boost. It was much easier to feel good when she bought cute outfits in her size and stopped trying to hide behind her oversized or black clothing. She looked so cute and fresh for her date, and she felt a tingle in her chest that confirmed she was on the right path for her future. One where she would stop hiding and start living in the incredible world that existed right outside her door.

She rolled her eyes, remembering how Gregory had called this a mistake. It was too risky.

She could feel the jealousy emanating from his every pore. And she loved it.

His possessiveness, whatever it meant, made her feel giddy. And powerful.

Nothing empowered a woman like teaching a man a lesson.

She smirked with delight. A touch of red lipstick on her full lips and she looked ready to conquer the world. She was ready to make big moves and do something a little risky.

Louise left the house, saying goodbye to Georgie and leaving her details of the man she was meeting and her location. She was no fool and still paranoid enough to be extremely cautious when meeting a new man. Her eyes were protected from the warm sun by her large frame grey tortoiseshell shades. When she put them on and started walking to the café, she felt just a little more fabulous. Even if boosting her confidence was a work in progress, she had made a deal with herself to fake it until she truly felt it. She grinned and nodded at the officer in the squad car parked down the street from her house, recognizing him as one she had seen before. It was her sincere hope that she wouldn't need this watch on her house soon. Gregory might not be the greatest in relationships, but he was one of the most dedicated officers she had ever seen. She knew he would catch his prey.

Louise rounded the corner into the community square, enjoying the feel of the sunshine on her face and feeling the nervous excitement brewing inside. She checked her messages from Brandon again, reminding herself that he would be wearing a blue-collar dress shirt, a brown sweater, and dark blue jeans. His outfit even sounded handsome. She liked a man who knew how to dress and took care of his appearance. The image of Gregory flashed in her mind, and she frowned, willing her mind to stop trying to compare every man to a certain handsome detective. The reality was that ship had sailed, and she was ready to welcome another one in her port.

Brandon sounded like a great guy on paper and if she wasn't interested, he could be blocked on the app. She hadn't really given him that much personal information beyond her name. She had watched enough *Dateline* that she would not make that mistake.

42

When Louise pushed open the heavy door of the café, she could see Brandon sitting at a marble bistro table with a glass of water. She waved at him and signaled to see if he had ordered. He shook his head and came to join her at the counter, where Louise could see Logan waiting to take their order. There, she was safe. Logan was here. There was hardly any risk involved.

Brandon was very clean cut and handsome, shaking her hand as he came up to her and flashing her a charming smile. They ordered their coffees and sat down at the table. He looked familiar. In person, he reminded her of every clean cut, fit, and good-looking dark-haired man she had seen on the Meet Cute app.

Brandon broke the silence. "Great suggestion for a meeting place, do you come here often? I like it."

Louise cleared her throat, feeling the strangest sensation come over her. Shivers. She felt so nervous meeting him. She quickly reminded herself that check, he was handsome and check, he was clean. He also paid for her coffee, which was a good sign.

"I like this place a lot. I've been a regular here since it opened, and it's such a cool place to work on my computer or hang out with friends. Do you live in the neighborhood?" she asked.

Brandon nodded, explaining that he lived close by, but not revealing anything more than that. An awkward silence came between them, as Logan walked over to them with a grin and brought them their coffees.

Louise took her coat off, realizing she hadn't done that yet, and hung her purse on the back of the chair. She cleared her throat, which felt so thick all of a sudden.

"So, Brandon, where do you work?" Louise tried to swallow the sensation she felt that she wanted to throw up.

Maybe this was too much, but she was overcome by nerves that could not be suppressed. She groaned inwardly thinking she might have to go to the bathroom just to take one of her pills, which she hadn't done in a while. She held off, knowing the pills would make her drowsy and essentially end the date.

Brandon explained he was an investment banker who worked downtown, in a building near hers, which seemed providential. He worked in a successful firm that catered to a very wealthy clientele. Louise thought Simone would love this guy, so polished and professional. He seemed a little too slick for Louise. Too perfect. It made her uncomfortable for reasons she could not explain.

She cleared her throat again and reached for her coffee. It was very normal to be feeling nerves, since she wasn't quite over Gregory, and she was pretty paranoid. Did Brandon's voice sound familiar? Surely not.

Louise explained her role as a law librarian, sketching out a little of what she did every day providing access to legal information resources and legal research to the lawyers in her firm. While he spoke, she took a moment to add a sugar packet to her latte, watching the sugar as it slowly penetrated the foam and sank to the bottom of the mug. She stirred the coffee, knocking her napkin by accident as she put her spoon back down on the table. Louise reached down to retrieve it at the same time as Brandon. She thought they were going to romantically bump their heads together if not careful and she pulled back, allowing him to grab the napkin.

As she brought her head back up, she was able to smell his hair and was hit by a familiar scent that filled her with dread. Vanilla cupcake scented hair. Her blood turned cold, and she felt goose bumps cover the surface of her skin.

Damn.

She sat back up, quelling a feeling of nausea that was rising in her chest. She told herself many people used vanilla scented hair product, and she couldn't forever be frightened by that scent. She placed a hand on her heart to still the furious beating she was certain Brandon could hear. She gave him a reassuring smile. Surely it wasn't possible.

"So, Brandon, I haven't seen you in the area much, where do you like to hang out? What do you do in your free time?" she asked.

She didn't want to indulge in constant fear and refused to believe the smell was anything but a coincidence.

Gregory had frightened her.

His warnings made her extra paranoid.

Giving in to his fear mongering would only achieve what he wanted, a failed date with another man. Louise snorted, causing Brandon to look up from his coffee cup with a questioning expression. She smiled sweetly at him.

This was a nice, perfectly normal guy that seemed to have everything she could want in a partner. He told her about his obsession with fitness and health. He had very high standards for himself and his appearance. She considered this a bit of a turnoff, given that she had just jumped off the diet bandwagon herself and was taking time to heal her relationship with her health and increase her overall wellness. He was an avid jogger, which she found appealing, since it was something they had in common.

Louise tried to focus on his conversation, though the unfortunate hair smelling had set her mind on a furious track that she couldn't derail from. She tried to calm the roiling feelings inside, telling herself she was jumping to conclusions, trying to talk herself out of this date.

Brandon asked her a question, which she totally missed, so she had to come back to reality and ask him to repeat the question.

"What do you like to do in your free time?" he repeated.

She explained that she also liked jogging, as well as watching reality TV, and cuddling her cat. She giggled nervously, guzzling her coffee like it was going out of style, trying to act normal. She cleared her throat again, unable to stop it from feeling like it was closing in on her.

"Do you like cats, Brandon?" she asked distractedly. She brought a hand to her neck instinctually, because she couldn't clear her throat. Brandon's dark eyes followed the path of her hand as he spoke slowly, mesmerized.

"I don't know. I haven't really met a lot of cats. They seem mean. Are you feeling okay?" he asked her, with a look of concern abruptly appearing on his face.

She chalked it up to nervousness and explained that she had

not been on a proper date in a long time. Brandon empathized, explaining that he had been in a few relationships, but they never lasted beyond a few months. They both agreed dating was hard, especially online dating. He regaled her with a few funny stories of past dates that had not gone well, and Louise felt herself relax a bit, though she could not stop thinking about his hair. At least her throat had cleared.

Though she wanted this date to go well, Louise couldn't help a morbid curiosity tickling her brain and making connections she couldn't believe as reality. She braced herself and took the risk, needing to satisfy her suspicions. She glanced around and laid eyes on Logan, chatting up a customer, as well as the other baristas she recognized and the familiar faces of the estheticians on the other side of the wall separating the café and the spa. She was safe. Time to be risky.

"I don't want to sound weird, but your hair smells nice, is that vanilla?" she asked, trying not to sound like she was interrogating him.

"Oh, you like it? Yeah, it's vanilla. It's a special product I get at my salon. I find it smells like a vanilla cupcake. At first it was a bit off-putting, but it works, so I keep using it," he explained.

She nodded and smiled reassuringly, telling him she liked it, even though the scent actually made her nauseous. The barista brought her a glass of water, which she delighted in, thinking she would have something else to awkwardly sip.

As they finished their coffees, Louise began to look for an out, given the sun was starting to set and she knew she would have to walk home alone. If she walked home in the dark, it would make a certain protector unhappy with her. She rolled her eyes, not happy to be giving that detective any more time in her thoughts.

"Well, Brandon, it's getting late, and my mum is expecting me soon for dinner. What are your plans for tonight? Maybe we should do this again?" she asked awkwardly, regretting saying the sentence as soon as it came out.

She definitely could not imagine doing this again. Brandon pulled out his phone, as well as a tin from his pocket, asking her to confirm her phone number before she left. He pulled out a pink breath mint and popped it into his mouth.

A pink fucking breath mint.

She hadn't tested a pink fucking breath mint like that one.

For a moment, it felt like time stood still as Louise gaped at the mint being placed in Brandon's perfect mouth, on his perfect tongue. He gave her a charming grin as she observed how fixated she was on his mints. He offered her the open mint box so she could avail herself of one.

With a tremble she tried to disguise, she selected one, and quickly got up, saying she should go to the washroom before going home. The washrooms were at the back of the café past a bunch of comfortable pedicure chairs and a counter with bar stool seating where patrons would sit for their manicures.

She walked quickly past a few salon chairs where some clients were having their hair washed and styled. She held the mint tightly in her palm, the pink lump beginning to moisten with the nervous sweat accumulating there. She used the key for the bathroom, which was sitting on a tray by the doors. Once in the bathroom, she locked the deadbolt behind her, finally catching her breath. She opened her hand and looked at the pink circular mint, with the word CANADA written on it.

Canada mints, the smell of pure terror in her hand. For all the mints that existed out there, the wintergreen scent was so distinct, she trembled with the fear she had been suppressing. Louise looked at her reflection in the mirror in disbelief, not being able to conceive what this meant for her. She had been assaulted by a symphony of vanilla and mint.

Louise rested her head against the wall and closed her eyes, attempting to clear her thoughts. She practiced her calming breathing exercises, but they weren't working. Her skin crawled with recognition. She was vibrating. If her mind couldn't believe it, the memories of him were stored in her bones. Could she have been sitting with her attacker all along?

43

Life was all about making big moves and so far, Gregory had made only a few of them. When he was a kid, he always enjoyed sports and math because he loved the rules. As long as you followed the steps and played by the rules, your results could almost be guaranteed consistent. Stick to the path and you won't get lost.

Gregory was a guy who could be counted on the follow the strict rule of the law, act with honor and do the right thing. His dream to become an officer had always made sense to him. Help make a better society by upholding the law and maintaining order. Of course, being an actual officer made him realize the naiveté of his original optimism.

There were often more crimes being committed than the police force could ever handle. The rules blurred when one had to choose between the most immediate threats and the crimes that could be ignored or dealt with later.

Gregory saw himself residing somewhere in the grey area now, having committed an offense, but somehow knowing that by doing the right thing and coming clean now, perhaps he would avoid the worst of the consequences.

At least, that was what he hoped.

He blew the breath he had been holding in his cheeks and nodded. He covered his face with his hands, leaned his elbows on Antonio's desk and groaned as his supervisor absorbed the information he had delivered.

"I don't believe it." A look of shock and disappointment etched itself on Antonio's face.

"Well, it happened," he repeated in a breathy, defeated tone.

"Are you sure? Upstanding, ethical to a fault, Detective Gregory Band? You fucked a witness in an open case?" Antonio said, excruciatingly slowly and with exaggerated hand gestures, as though to draw out Gregory's discomfort more than it already had been. "This job never gets boring."

Gregory wasn't sure that Antonio was more surprised by his having compromised a witness or that he had actually had sex with someone. Antonio kicked back in his chair and rested his head in the hands he placed behind his head. His supervisor let out a pensive whistle. Gregory nodded once more, his gaze traveling downward.

"Oh boy. You fucked a witness," Antonio repeated to himself, as though his thought process involved repeating the same statement over and over again.

"It's more than that. We dated in university. I hadn't seen her for maybe…nine years? We started working together on the case and, well," Gregory said with a nervous chuckle. "I just liked spending time with her, and one thing led to another…"

Antonio held up a hand, stopping Gregory from emitting another word.

"Sounds romantic, sweetie, but this a problem. You aren't sup-posed to do anything beyond *interview* a witness, maybe comfort a witness. Definitely not sleeping with a witness." Antonio brought his arms back on his desk and sighed. "You know what this means."

Gregory nodded, resigned. "Am I fired?"

"Well, no. I don't think we need to go that far, but I'm taking you off this case. You'll compromise our investigation if you stay involved. There is way too much at stake with this one." Antonio pressed a button on his phone and called his assistant to send Detective Selena Blair to his office. "The public is clamoring for details about this case, and I cannot imagine what this would do if they thought we were bumbling up this investigation."

Gregory resented the implication but nodded in understanding. The perception of police competency maintained trust with the public. When that trust was eroded in any way, it usually spelled out scandal for the force.

"You have to give Selena all the details. Tell her what you know and hand the case over to her. I know she won't make a pass at Louise."

Though he knew it was a logical consequence, Gregory felt the dagger in his heart, thinking of handing over his first big case to someone else. This had been his obsession, his baby, for months now.

But perhaps it would be worth it. He thought of warm hazel eyes and a familiar smile, and it gave him courage. This move, however painful, was an essential step that must be taken if he was to make things right with Louise. If he had to hurt himself to save himself, he invited the pain. There was plenty to be had.

"Selena, you're going to be working with Marty on the Marda Loop murderer case now. I'm going to let, Loverboy here fill you in on all the details you need."

Gregory could feel Selena coming up behind him and he looked up at her with determined eyes. Antonio could not have picked a better detective to take over the case. At least if Gregory couldn't enjoy the glory of solving this complex case, he was happy to see it going into the hands of a capable and determined detective. Gregory knew that Marty would work well with her as well.

"As soon as you're done catching up Detective Blair, check in with the Missing Persons department. I want you hidden away somewhere safe until this whole thing blows over. They've got lots of work for you over there."

Gregory accepted his new assignment and led Selena to his office, where he handed her the stack of his notes and files to look over. Major crimes was where he belonged, but he would hopefully make a dent in the cases needing to be investigated in Missing Persons while he waited for Antonio to trust him again. He loved solving puzzles, and that particular department provided some challenging ones.

They sat beneath the small pool of light provided by his desk lamp and went through each page, each interview and each minute detail until Gregory was satisfied the murder victims would be well represented and the hunt for justice on their behalf just might be successful.

44

LOUISE THREW THE MINT IN THE GARBAGE and washed her hands, taking a moment to catch her breath. She had to call Gregory. He would know what to do. She picked up her phone with trembling hands and dialed. After two terribly long rings, he picked up.

"Gregory," she whispered, though no one would hear her phone call through the bathroom walls.

"What, what is it? Why are you whispering?" he replied in a whisper.

"I'm in the bathroom at Distilled. I think I'm on a date with my attacker. Can you come get him or something?" she asked, feeling trapped in the bathroom, unable to escape without arousing Brandon's suspicions.

Louise worried that he already knew who she was. Maybe he thought he was playing with his prey before killing, as does a cat. He had a propensity for toying with his victims, then murdering them. Wait, had he put anything in her coffee? No, Louise was still feeling fine.

Gregory was quite a distance away, questioning a witness for a new case, and he told her to stay in the bathroom until someone came to get her.

"I'm scared. I can't go back out there." Her breaths began to speed up, her heart pounding its way through her rib cage. Her stomach churned with nausea.

"Don't let anyone in the room, unless they show you a badge. I'm sending someone over right away," Gregory said. "I'll come to you as quickly as I can."

They couldn't arrest him on suspicion, but they could take him in for questioning and DNA testing. The police would take care of it from there, as long as they got him in custody. Even though she had never clearly seen his face, she knew the DNA testing results would be conclusive. She recognized the timbre in his voice, the scent, even the leather gloves she could remember him wearing. Were they the gloves he had on his hands when he wrapped them around her neck? Her fingers grazed her neck, feeling sick at the thought. While she waited to be alerted in the bathroom, she looked at herself in the mirror bracing her hands on the counter. She had been ready for this moment for so long.

"Come on, Lou. This is your moment. You will make him suffer for a change. He will not steal your power." She braced herself on the counter and stared at herself determinedly in the mirror. Following what seemed like an eternity, a knock came at the bathroom door, and Louise nearly jumped out of her skin. She heard the voice of a woman outside the door.

"Hi, Louise, are you in there?" the person on the other side of the door asked.

"Yes, who is it?" she asked.

"This is Officer Serena Blair, and I'm here to escort you to your car." The officer slipped an identification badge under the door to verify her identity.

Louise opened the door with relief, knowing she could get out safely. As she came out of the bathroom, Officer Blair asked her to go get her jacket casually to indicate the table where the suspect was seated, then make her exit as calmly as possible. Other officers would be waiting outside to pick him up as soon as they knew Louise had been removed safely from the situation.

"Can you handle this, Louise?" Officer Blair asked to which Louise nodded silently.

Though she was afraid, in this environment and with Officer Blair close behind, she would be safe. Louise walked calmly down the hallway from the washrooms and stared into the café area and her heart sank.

Brandon was gone.

She went back to Officer Blair and declared that he had already left while she was in the washroom.

"Not to worry, we have officers watching the door for anyone trying to run out, and with any luck, they will grab him. Do you need to be escorted to your car or do you need a ride home?" Officer Blair asked.

Louise explained that she had walked there, and her home was close by. Once Louise had indicated the table where they were sitting, Officer Blair grabbed the glass the suspect had used and put it in a bag to get preliminary DNA testing done. The officer guided Louise to the patrol car outside, where she sat in the passenger side.

Officer Blair sent a radio message describing the suspect and send out a "be on the lookout" for the area of Marda Loop. As they arrived at her house, Louise could hear the radio blaring, with officers declaring they had captured the suspect running on the pathways close to the coffee shop. Louise's heart lightened. They had caught him.

As the car pulled up to the Cambrai Cottage, the lights were on, and Louise imagined Georgie was in the kitchen preparing dinner. She sighed happily.

"I'll walk you into the house," Detective Blair said, her gaze determined.

"You have to go get him. He needs to be put away for good," Louise insisted.

"Louise, I need to make sure you're safe first."

"I'm good. Trust me, there's an officer right over there, and my mum is home. See? The lights are on. I won't be alone. I don't want to frighten her. I just want to tell her the good news."

Detective Blair agreed reluctantly when Louise promised to call if anything was amiss. They would need to bring her in later to identify Brandon, so Detective Blair would be back. The faster they could have this man in handcuffs, the better.

Louise opened and closed the door, taking a moment to lean against the door and inhale the comforting feeling of home. She was struck immediately with the stillness, a charged silence she recognized. A familiar silence. Louise shook her head, no, they had caught Brandon. He was in police custody.

Louise looked for her mother in the kitchen, then called out for her. Her chest burning with apprehension, when Georgie did not reply. She looked for Cosette, who had mysteriously disappeared from the cozy spot she had been in before Louise left. She texted Gregory to hurry because she was frightened. Something wasn't right about the home. The air was charged with a familiar danger.

Louise only had moments to decide and before she could think, her feet were walking up the stairs.

Her mother could be in danger and the time she took to go outside and flag down the officer could mean life or death to the woman that meant the world to her.

Louise couldn't take that risk.

Seconds mattered.

She could be overly paranoid.

It could be nothing.

She didn't want anything horrible to happen because she had tipped Brandon off that she knew he was in the house.

It was also very possible that she was paranoid, and her mother was upstairs with the cat folding laundry and listening to a show on her iPad. She crept silently up the stairs, taking a brief moment to stop in her room for some backup. She closed her hand around the firm length of her trusty baseball bat, one she had stolen from her brother when he moved out many years ago. She opened her closet door and stabbed into her clothing quietly with the bat, finding nothing. He wasn't there.

Louise exhaled, beginning to feel foolish. Well at least, if nothing else, she might appear crazy to her mother, but she would not be caught unaware. The bat nestled within the folds of her peacoat and continued on to her mother's room. Oddly, the door was closed. Louise could hear no sounds of a television show inside the room. Her heart was hurting as it was pounding so hard and Louise worried she would pass out before being able to see her mother.

Georgie usually left the door open, allowing Cosette to come and go as she pleased. Louise walked silently up to the door, seeing a light shine through the bottom section, alerting her that the room could be occupied. She thought for a split second, maybe this was silly, maybe Georgie was changing her clothing and Louise was about to give her a heart attack. She calmed herself and knew she had to keep her wits about her. She took a deep breath and pushed open the door.

45

In her bedroom, Georgie lay sprawled out in a star formation on the bed, seemingly asleep. Her mother never slept like that, and Louise hoped and prayed she was still breathing. She crept in the room and walked up to the bed, checking for a pulse on her mother's neck. She smelled a strong sweet odor permeating the room which she could not identify. Her mother must have been knocked out somehow. Louise could see her chest rising and falling, a sign of shallow breath. She barely enjoyed a moment of relief that Georgie was alive when she heard the closet door creak open and felt his hands on her arms. She kept a hold on her bat, which Brandon seemed unaware of yet, as it was well hidden in her coat folds.

He nuzzled his head in her neck, saying "Hi, Louise. We have some unfinished business, you and me. You didn't think I would forget about you, did you? I've dreamed about you," he said with a breathy panting voice.

Brandon ran his hand down the side of her body, opposite the arm that held the bat. Louise shivered in fear, which seemed to excite him. He brought his face to the nape of her neck and inhaled deeply, as though triggering his memories of their night spent together long ago. Louise was chilled with a sense of déjà vu. A ball of dread made her stomach feel like it was retreating into her legs.

"Mmm, my sweet rose. You have no idea how excited I am to be with you again. My dream girl," he inhaled again. His hands tightened around both her arms, attempting to trap her. He was so damn strong.

Frozen in shock, Louise felt the power drain from her body. Her moment had come at last, and she was utterly useless. Brandon pulled her to his chest and held her with one arm while he rooted in his pocket. His routine had not changed. A few devastated tears squeezed from her eyes, as her breath stuttering out, and her heart raced to keep up with the energy coursing through her body. She closed her eyes and shook her head, her breath rattling in her chest. She could hear the clicking plastic of the zip ties as they came from his pocket, and he squeezed her with both arms once more.

"No, you will not have me," she said, a sob escaping as she struggled to move her arms.

She gripped the bat in her hand as he pressed her arms against her body painfully, showing the extent of his might. "I belong to no one." She held the bat, but hesitated to reveal the weapon until she could use it without him being able to take it from her.

"Louise, have you forgotten?" He shook his head, chuckling at her defiance. She turned to the side, and her eyes connected with his, the black circles of his pupils dilated like that of a predator in the moment before pouncing on his prey.

"You're mine."

"No," she breathed out, causing a smile to curve on his perfectly wide mouth.

"Louise, I have my ways of making you cooperate." His gaze, warm and charming, his face a picture of triumphant delight. "I have you right where I want you. Now turn and look at me," he murmured and loosened his grip to turn her around in his arms. Louise felt the resistance of the smooth firm wood handle of the bat in her palm.

"I'm not your dream. I'm your nightmare," Louise spat out, squeezing the bat as though it suddenly filled her with renewed power.

His change in grip had forced her out of her temporary stupor, and she bent her knees to drop out of his hold for a mere second, as she had learned to in her self-defense classes. She backed away a step, stepping between Brandon and Georgie, and lifted the bat over his head. His eyes connected instantly with the bat as she hurtled it in his direction without looking. She pounded against Brandon, screaming as each hit connected with his body, though she could not keep track of her hits being successful or not.

Brandon kept desperately grabbing for the bat and was almost successful a few times, yet Louise held on for dear life. At times, she swore she could almost feel the spirits of the women he had killed giving her strength and not allowing her to give up. Hit harder. Stop the monster. Louise knew she was not only fighting for herself, but for Georgie, and the countless victims he had assaulted and murdered.

Louise barely registered the sound of Gregory running into the house, most likely following the sound of her screams, going up the stairs in record speed, followed by Officer Blair.

"Louise!"

"I'm in here, Gregory!"

Louise finally silenced Brandon with one good wallop, which sent him backing into the bedroom wall. She kept hitting him until he lay in a crumpled heap perched against the floral wallpaper. He seemed incapacitated, with quite a few good hits to the head to show for her efforts. Louise, not taking his inaction for granted, waited for Gregory to come up the stairs, gripping the bat as though to pounce at any moment, her breath heaving in her chest.

Gregory burst into the room, breathing heavily, with Officer Blair close behind him. Louise dropped the bat and ran to them, begging them to call an ambulance for her mother.

Officer Blair checked to see if Brandon was awake, and he was knocked out cold. She handcuffed Brandon's hands behind his back and sat him up against the wall, waiting for him to also be carried out on a stretcher by the paramedics.

Gregory wrapped his arms around Louise and looked her over for injuries. "Are you okay? Are you hurt?" His eyes darted frantically over her face, as though her face would reveal the extent of her injuries.

Louise shook her head in response, closing her eyes at the feel of his hand caressing her face gently.

"The ambulance is on its way. I'm sorry you had to do this alone," he said, pulling her closer.

Louise turned and looked at her mother, who still hadn't shown signs of movement on the bed.

"I need to help Georgie," she sobbed as she left his arms and sat on the bed, feeling her mother's neck for a pulse. Georgie's skin was warm, and her chest was still rising and falling, filling Louise with cautious optimism. She spoke to her mother with reassurances and held her hand as they waited.

Officer Blair read her attacker his rights when he came to and hauled him down the stairs to meet the first responders.

When the two ambulances arrived, Louise climbed in with

her mother, who was still unconscious. Georgie was put on oxygen and taken to the hospital. Gregory waved her off and turned to his police cruiser.

He promised to meet her at the hospital.

Gregory wouldn't let her go through this alone.

As the ambulance drove off, Louise left the cottage with a sense of relief in her heart, though she knew the work was only beginning. Red and blue lights flashed from outside the ambulance, reminding Louise that she would be unable to return home for a few days at the very least. She would be bedding down with Georgie at the hospital, their home could wait. Seeing Georgie on the plastic mattress covered in a sheet, Louise fretted over her mother's ability to recover from whatever poison he had used on her. She shivered, thinking she had come so close to being incapacitated herself. Her mother had to survive. She had to. There would be no home without Georgie.

46

"Watch the ice, Mum. You have to take it easy," Louise said as she held Georgie's arm and helped her walk on the icy sidewalks to her house. While Georgie was in the hospital being monitored for a few nights, police examined Cambrai Cottage with a fine-toothed comb, leaving a mess in their wake.

Gregory refused to leave her side until she forced him to go home for a proper meal and a shower. They hadn't discussed the status of their relationship, since Louise needed to focus on her mother.

She dreaded discussing it, so she avoided it. Her last message to him had been to let him know Georgie was doing well. Though he tried to talk to her, she had asked him for more time. Her own recovery from the night with Brandon would take as long as it needed. She wanted to give herself processing time to absorb all that had happened in such a short time.

Louise had no idea how long she needed. She just found ways to keep busy while Georgie recovered. The house was scrubbed from top to bottom, making it nice and welcoming for her mother when she returned. Georgie had been rendered unconscious with chloroform, which explained the sweet smell in the room. Louise had found it necessary to air out the rooms, even though it was cold outside, just to rid themselves of the odor and the memories. She filled the home with flowers and tried to erase any signs of their horrific night. Georgie's only lingering side effects had been mild headaches, and she seemed to be suffering less and less from them now.

Louise opened the door and settled her mother on the sofa with a giant pile of pillows and blankets.

"How do you feel, Mum? Can I make you some tea? Are you okay being here again?" Louise asked, tears welling up in her eyes. "We can go stay somewhere else if you aren't comfortable." Simone had offered for them to stay at the Cormiers if they needed a place to relax and recover. Seeing Georgie back in the house made Louise wonder if perhaps she should have accepted the offer.

Georgie patted Louise on the cheek and shushed her. "I'm feeling okay now. He is locked up in a jail cell. We can all breathe easy now. He can't hurt us anymore. I will always feel happiest in my home."

Louise leaned over and rested her head in her mother's arms, recognizing the irony that her patient was the one providing the comfort. Georgie always made her feel like everything would be alright. It was time for a cup of tea and some Christmas movies. Cosette jumped on the sofa, ready to nestle in next to Georgie, and started bumping her arm for some cuddles.

"Oh, how I have missed you, my kitty," she said, petting the grey tabby until she purred happily. Louise frowned, thinking it was going to be difficult for her mother when she actually did move out, since Cosette would be coming with her.

Louise spent the rest of the week overseeing Georgie's recovery and preparing for the upcoming family holidays that would happen in the next few days. Anika and Simone helped fill the fridge with foods to sustain Georgie and Louise when they returned from the hospital. Well, Simone specified that she had hired someone to make her contributions, but it was all the same in the end. Georgie and Louise wouldn't have to lift a finger for meals for weeks to come.

Louise washed and folded the bedding for the pull-out sofa, since her brother would be crashing there for a few days while spending time in the city. Her brother worked out-of-town most of the year in the Northern Alberta oilfields and spent the rest of his time traveling with the money he accumulated. Louise looked forward to the crowded cozy nights when the tiny house would be full to the brim with visiting friends and family. Anything to keep her distracted from thoughts of Gregory.

She would call Gregory.

Eventually.

Louise was struggling to find the words to speak to Gregory again. He had literally ripped her heart to shreds, and she was so afraid to take any kind of leap again. The pain in her chest was staggering. As a distraction, she helped her mum plan a Christmas party for her canasta group, which sounded absolutely adorable. A group of sixty-five-year-olds getting drunk on one or two glasses of wine and leaving by eight.

The ample amount of neighborhood gossip Louise would hear made all her efforts worth it. Louise dreaded the questions about why she was still single, and she was sure they would have many helpful suggestions about who she should date.

Who could she trust, if not a group of thirsty seniors?

They knew the dirt on everyone.

Louise planned to escape to her room with a spicy Christmas romance novel if things got too personal, but only after writing down a few notes. After her ordeal with Gregory, then the Marda Loop murderer, she had deleted her Meet Cute app and sworn off dating for a while. Time to focus on new things.

Like herself.

She hadn't spent enough time thinking about what she wanted. Louise needed to spend some time goal setting and giving her life new meaning. With her attacker in jail, the fear was no longer going to be enough to fulfill her thoughts and steal her energy. Louise wanted to have big dreams again.

So she would.

It was time to write a new list.

* * *

The normal life of a retiree resumed once Georgie began meeting her friends for cards and mall walking once again. She enjoyed the attention when she shared her story, multiple times, to anyone who would listen about being knocked out by chloroform. Georgie loved to brag that it was "nothing" and that her daughter "taught that guy a lesson" by knocking him senseless with a baseball bat. They were both grateful there were no residual aftereffects from the attack, save a few emotional scars that would take time to heal. They reveled in knowing they were safe and, regardless of which case Brandon was charged for, since the police had solid evidence against him.

Louise hoped to eventually get an update on the case, but she was still not picking up Gregory's calls. Each time his name popped up on her phone, she felt a rush of fear and shame and that emotion she wouldn't name. That conversation would have to wait for another day. She wasn't ready.

There was no part of her that wanted to spend time with Gregory yet, and certainly not "as a friend". Being around him would hurt too much, given how strongly she felt toward him. It was so embarrassing to carry a love that was unrequited. And so painful.

Louise opted to avoid the feelings and tuck them away in a section of her heart, just like she tried to do so many others. Hide them away so the pain would eventually stop. Cauterize the wound to stop the bleeding.

47

AFTER A FEW DAYS CARING FOR HER MOTHER, Louise returned to work and finished up her projects, even though it felt like she was always distracted by intrusive thoughts about a certain detective. She wondered where he was at certain times of day as she gazed out her office window and saw the city teeming with life around them.

Simone tried to convince Louise to go after what she wanted a bit harder, if Gregory was the one occupying her thoughts and her heart. Louise couldn't. She had been dumped by him twice. Twice! Louise may not have much, but she did have her pride. She didn't want Gregory to be with her because of a relentless pursuit. She wanted Gregory to come to her, ready to make a lasting commitment, and she feared that was too much to expect.

"You could just hook up with him for a bit to get you over your dumpy mood. I mean, why define the relationship if it's working for you? We're trying to get work done over here and all you can think of is him," Simone grumbled with a resigned shake of her head. "Face it, lady, you're addicted to Gregory. There is nothing to be done for it."

Louise shrugged, choosing to do nothing rather than complicate her life with more drama. Love engendered strong feelings, which then increased her chances of getting hurt. She sighed and turned back to the computer screen in front of her.

"I think it's just the holidays that get me a little distracted. Tell me what you're working on. Happy to help if I can, I'm just about done this research project. I promise to stop being in my head," Louise said with a hopeful expression.

Simone rolled her eyes and turned back to her computer, unconvinced.

Louise always took time off around the holidays. She hadn't been a huge traveler over the last few years, so it was a good time to use up her vacation days. Next year would be different, she promised herself. Anika was planning an outstanding wedding somewhere in Hawaii and she would be taking a few weeks off to enjoy a holiday in the tropics.

As she had known before her fling with Gregory, she had the power in her hands to rebuild a beautiful life for herself and she planned on doing just that.

As evening fell, Louise and Simone decided they had done all the work they could accomplish for that day. They collected their coats and purses, turning the lights off in their office as they went. Before they parted in the parking lot, Simone handed Louise a crisp vellum invitation card with silver writing on it.

"What's this?" Louise questioned.

She opened it carefully and pulled out an embossed invitation on thick creamy paper with a silver gilt snowflake border. It was so delicate and pretty. Louise read the invitation, instantly remembering what it was.

"The Cormier New Year's Eve party! Wow, thanks for the invite, I totally forgot that you guys do this every year. It's been a while since I've been."

Simone nodded in agreement. "Yes, I figured you had crawled out of your hole these days and were joining the rest of us here in the world of the living. You'll have to go shopping for something sparkly, and I already went to Adorn to pick out some dresses for you to try on. Let's check it out this weekend before the Christmas blitz begins at home!"

They arranged a time to meet up and Louise drove home, in a slightly better mood than she had been before. Georgie had started dinner when she arrived and the house smelled like beef stroganoff and roasted broccoli, one of her favorite meals. Two glasses of pinot noir had already been poured and Louise let out a big sigh when she put on her grey sweats then took a big first sip. She held the glass against her chest and inhaled the life-giving aroma deeply. Wine tasted better when one was on vacation.

"Ah, I needed that. I'm glad I have a few weeks off now; I am feeling so checked out from work. I need a reset." Georgie nodded in agreement, wringing a dish towel in her hands, then placing said towel back over her shoulder. She turned back to the stove and hummed as she added the finishing touches to Louise's dinner.

"I'm glad Sebastian is coming; I've missed seeing him so much," Georgie said, a small smile on her face, "besides, you're going to need his help." Louise screwed up her face in question, not understanding the meaning of her mother's comment.

"What do you mean I'm going to need him?" she asked.

Georgie smiled at her, excited as though she had been holding a secret.

"Well, if you have to move into your apartment January first, you might need help getting packed up and moving boxes, right?"

Louise looked at her blankly, unable to make the connection to any apartment she had looked at recently. "Mum, I haven't picked a place yet. I can't move by January first. Maybe February first?"

Georgie shook her head, smiling happily. "Nope, you get possession of your apartment January first. I put a deposit on Myrna's apartment for you, thinking you were being too hasty, and I felt it was the perfect safe place for you to live. If you don't like it, we can do something else, but I felt in my heart that you wanted that place."

Louise looked at her mother, aghast, but terribly pleased that her mother had made this decision for her. She hugged her mum with joy, happy tears gathering in her eyes. "Thank you so much, Mum. I'm so lucky you know me so well. I loved that place, and it felt so perfect for me. I guess my break is tonight, and tomorrow, I start packing!"

Georgie explained that she had been given the keys to the apartment and they could start moving in slowly during the holidays, since the last tenants would be moved out to be in their new house for Christmas.

Louise and Georgie clinked their glasses to celebrate. There wouldn't be too much to pack up, Louise could order some new pieces of furniture to be delivered in the new year. She mainly had clothing, her treasured collection of romance novels, a few bits of old furniture, and a few personal items.

Before moving in, she would give the place a thorough cleaning and paint that horrid orange bathroom, which would ease her mind considerably. It was the best Christmas present she could ever have hoped for. Her surprise new apartment was an important part of that fresh start she was grasping for.

For the first time, Louise felt like she was back on track, or at least on a track that was leading somewhere amazing.

48

"Ah, perfect, all set up to watch the finale." The scent of the gorgeous red wine she had treated herself with for this special occasion wafted and tantalized her as she poured. "Are you sitting down with me, Mum?" Louise called out to Georgie, who was finishing up doing the dishes after a delicious home-cooked meal. It was nice that her mother was feeling up to cooking again. It was a sign that she must be feeling better.

"Pass," her mother said in a snarky tone.

Louise shook her head. "Your loss. This wine is amazing," Louise said. "I picked it up from that cute little wine shop near my apartment. I'm gonna develop a drinking problem if they keep recommending wines this good."

Louise smoothed out the blanket over her legs and reached over to pat Cosette, who purred softly next to her thigh. Yep, this is the good life. No man, no complications, only good wine and the final contestants on *The Bachelor* for company. There had been a lot of tears in the preview, so Louise was looking forward to enjoying a few hours of chaos. She rubbed her hands together in excitement.

She heard the familiar crunch of snow outside the window, indicating someone was walking by, and she looked out the window to spy on whichever neighbor or dog walker was out this late. Her smile faded instantly as she spied Gregory making his way up their walkway. She got down on her hands and knees in front of the sofa, hoping he wouldn't see her.

"Mum, tell him I'm not here," Louise said, not prepared in the least to deal with the handsome officer again. Her heart was too raw. He made her feel so weak. Georgie peeked around the corner from the kitchen and shook her head.

"Nope, you need to deal with him sooner or later, Louise. Maybe he has news about the case," she suggested, abandoning her daughter.

Louise swore under her breath, wondering if she could wait long enough for him to ring the doorbell and assume they weren't at home. Damn the lights that were shining so brightly in the living room. The doorbell rang once, then twice.

"Louise," Georgie said. "Go answer the door. I know he's not here to see me."

A frustrated growl filled the living room, and she stood up, walking to the door and certainly releasing a cloud of steam from her ears. Imagine her own mother betraying her like that. There was no loyalty in this house.

Louise opened the door a crack and locked eyes with Gregory. She hated how her insides melted at the sight of him, his glasses fogging over from the warmth of the house and hair slightly mussed by his hood. It occurred to Louise that despite the fact that she had told herself she had moved on, her heart had not. It basically stopped as soon as she laid eyes on him.

There was no way she was going to show him that.

She gave him her most pleasant smile.

"Hi, Officer Band. How can I help you?" She used her most pleasant tone, to ensure he would still know she was furious with him and definitely *not* missing him.

"Louise, we need to talk. You're not answering my calls. I can't eat, I can barely sleep, I miss you so—"

Louise cut him off with a hand, nodding toward the kitchen where Georgie was working. They could hear the rush of water and the clatter of dishes in the sink. Gregory merely gazed at Louise, his hands up in question.

"Can we go somewhere to talk?" he whispered.

Louise looked down, taking in her "less upsetti, more spaghetti" sweatshirt (she wore it because Georgie hated it) and grey sweatpants with a hole in the crotch.

"Maybe another time? When I can, you know, look a little more put together?"

He brought his mouth to her ear so that only she would hear. "I don't give a shit about that. I can barely see you as it is. I just need to talk to you."

He reached a hand to touch hers, rubbing his thumb along the top of her hand. She rolled her eyes at the sheer pleasure she felt, embarrassed at her body's willingness to forget, when her heart was in a million pieces.

"Please, I'm desperate." His pleading tone convinced her to reach into the closet for her puffer coat.

"I just want you to know I'm missing *The Bachelor* finale for you. This had better be worth it."

Gregory's face split with a huge grin as he laid a hand on the small of her back to guide her to the car. He opened the passenger door, and she sat, appreciating that the car was already warm.

"So, where are you taking me?" Louise asked, as they pulled away from her mother's home and headed toward Mount Royal, a neighborhood filled with megamansions and beautiful Christmas lights left over from the holidays. Not far from where Simone lived in a guesthouse on her parents' compound.

Gregory drove to a secluded street which overlooked downtown, giving them a 180-degree stunning view of the city at night. He left the car running as Louise waited for him to speak. She gazed out the window in wonder at how her beloved city sparkled at night. That view would never cease to fill her heart with happiness.

Gregory cleared his throat behind her, and she turned. Her chest physically hurt at being in the same space with him and not being able to love him, to touch him. The walls she kept up prevented her from reaching across and seeking that comfort, the warmth that he could provide.

"Louise, do you remember that night, when we were badass university students, and got super drunk at the Wild Rose Saloon?"

A creep of a blush bloomed in her face at the memory, and Louise was grateful for the darkness that hid it. Of course, she remembered. The night had been warm and seductive. The air was warm like bath water. Gregory had walked her back to Georgie's place, since she was living with her mother at the time.

Louise was trying to forget her family problems with a night on the town. Forget the messy divorce, the betrayal, the constant sound of her mother weeping, which was so unlike Georgie. On the way, they had started making out and decided to take advantage of the warm night and the semblance of privacy to enjoy a moment in the cool grass. They had walked through a hilly park on the way up to their neighborhood and stolen a moment sheltered by a surrounding grove of trees.

A moment of hot, moist kisses.

A moment of being pressed against the grass, feeling simultaneously connected to the earth and Gregory's body.

A moment of drunken lust and fulfillment.

She sighed at the memory.

"I'm not that girl anymore, Gregory. There were moments back then when I could be wild, impulsive. That girl doesn't exist anymore."

"I'm just trying to remind you that we have a history. And that complicates things. But it can also simplify things. When I stopped seeing you, I had my reasons, but they were never that our connection wasn't real. Our connection was almost too strong. Too distracting. I broke up with you back in university because I knew I had to leave you for a while and couldn't stand the idea of you waiting for me, and being disappointed by me when I couldn't give you what you wanted."

Louise pressed her lips together and stared out the window. A heavy sigh emerged from her lips. "What is it you thought I wanted?"

"You wanted a boyfriend. A guy who wanted to get married, have a family, I don't know. That freaked me out. I wanted my house in order before ever dreaming about any of those things." He reached a hand across the console and laid it on hers, stroking her hand softly.

"Well, you got that wrong. I wasn't going to let some man get in the way of my education or my career dreams. All I wanted was to be with you and be with someone who understood me. Maybe even love you a little." Her gaze traveled from their hands to his face, and he dragged a hand through his hair.

"Right, well, I screwed that one up royally."

"And you did it again."

"Listen, I've had an epiphany. I keep making these decisions thinking I know best what you need. I know best how to protect you, but I've been a fool. I mean, you beat the shit out of a perp I've been trying to catch for months. You don't need me to protect you. I don't want to save you." Their gazes locked. "I just want to love you."

Louise looked away, incapable of absorbing the pain and vulnerability she saw in his eyes. She gave a breathy little laugh at his comment about the murderer.

"Well, I did help catch the Marda Loop murderer."

"Yep. You fucking destroyed him, Lou." She turned at his comment, and saw him beaming with pride.

"That's a pretty big flex," she said, blushing.

A smile tickled at the edges of Louise's mouth. She took Gregory's hand from her lap and placed it on her heart.

"You know, I don't mind having a knight in shining armor, as long as he knows when to step aside and let my light shine. I can be brave too."

"Don't I know it." His lip quivered, as though remembering the day he had swept in and apprehended the Marda Loop murderer. Louise wondered if he could feel her heart thundering in her chest. They had been through a lot together.

"You know, I'll consider letting you love me, as long as you understand there is no going back." She brought his hand to her cheek and kissed his palm. The electricity of their connection shooting sparks through her. She closed her eyes to savor the warmth of his skin.

Was she a fool?

Yes.

A fool for love.

"You got one thing right. I am brave. It takes bravery to trust a man who dumped you twice," Louise continued.

A hopeful smile emerged on his face. "I deserve that."

Her eyes connected with his. The look of absolute devotion in them was terrifying. Louise looked out the window once more, pretending to consider her options, as though she had any. The silence stretched out between them as her brain seemed to process. She desperately wanted the love he was offering, yet she was terrified of having her heart broken.

Again.

She wasn't good at love. She chafed at needing someone so desperately. There was a cavern of need burning inside her. Love hurt. Desire tortured. Longing devastated. Gregory could be the cure to the burning ache that throbbed in her chest. She wanted to find out. Louise didn't love doing scary or risky things. Yet here she was, jumping off a cliff with her eyes open.

"I'm not making any promises, but I am going to allow you a fresh start. I will permit you to take me on a proper date. It better be fucking dazzling."

Gregory chuckled and kissed her on the cheek. "Oh, it will be."

He pulled away, and she leaned in for more, the attraction irresistible. Her lips begging to touch his once more. She brought her hands to his hair and relished the delicious feel of messing it up and steaming up his glasses all on her own. She pulled away, a playful gaze dancing in her eyes.

"Does this mean I get to help you on future cases?" she asked with a little giggle.

Gregory considered. "Well, you did pretty much solve my last big case on your own."

"I basically have a degree in *Dateline*," she said with a serious face.

Gregory rubbed his chin in one hand, a mock look of pensiveness on his face.

"That's something," he said. "How about you solve the mystery of how I went this long without you? God, kiss me one more time, then I'll take you home. You need to finish that *Bachelor* finale, right?" He swallowed a laugh as he brought her face to his and enjoyed her lips slowly, savoring their kiss as though it would have to last him a little while.

Her lips traveled along his soft, freshly shaven cheek and drew a path down his neck, enjoying a nuzzle and inhaling the scent of him. The cold air mingled with lemon and cedarwood was purely intoxicating. She inhaled deeply, unwilling to break the connection yet. Her hand traveled up his thigh, discovering the proof of his desperate need pressing against his dark blue jeans. Her hand rubbed against him playfully, and he put a hand to hers to stop it.

"Cease this torture. I wanted to make this about us, not about *you know*."

"Yeah, but don't we technically have to have makeup sex or something?" she asked, sticking her tongue out and tasting his warm, salty skin. Gregory moaned in response. His resistance clearly being tested.

"Louise, I'm taking you out on a dazzling date and we are starting this relationship off properly."

She pulled away, her eyes narrowing in challenge. "Are you saying that if I go into the back seat, you're not going to join me?" She softened her eyes into the most seductive look she could muster. Her lips hovered over his, whispering her plea.

"Please, Gregory. Let's turn the car off and steam up the windows the old-fashioned way. We can start off our relationship properly after that." She kissed a trail down his neck and allowed her hands to travel freely up his leg and slipping under his shirt, where it was warm and toasty. His stomach started at the invasion. He stilled her hand with his.

"Are you sure you want this? You want me?" he asked, tender desperation fresh in his eyes.

She rolled her eyes and opened the passenger door to quickly dip into the backseat. "Gregory, are we going to do this or what? Hurry, before the cops catch us." She winked and took her sweatshirt off, revealing that she wasn't wearing a bra. His jaw dropped, and he swallowed, nodding uncontrollably. He turned the car off and dashed to the backseat, trying to let in as little cold air as possible.

"I thought you said my wild girl doesn't exist anymore," he said, shaking his head and kissing her as he tugged his shirt off and pressed her gently against the door. "I think she's making a comeback." He pressed his lips against her skin as he pulled her sweatpants down and kissed a trail to her striped lace trimmed cotton underwear. "Damn, these are so naughty."

They were definitely *not* naughty.

She gave a warm laughing sound and surrendered to the night, the moon, and the heat of their bodies. "I can't help it; you make me wild."

Gregory groaned as his finger traced a path along her inner thighs and sought the warmth between her legs. Louise tossed her head back with a moan and let him do as he wished to her body. She had missed him. And he did have to earn her forgiveness, after all.

49

LOUISE SHEEPISHLY USED HER PANTS to wipe the front windshield of the car. She was immune to the damp coolness of them, as she basked in the glow of warmth rippling between them. She had taken a risk yes, but she had no doubts. It wasn't really a gamble. Gregory's heart had always answered the call, he just had to make his brain listen to the inevitable. She could hear Simone's voice in her ear telling her that boys could sometimes be blind like that, and women were here to make them see what they needed.

They drove rather slowly back to Marda Loop, hands intertwined, sharing secret smiles. Gregory looked still in disbelief, grateful that the conversation had happened and that he had managed to convince her to be his. As though she had any choice.

Louise looked to him in bewilderment when the car stopped in the grocery store parking lot. It was almost eleven at night and Louise could not imagine why Gregory wanted to stop here before dropping her off.

"I just need to go get something really quick," he explained. "Can you wait here for five minutes? I'll lock the door."

She nodded in confusion and watched him disappear into the grocery store. She hummed a tune to herself as she kept her eyes glued to the exit doors, trying to keep her nerves at bay. Louise forced herself not to think about the fact that their car was one of very few in the deserted parking lot. She twiddled her fingers nervously and her chest filled with relief when he emerged after a few minutes.

He had the biggest grin on his face, and she looked down at her hands, wondering what he could possibly need at the store this late at night. He was hiding whatever it was he had purchased behind his back and Louise was dying of curiosity. The driver side door opened, and he sat back down, a mischievous look on his face.

"I have a surprise for you."

Louise made a wary face, curious as to what he had planned. He unwrapped a plastic covered object gently to reveal a single red rose. Her heart stood still in her chest. Could it be possible? Her own *Bachelor* finale happening right now?

"Louise Dubois, I have spent years loving you, even though my own brain took a long time to figure things out. I can't imagine having pizza dates, back seat cuddle sessions, or holding hands on late-night walks with anyone else. Will you accept my final rose?"

Louise's hands traveled to her face as she gazed at the perfect red rose in his hand, surrounded by layers of crinkly cellophane, her mouth agape in surprise.

"Gregory, I'll accept your rose, but a word of warning, a final rose is *Bachelor* speak for a proposal. Let's go on that date before getting engaged, okay?"

Gregory's eyes widened. "Yeah, okay. One step at a time. But just so we're clear, I'm not handing out roses to anyone else." He smiled, a handsome glow traveling up to his eyes, sending shivers down her spine. Their lips met in time with their hearts, sealing their fates with a simple kiss.

When Louise walked into Cambrai Cottage, floating on a cloud, Georgie had already gone up to bed, leaving a few lights on for her daughter. Louise tossed her keys on a side table and hung up her coat. She filled a small vase with water and lovingly trimmed the rose at the bottom and walked it up to her room. Louise had no need to watch the finale, she would catch up another day. One happy ending was enough to savor for tonight.

50

DETECTIVE BLAIR CAME TO CHECK ON GEORGIE a few days before Christmas, since she had been unable to stop worrying about the ladies after the night of the attack with Brandon. Louise and Georgie were pleasantly surprised once they opened the red door of the cottage, and the officer strode in. Her dark curly hair in a tight low bun and a light pink lip gloss on her lips which complemented her brown skin. She had intelligent, dark brown eyes and a reassuring strength that made Louise feel safe whenever she was around.

Louise would never forget how the officer had cared for her and her mother after their time with the Marda Loop murderer. Serena had kept tabs on them at the hospital and let Louise know as soon as possible when Brandon had been put in jail, after his own brief hospital stay.

Officer Blair came into the living room and settled on the sofa, automatically starting to pet Cosette, who was rather aggressively seeking some love once again. Georgie settled on the sofa next to them and Louise sat across in a cozy, cream-colored stuffed chair.

She had served them each a warm mug of tea with milk and sugar.

On the coffee table sat an antique floral plate filled with assorted cookies and sweets from the Christmas baking Louise and Georgie had been doing. Serena took a sip of her tea and nibbled on a cookie, as Louise and Georgie waited with bated breath for what she had come to see them about.

"Ladies, I come here with some good news. We were able to put a rush on that DNA evidence and, as of today, the Marda Loop murderer is charged with multiple murders and assaults. I wanted you to be among the first to know. He has been identified as Joseph James, not Brandon, as he was going by on the Meet Cute dating app."

Louise piped up, unable to resist her curiosity. "Were you able to connect him to all the cases in the area?" she asked.

Serena paused for a moment, as though deciding how much information she could give them. "We were able to link him to cases near his own home, in Signal Hill, a neighborhood west of here. I've been studying his pattern, and he seems to have begun with break and enters and assaults in his comfort zone, then he moved on as people in the neighborhood became more aware and more vigilant," Serena said as she nibbled on a cookie, giving them time to absorb the information.

"When he changed neighborhoods," she continued, "he escalated his behavior. I'm just glad we caught him before he could hurt anyone else. There are no indications he would have stopped at two murders, especially since he intended to go after you ladies." Serena explained how much she enjoyed writing up the report on the incident at Cambrai Cottage. She beamed with pride as she looked at Louise.

"You cannot imagine how satisfying it was to write how the victim of a crime had knocked her attacker senseless with her baseball bat. I loved every minute," Serena said and chuckled with satisfaction, then quickly returning to a serious face.

Her eyes gazed with admiration upon Louise, who was still uncomfortable with the reality of having used her self-defense training to save her mother and herself. They all sipped their tea at the same time and took a deep breath. Serena cleared her throat once more and placed her teacup on the table.

"Louise, there is one more delicate matter I need to communicate with you." She looked from mother to daughter and waited for a nod before continuing.

"We found some, trophies. We'll analyze where they all came from, but I'll need you to come to the police station and identify if any belong to you."

"Trophies? I'm not sure I understand," Louise said, a frown creasing her forehead.

"He stole small things that wouldn't be noticed. We assume during his prowls, um," Serena cleared her throat again. "He had quite a collection of panties. The amount he stole gave us the impression that he had visited many more women's homes than we have known victims." Serena shook her head, while gazing at Louise.

Georgie's hand came to her chest and silence filled the room as the information sank in. A familiar chill ran though Louise's body, the memory of him causing an involuntary reaction. She had to remind herself that Joseph James was in police custody now and wouldn't be coming after her ever again.

Georgie, never one to hold back when her curiosity was piqued, questioned Serena further. "Detective Blair, I'm so happy you have come to see us, but I can't help but wonder where is Gregory? Wasn't he working on this case?" she asked.

Serena paused as if trying to formulate an adequate answer. "Detective Band was removed from this case for personal reasons. He was worried about appearances when it came to his time spent with you," she said, nodding in Louise's direction. Louise choked on her tea and put the cup down.

"You mean he was taken off the case because of me?" Louise asked, shaken. He had never told her.

Serena shook her head. "Not exactly. He removed himself from the case, so as not to interfere with the lawful prosecution of the suspect," she said. "It was the right thing to do."

Georgie and Louise both looked at each other across the room. Detective Blair finished her cookie, and got up, brushing a few invisible crumbs off her pants.

"Well, I should head out. Merry Christmas, ladies, I wish you a safe and happy holiday," she said as she walked toward the door.

Georgie and Louise wished her well as Serena let herself out the front door. They stared at each other in silence.

"Well, that was interesting..." Georgie mumbled, walking into the kitchen. "Did you know this?"

"No, I just assumed he was still working on it, but that makes sense."

Louise breathed a sigh of relief, feeling a weight come off her shoulders with the knowledge that Joseph James was on his way to a life sentence in jail. She pressed her hand on her stomach, wondering why she felt a knot lingering there after having heard such happy news. Knowing the killer was where he belonged didn't take away the feeling that Louise had survived — when the others didn't. It bothered her that she was the one that got away.

The ache of guilt thrummed within her, as she wondered if the trophies would reveal there were other victims, more that didn't survive. Louise would forever feel connected to these women, even though she lived, and they were buried deep in the ground. They belonged to a sisterhood to which no one wanted to be a member. She thought of the innocent women, snatched away before their time and wondered how she had been so lucky to survive. If she didn't take advantage of the second chance she had been given, would she even be worthy of the gift?

She took another sip of tea and enjoyed as it filled her mouth with precious sweetness. Her eyes closed in a moment of worship. Louise loved tea. Louise loved life. It tasted so fucking good.

51

The Cormier home positively glowed, a welcoming sight for the party guests trickling in for their yearly New Year's Eve celebration. The white lights strung along the windows and roofline gleamed beneath the white banks of soft fluffy snow that had accumulated by the end of December. Snowflakes gently danced in the air, resting themselves upon the lavish hairstyles, fur jackets, and eyelashes of the guests arriving for the party.

Louise was thoroughly enjoying herself, gazing at the busy ballroom from her place on the outskirts of the dance floor. A big band was playing Frank Sinatra songs on one end of the ballroom, which caused her hips to sway. This was the perfect party for her, the music was calming, and the ambience was enchanting.

A crowd had gathered around the musicians, taking in the beautiful music as it drifted around them like a warm blanket. The ballroom had dim, romantic lighting that create a relaxing party atmosphere. Louise delighted at the sounds of laughter, tinkling glasses, and music that mingled to create a magical symphony for her ears. She was glad she and Georgie had come. She surrendered to the prodding from her mother and Simone, who had helped her choose the iridescent black sequin puff sleeve mini dress she was wearing, with an open back drawn closed by a velvet bow.

A rush of air entered Louise as she felt a touch from behind on her waist. She felt the press of sequins into her skin, slightly irritating, but she had an idea who was standing behind her.

"You better watch it when you sneak up on me. The last guy who did that barely lived to tell about it," she said, turning around to gaze at Gregory, feeling a turmoil of joy and sadness inside her.

It was a punch to the gut, seeing how handsome Gregory looked in his tuxedo, she almost had to wipe the drool from her mouth at the sight. She attempted to be covert as she took in his perfectly styled hair and his pale blue eyes behind his glasses, which gazed upon her with warmth and love.

"I didn't know if you were going to show up," she said. "How did you get away from work?" Louise chewed the inside of her lip at the reminder. She wondered what Gregory was working on now, if not the Marda Loop murderer case.

Their hands found each other as they strolled around the ballroom. They took in the beautiful decorations around the Cormier house. It was a stunning mansion, and the Cormier family had decorated it beautifully for the holidays. The herringbone hardwood gleamed, reflecting the glow of the lights on the trees in the room. There were multiple clusters of white and green Christmas trees dotting the ballroom, casting a romantic light for the party guests. From the ceiling dangled an array of many sized snowflakes that sparkled in the light. On one side of the room was an inlaid wood antique bar with a dark granite top, where the family had hired bartenders wearing white shirts and black bowties for the evening.

Louise ordered a soixante-quinze, a mix of champagne, gin, a dash of lemon juice, and simple syrup. The bubbles danced around a beautiful, sugared cranberry floating on the surface of the champagne, adding a festive touch to her drink.

"I heard some interesting news the other day," Louise began as they strolled away from the crowd.

"Oh yeah?"

Louise was eager to hear from him if he truly had been reassigned and was no longer working on the case. "Serena told me you are not working in Major Crimes anymore. Is that true?"

Gregory's mouth tightened, his eyes looking bleak, though he quickly shook himself out of it. "I made the decision to come clean and I've been reassigned."

"Why didn't you tell me?"

They walked through the main ballroom to find a place to discuss the case a little more privately. A short hallway led to a conservatory where they could gaze at the evening stars through the floor to ceiling windows. The room had few comfortable areas for sitting and lounging, as well as the large potted plants strung with sparkling white lights.

"Louise, I slept with a potential witness. I wasn't going to shout it from the rooftops," Gregory said, a slight pink blush tinging his cheeks. "I needed to make things right. I came clean to my supervisor and obviously, he wanted my name off all the cases related to Joseph James and had them reassigned to Officer Blair and Officer Tall to tie up all the loose ends. I would do anything to avoid screwing up the trial, but you already know that."

"Gregory…I'm so sorry you lost your dream case because of me."

"Nah, don't look at it like that. I feel good knowing that this guy will be put away for a long time. No mess, no complications. I don't even care that I don't get the satisfaction of being the cop that caught this guy. Once I figured out what I actually wanted, nothing else really mattered."

Louise was speechless, glossy tears threatening to ruin her carefully done party makeup. She sniffed and placed his hand on her heart, so he could feel it beating. She wondered if he could feel all the love inside there.

"I'm just not good at this relationship stuff. I have so much baggage, you don't even know. But that's the sweetest thing anyone has ever said to me, Gregory."

"I'm strong. Let me help you carry your baggage. Maybe I can help you unpack and over time, we can decide what to keep and what isn't serving you anymore."

Louise closed her eyes and turned away, feeling his words touch a place inside her that had once felt so empty. Maybe they were perfect for each other. She sighed and took a moment to gaze outside.

Louise admired the starry sky sparkling above the perfect bed of white snow covering the Cormier's backyard and prayed that she could be filled with as much peace as the image instilled. The stars, which could be seen above them through the conservatory glass, mixed with the softly falling snow and gave the impression they were standing in a snow globe.

"So beautiful," he said.

She turned to him, noticing that he wasn't even looking at the view. "It's enchanting," she said, a smile forming on her face.

"I wasn't talking about the view," he said as he brought a hand to her cheek.

She pressed her face into it, loving the feel of his warm hand touching her again. Her gaze traveled slowly up his face, and he pulled her face closer, unable to wait any longer to give her what she needed. They deepened their kiss. His tongue taking freely what she was offering, as he pressed her gently against the small section of wall between the windows. She pulled away to guzzle her drink and put down her glass, returning to taste the champagne bubbles on his tongue. Their kisses became more demanding as he made his way down her neck with his lips and brought his hands up to fondle her rear, pressing his erection into her sequin skirt, leaving no doubt to his level of arousal.

"Gregory," she breathed. "We should stop. People will notice."

He continued to work his way down her neck, grunting in acknowledgment, but not ceasing his kisses. His hand began to travel up her black thigh-high pantyhose, to the warmth that resided between her legs. She moaned at the sensation of her lust burning inside her stomach as he slowly made his way to the apex up her dress. She was jolted back to reality and pushed him away playfully.

"Sorry, it's just been a while since our date, and I missed you."

"Ah yes, our dazzling first date. I was very impressed by our dinner at the Calgary Tower. The views were stunning."

"Not to mention the views afterward," he whispered in her ear, clearly trying to break her resolve.

Louise giggled and shivered as he nibbled ear determinedly. "Gregory..."

"No one's going to notice a guy making out with his girlfriend on New Year's Eve. Who cares?"

Louise froze at his last words. "Wait... since when am I your girlfriend? That sounds so serious," she said with a grin.

"I'm pretty serious, Louise. I knew you were my girlfriend the minute I watched you demolish half a dill pickle pizza. Only my soulmate would be able to do that."

Louise blushed at the compliment.

"I fell for you so hard that night, I just needed my brain to catch up with my heart." His words sent a current of warmth radiating throughout her body. She giggled at his silly declaration of love. It was so deliciously charming.

She cupped his cheeks and met his joyful gaze. "Well, I knew I loved you the minute we danced in our underwear. That's the kind of thing you can only do with your true love, right?"

Gregory grabbed her bottom and pressed her up against him, seized by a fever of passion. "That's the most romantic thing anyone has ever said to me."

He pressed her up against the wall and claimed her lips for his own, her resistance having dissolved at their words.

She let out a whimper as he ran his hands up her skirt, pushing it up as he pressed her gently against the wall. She wrapped a leg around him, feeling the shape of his erection pressing against her sex, creating a heady, drunk sensation within her. Their lips collided hungrily, a tangible heat rising from their bodies clinging to each other.

"We need to leave," she panted as she came up for air. She unwound her body from his and tugged at the sides of her skirt to fix her outfit. Her wobbly legs struggled to walk away normally in heels, given her heightened state of arousal. When she turned to look back at him, her hand reached for his and he stopped her.

"I need a minute. Go get your jacket and meet me outside," he said, looking slightly embarrassed, and he turned to glance back outside the conservatory windows.

She nodded in understanding and started to walk off.

"Louise," he said as she turned to face him once more. "I love you."

"Gregory. I love you too." Her shoes clicked on the tile floors as she went to grab their things and saying goodbye to Simone.

"Wait, what? It's not even midnight yet. How are you leaving already?" Simone asked, slightly perturbed by Louise's sudden exit. Louise gave her friend a conspiratorial look.

"Gregory and I have to go, if you know what I mean. Take care of Georgie for me, okay? Tell her I had to make a French exit. She'll get it." Louise winked at her and nudged her with her elbow.

"Ah, I gotcha. Get out of here. And don't worry about me, I've got a real charmer with me tonight. His name is Trevor, and he's a rich lawyer. Sounds like a match made in heaven, right?" Simone grinned, pointing to her latest conquest. "Isn't he cute?"

"He sure is! Maybe we'll both enjoy some New Year's Eve fireworks," Louise said.

She hugged Simone and kissed her on the cheek, saying her goodbye. Louise put on her coat in the foyer, and could hear her heels clicking on the marble tile loudly as she rushed. They reminded her to slow down to maintain the illusion that she wasn't escaping to have a sexy hookup with her...boyfriend? The word felt foreign in her mouth, but the rush of excitement it engendered told her it was right. When the door opened, Gregory was there, cheeks and nose turning pink in the cold. She wrapped her arms around his waist and kissed him. He pressed his face in her neck, inhaling her fragrance, unable to resist the rose perfume she had spritzed on before leaving the house. He grunted in appreciation.

"You sure we should leave the party early? Things were pretty bumpin' in there," she said.

Gregory looked up at the sky. "Oh my God, yes. It's been like two days since we were alone and that's just too long. If I have to spend another night away from you, I might die," he said.

Louise smirked and shook her head. "A touch dramatic, but I don't want your death on my hands."

He kissed her once more before they turned to find his car, joining hands beneath the starry winter sky as the snowflakes danced around them. Louise nestled her head on his arm, and Gregory brought his arm around her shoulders, squeezing her tightly against him. She could get used to this. The moon, the stars, and her beloved were all she needed.

52

The few boxes Louise had brought with her were piled up in the living room and kitchen of her new apartment in the Marda Point building. Myrna had come by and left her a bottle of wine and a beautiful flower arrangement from a nearby flower shop. Louise loved the reminder of how close she was to so many amazing businesses: a French wine bistro, a romance novel bookshop, one of her favorite coffee shops, and her precious Marda Loop Brewing, where she had been enjoying drinks with her friends for years. They planned to pop in there for dinner this evening once they finished unloading the last few boxes from the car.

She gazed at the antique bed frame from her old bedroom in Georgie's house as it leaned against the bedroom wall. It was meant to be used temporarily while Louise waited for a new bed frame to be delivered. The door opened slowly as Gregory popped in to drop off a few more boxes.

"Who is giving you flowers? I thought I was the only one allowed to get you flowers from now on," he grumbled, noticing the arrangement of roses, sweet smelling freesia interspersed with spray roses and magnolia leaves. It was really a stunning bouquet. Louise rolled her eyes at him.

"Relax. Myrna stopped by while you were getting the last load of boxes. No one is trying to romance me, you can stop being jealous," she admonished.

Gregory looked skeptical and grumbled but accepted the response. He dropped the boxes of books in her bedroom where her cream-colored antique bookcase had been set up.

"So, have you thought of a solution to my bed problem?" Louise called playfully from the kitchen, where she was unloading more dishes from boxes. Her mother had accumulated a large number of cute dishes from her second-hand shopping and if Louise hadn't known they were all for her, she would have thought her mother was a hoarder. In fact, there was most likely sufficient evidence that Georgie had a slight accumulation problem, but Louise was grateful for it now that she needed new stuff for her apartment.

"Yes, you already ordered the new bed, so we are good. Antique beds are so unreliable, I cannot believe it couldn't handle us for one night. This is why I say no to antique furniture."

Louise smiled and shook her head, looking at the broken bed frame standing against the wall and the mattress sitting on the ground, with cream sheets, a fluffy duvet and a cream waffle throw spread across the middle.

"Hm, well someone is going to have to explain to Georgie that the bed frame is broken. I don't want to be the one to tell her how we broke it," she said, slightly worried. Louise wrapped her arms around his waist, looking at him for the solution or perhaps hoping he would be the one to tell Georgie.

"I'll tell Georgie the bed didn't make it in the move, and we'll just leave it at that. Besides, we might be able to fix it. We just can't, you know, test it again," he said, lowering his head to kiss her. He began to push her toward the bed.

"Mmm, maybe we need to test the new mattress again. It looks awfully nicely made up," he suggested.

Louise, concerned they would never finish moving if they started down this path, pulled away. "Gregory. Let's finish unloading those boxes out of my car and go get dinner. We've got lots of time to do that later. I'm too excited to get started on my new life in this apartment. My new life with you."

Louise checked her phone for messages, since her friends were eager to meet them for drinks and a tour of the apartment once they were done bringing boxes. The group chat was alive with Simone, Anika, Roger, and Tom making plans to meet up at the place down the street.

She wrapped her arms around his neck and kissed him again, secure in the knowledge that her new beginning was here. She looked around at the empty apartment and pictured the new furniture and art she would fill it with and the housewarming party she would throw.

This place, like her future, would be filled with lots of happiness. No shadows had followed her from her past life and though her future was sparsely furnished for now, she and Gregory would find ways to imbue each corner with a sprinkling of joy.

WHAT'S NEXT FOR LOUISE AND GREGORY AND
THE MARDA LOOP MYSTERIES CREW?
JOIN US FOR ANIKA AND TOM'S WEDDING IN

Death at the Luau

COMING IN 2025

Acknowledgements

There are so many people to that helped make my first book possible.

To my husband: Thank you for forcing me to buy a computer, even though I didn't think I was worth such an extravagant gift. I found the pressure to write a book would be crushing if I got one, but you made me do it anyway. Thank you for believing I could write a book, even when I had almost decided it wasn't going to happen for me. You are my true love and definitely a great guy.

To my mother: You were my first example of what a strong woman should be. You reminded me that I could do it, even when I was placing obstacles in my own way. I strive to be as wonderful a mother as you one day.

To my daughters: Thank you for giving me the time and the space to write my novel. Thank you for always believing in my characters and loving the parts of the story I shared with you (not the spicy ones!). You are my *raison d'être*.

I would like to thank my romance novel writing teacher, M. Jane Colette. Your course was the key to unlocking the stories I had trapped in my mind. I had the ideas, all I needed was the tools. It is one of the greatest gifts anyone has ever given me.

I would like to thank my beta readers for giving me amazing

feedback and support. Naomi, Alexandria, Ellory, Ivy, Kelsey, Corinne and Charles. Thank you for believing in the story of Louise and Gregory.

Thank you to my police liaison Rad, your information has been invaluable.

Thank you to Luna Day for your constant mentoring and support. You helped me write a banger of a book blurb.

Finally, I would like to thank my editor, Jennifer Herrington and my cover designer Claire Brown. You have both been instrumental in helping me bring my vision to life and for making it better than I could have ever imagined. Jennifer, the answer is yes. I will always murder another character for you.

VISUAL HUES PHOTOGRAPHY

About the Author

Mimi Gunn writes from the unique perspective of an Ottawa region born French-Canadian living in Calgary, Alberta. Stories have always been an important part of her culture growing up, from hilarious tales shared around the kitchen table to ghost stories told around the campfire. She is passionate about cooking meals that bring people together and spending time with her family. In her free time, she hoards romance novels and feeds her addiction to travel and adventures, with a strong penchant for Disneyland as a destination! She loves to pay homage to the romance genre with her excessive reading and book photography. Mimi is delighted to share the stories that have been living in her mind with you and hopes you enjoy her strong heroines and dashing heroes.

Visit her at @mimigunnbooks and at www.mimigunn.com for romance book recommendations and updates on the next book coming in the series. Follow her Goodreads at Mimi Gunn.

Manufactured by Amazon.ca
Bolton, ON

46250188R00213